WATERPROOF

With sincere best wishes

Chris Crowther

WATERPROOF

Patrolling the Norfolk Broads as a Navigation Ranger is, to ex-Scotland Yard detective Jack Fellows, the perfect job.

That's until the cold hand of violent death touches even this idyllic corner of East Anglia. Murder on the Broads is rarer than a bittern but the police soon have their man. Or have they? Jack is sure they've got it wrong and sets out to prove it. Amongst the tranquillity of this unique setting he discovers a simmering cauldron of bitterness and deceit with suspects aplenty.

Relationships, livelihoods and reputations are in jeopardy but whose will be sacrificed as he pursues the truth?

British Library Cataloguing in Publication Data.
A catalogue record is available from the British Library.

ISBN 978 0 903094 23
EAN 9780903094238

First published in this edition in 2007
by

Hamilton Publications,
9 Marine Parade,
Gorleston on sea,
Norfolk. NR 31 6DU.

www.chriscrowther.co.uk

Printed in Great Britain by Barnwell Print Ltd., 2 - 6 Penfold Street, Aylsham, Norfolk. NR11 6ET.

Cover photograph: Sue Crowther

WaterProof

Chris Crowther

FOREWORD

There is often a great power in being locally creative. I admire novelists who have the courage to set a story in their own territory - one mistake and their credibility disappears.

WATERPROOF unfolds its story in an accurate setting of the tranquil Norfolk Broads and like those famous rivers, there are plenty of twists and turns in a plot that makes the reader want to turn pages.

WATERPROOF is unusual in three aspects: its writer is local, the story is local and Chris Crowther, a former commercial pilot, designed his yarn specifically for local people and the many tourists who visit the Broads each year.

I am sure they will enjoy it.

Ian Masters

Broadcaster and Chairman of the Creative Industries Board.

Chapter One

IN THE EARLY MORNING LIGHT, the broad lay calm and still. To Navigation Ranger Jack Fellows, it seemed almost desecration to be cleaving its mirror-like surface with the lean bows of his patrol launch. This was his favourite time, a moment in his routine when the peace of the night still worked its magic on the emerging day. As if to emphasise life's new awakening, a squawking flight of Canada geese came banking in over the reed beds, the ripples from their formation landing reaching the few boats lying to scattered anchorages just out of the main fairway. Another day on the Norfolk Broads had begun.

For Jack, this one, like every other, would be spent patrolling his own sector of these enchanted waters. His presence would be that of guardian, enforcing the rules and by-laws of the waterway but offering assistance and advice along the way. It was as close to the perfect job as he could imagine and even reprimanding the odd skipper exceeding river speed or stereo decibel limits, was pretty tame stuff for someone who'd known the worst side of human nature.

He'd grown up in London's East End, done well at school, gone straight into the Metropolitan Police and after the statutory period on the beat, gained assignment to the coveted Thames Division. London's river in those days was a commercial artery and the continuous passage of shipping a source of fascination for young Jack. A rewarding decade piloting police launches had stimulated a deep love of boats and all things nautical. Only career ambition had led him to apply for transfer to CID. The Met. didn't encourage such changes but an award for gallantry and two commendations earned some preferential consideration and he got his transfer. Twenty more years distinguished service and the rank of Detective Superintendent had shown that decision to be right for the force, but not always for Jack. Fighting London's crime meant an unending exposure to life at its most sordid and by the age of forty-eight, he'd had enough. Besides, he missed boats. When word came through that the Broads Authority were seeking to fill a Ranger position, he'd taken early retirement and the job. Jack and his wife had spent holidays on Broads hire cruisers so the move to Norfolk had been perfect. Back on boats, patrolling waters he truly loved, Jack felt his career had surely gone full circle.

And now, the early summer sun was reflecting off the white hull, varnished cabin and stainless fittings of his launch. Virtually identical to a standard police launch, this boat differed only in that it was diesel-electric and capable of running on either. At low power the engine only emitted a background rumble, but even that would be a seeming intrusion on this scene's timeless tranquillity. So Jack ran with the diesel shut down, ghosting along on just the electric motor with only the satisfying chuckle of the bow wave to compete with the odd cries of awakening wildlife. From its domain atop a channel marker, a grey heron, head retracted into its hunched shoulders, seemed to almost nod approval.

Others who would appreciate his silent passing were the occupants of boats anchored for the night. The first were coming abeam now, lying just outside the fairway with their bows facing south into the early flood tide. There were some motor cruisers and a traditional gaff-rigged yacht, but even the latter appeared modern compared to the boat lying apart and ghostlike at the north end of the broad.

This was *Raedwald*, a replica Anglo-Saxon galley whose lean clinker hull and single mast with its crossed yard and furled sail, produced a look very akin to a Viking longship. In fact, the period she represented predated the Norsemen by three centuries. She lay alongside a larger, luxurious motor cruiser, *Aethelberht*, whose lines were as modern and high-tech as her charge was basic. Jack knew these boats well. He also knew their owner, the man standing in the cruiser's bows beckoning him with lordly waves. It was Professor Rupert Stack.

THE ACADEMIC GLANCED AT his watch. 'What time are you supposed to pass through this broad, Fellows?'

Jack brought his launch alongside *Aethelberht*, climbed on board and secured his bow and stern lines. 'Whatever time I decide.' Jack never wasted words with Professor Stack, finding it increasingly difficult to ignore the academic's air of intellectual pomposity.

Tall, heavily built and with a derisive Oxford accent, Stack had been an eminent scholar in his day, a recognised authority on Anglo-Saxon history. In semi-retirement, he had conceived the project of *Aethelberht* as a floating museum to that period. Although he had an apartment-cum-office in the nearby town, Stack spent most of the summer months living aboard his boat. Thus, with an assortment of artefacts, he meandered his way around the rivers, opening his exhibition to the holidaying public at whatever location he decided to spend the night. *Aethelberht* was a popular attraction in spite of her custodian, for Stack's intellectual snobbery ensured that many innocent questions were met with ill-disguised arrogance and offhand condescension. Complaints from visitors of the professor's rudeness came regularly to Jack, but the exhibition was undoubtedly unique and the Ranger usually managed to smooth ruffled tourist feathers.

Raedwald was Stack's latest acquisition; built locally and a crowd-puller wherever the museum flotilla moored for the day. Jack always felt it a shame that that was her only function. He would have loved to have seen the galley's big red sail gliding over the reedbeds, but never did. Stack's finicky nature fell short of ever as much as unfurling it and his selfishness ensured no other was even offered the chance. From *Aethelberht's* foredeck, Jack looked down on the forty foot wooden replica. *Raedwald* was certainly an impressive vessel evoking a great sense of history, though her own was less than happy. Many locals swore she was cursed and with good reason. She had been lovingly built only the year before by local boatbuilder Alan Giller. Now Giller's Boatyard was no more and, sadly, neither was Alan Giller. Jack had heard all the local rumours on why Alan Giller had taken his own life but shook away bitter thoughts, glanced at his own watch and asked: 'What did you want to talk to me about, Professor?'

Stack scoffed. 'The usual, of course: that young hooligan, Morecroft.'

'Peter Morecroft, the eel-fisherman? What's your problem with him now?'

Stack's sneer was almost audible. 'The same as last time, of course: threatening behaviour.' He pointed a lecturing finger at Jack's face. 'I shouldn't have to tell an ex-constable like yourself, Fellows, that the moronic likes of Morecroft never bloody well change their ways. Well, now he's compounding his previous felony and I want something done about it.'

Jack ignored the deliberate demotion of his previous rank. 'What sort of threat is he making, Professor? Verbal? Physical?'

Jack Fellows was a tall man but Professor Stack was even taller and he drew himself up now into a stance he must have used many times to intimidate subordinates. 'You police like to compartmentalise everything don't you. Threats don't have to be corporeal or spoken, Fellows; Morecroft's are psychological.'

'In what way?'

'He anchors his boat close to mine at night and just sits there until the early hours trying to scare me.'

Jack shrugged. ' He's a licensed eel fisherman, Professor, and entitled to anchor his boat wherever he wants, just as long as he complies with the rules of the Navigation. If he isn't making any direct threats against your person, there's little the police or I can do.'

Stack gave an exasperated snort. 'Typical; here's a man who has already been convicted for making threats against my life and no-one seems prepared to act until the damn thug actually murders me.'

Jack shook his head, smiling. 'Don't exaggerate, Professor. Peter Morecroft never threatened you with murder. You gave evidence that sent him to prison. I should think his "milk of human kindness" towards you evaporated long ago.'

'Yes, I might have expected you to defend him.' Stack, with seemingly little effort, was at his most pompous. 'It amazes me, Fellows, that someone with so many years in the police can't recognise a bloody villain when he sees one.'

'It's instinct honed by that experience, Professor Stack, that tells me young Morecroft was wrongly accused.'

'Is that so. Well, take care, Fellows,' the academic leaned towards Jack, eyeing him now through narrowed lids, 'if you so much as insinuate I gave perjured evidence, I'll have your job.' He drew away with a mirthless smile. 'I'm not without influence as you know.'

Jack's eyes met Stack's with an unblinking resolve that had weakened many a villain's. 'Indeed I do, Stack, but those who know me think carefully before throwing out spineless threats.' He took a deep breath and five seconds to scan the early-morning beauty of the broad; this lovely part of creation wasn't the place for hostility. He turned back to the arrogant figure beside him. 'All right, Professor, I'll have a word with the lad and ask him to keep his distance.'

'Good.' Stack's own manner moderated to one of mock confidentiality. 'Security is very much on my mind right now as you can appreciate...' he gestured below with a nod of his head, '... with the artefacts I've got on board.'

'Ah yes, the brooches.' Jack remembered the media announcements of the previous week. Stack had managed to obtain, on loan from the British Museum, some extremely rare artefacts. 'Quite a coup, I should think, borrowing those for your exhibition.'

'It's who you know, old boy,' said Stack, tapping the side of his nose. 'A bit of influence here and the odd favour called in there. They trust me, you know.' The latter was said with sarcastic emphasis as he gestured below. 'Want to have a look at them?'

Accepting favours from a condescending martinet wasn't high on Jack's priorities but goods being carried on these waters was, and besides he was intrigued by the history of it all, so he simply nodded and followed Stack below.

Aethelberht was a fifty-foot single-decker with the aft companionway leading directly into the exhibition space. Here, rows of glass cases down each side and along the boat's centreline, contained a varied selection of Anglo-Saxon coins, earthenware, jewellery and weapons, all professionally labelled and catalogued. One case however, central in a place of honour, with toughened glass and heavy locks, was significantly empty.

'This is where the brooches are displayed,' said Stack with a casual wave of his hand, 'though, of course, they're not kept here overnight.' He continued through the exhibition area into his quarters, passing between galley, shower and heads into a large comfortably furnished saloon. For'ard, portside of the cabin area, was the pilot station with wheel, engine controls and instrumentation but it was the aft, starboard corner that drew Jack's attention. Here sat a small but compact safe. Pointedly shielding it from view by the bulk of his body, Stack spun the combination dial, turned a large lever and swung open the impressively heavy door. With surgical care, the historian drew out a covered tray, placed it on the saloon table behind him and unwrapped the cloth. In the early morning sunshine came the glint of sparkling gold. The two brooches lay there for Jack to see and he realised immediately how they had generated such intense local interest. They were truly beautiful and exquisitely crafted, one in the form of an inverted crucifix, the other fashioned like a small shield, both about the size of a human hand.

Jack gasped. 'My goodness; what's the story behind these?'

'They were recovered from an Anglo-Saxon cemetery excavated near here,' explained Stack, obviously keen to display his knowledge, 'buried with a lady of obvious wealth in about 700 AD. The cross is of a type known as Florid Cruciform. They were normally worn in a central showy position and made from bronze but this one is solid gold.'

'So I can see,' said Jack, whistling. 'How about the other?'

'It's what's known as a "composite disc brooch" probably made in Kent in about 610 - 650 AD, of gold also with the cross in its centre formed of gold cells or cloisonné that contain garnets.' Stack turned the brooch over. 'Rather interestingly, the name of the maker is actually inscribed on the back.'

Jack looked at the simple odd-shaped letters. 'Those are names?'

'Yes,' Stack gave a small condescending laugh, 'but in runic script. It was the alphabet of its day but the runes weren't just letters; each symbol had a name and special meaning.'

'I wonder how many times our ancestors fought and died over such precious possessions,' mused Jack. He turned to the tall figure hovering protectively behind him. 'Just as a matter of interest, how much is this lot worth?'

Stack closed his eyes and shook his head. 'In the archaeological world we never like to put things into monetary terms but the simple answer is…' he opened his eyes again and shrugged rounded shoulders, '… priceless.'

'And the British Museum were happy with you displaying their treasure on a boat?'

'Of course. They came and looked at my arrangements and were satisfied for me to have them for just one month. I never let the artefacts out of my sight when on display and they're in the safe when not. I live onboard so they're in my direct charge at all times. If the truth be known, they're probably more secure here with me than in some provincial museum.'

Jack wasn't so easily convinced. 'But you must leave the boat at times, if only to do a bit of shopping.'

'Only for short periods and then they're in here,' explained Stack, covering the brooches again and returning them to the safe.

The professor had seemed unduly secretive when first opening it and Jack was intrigued to know why. This time, over the historian's shoulder, he purposely glanced inside and saw piles of what were obviously very old silver coins. Unaware of Jack's scrutiny, Stack continued, '... however, just to be yet more secure, I'm not mooring alongside at night while I've got the brooches on board. Instead, I anchor out on the nearest broad, which is usually this one. So, Fellows,' the historian gave a disapproving frown as he slammed the safe door shut and spun the combination lock, 'you should well understand why I'm nervous of that reprobate Morecroft being near this boat at night.'

'When priceless gold is involved, everyone should be nervous,' said Jack, walking back into the exhibition space with Stack just behind him, 'but Peter Morecroft should be the least of your concerns. With the media coverage you got for that lot, there are plenty of real villains around probably planning some heist even as we speak.' He fixed Stack with a questioning eye. 'I just hope it's all worth it.'

'Indeed it is,' said Stack, gleefully. 'With all the publicity these brooches have brought I have a continuous queue of people through the boat.' He glanced again at his watch. 'Which reminds me I must be underway: I'm due at Potter Heigham Staithe by ten.'

Jack climbed down into his launch. 'With free mooring on most broads, anchoring nightly must save you some money too, Professor?'

Stack unhitched the launch's lines and handed them down to Jack. 'Yes, indeed, though I won't be paying for moorings much longer anyway because...' he pushed the launch off with his foot, '... I'm buying my own boatyard.'

The dawn had given way to day with a slight breeze ruffling the waters of the broad. Already, boats were on passage through the fairway and, with the silence gone until evening, Jack started his diesel, eased the throttle ahead and pulled away.

So, the professor was buying a boatyard, was he. Where did the man get his money and which boatyard was he buying? Jack deliberately hadn't asked but had a suspicion which he just as quickly dismissed. Even Rupert Stack wouldn't be that insensitive.

Chapter Two

THE TELEPHONE WAS RINGING as Charlotte Giller came into the cottage from her morning paper round. Boatyard Cottage was an unimaginative but appropriate name for her small thatched home, snuggled as it was into one corner of the boatyard. Charlotte kicked off her shoes and padded into the small room at the cottage's rear that had once served as the boatyard office. It seemed a long time now since a ringing phone had carried the excitement of orders for the boat business she and Alan had run together. These lonely days the calls could only be for her and they were invariably bad. This morning's was no exception.

'Is that Mrs. Giller?' said the female voice at the other end. The tone was businesslike but not without an edge of sympathy. 'This is Gwen Fosdyke here, Mrs. Giller.'

Charlotte's sense of despair deepened. Gwen Fosdyke was a local solicitor, practising in the small market town just a few miles up river. She was also District Councillor and the appointed Receiver for the bankruptcy of Giller's Boatyard. Still handsome in late middle-age, she was one of those rare people who combined competency and professionalism with an empathy for those less fortunate than herself. It was a gift that had won her constant re-election over the years, but Charlotte's own relationship with the councillor was less than happy, for Gwen Fosdyke was now winding up a dream that had taken her and Alan a decade to build.

She swallowed hard and said, 'Hello, Miss Fosdyke.'

'How are you, Charlotte?' Gwen Fosdyke's voice was calming which Charlotte knew from experience meant she was being prepared for bad news.

'Oh... okay... as well as can be expected.'

'I know; it can't be easy.' The solicitor cleared her throat.

'Charlotte, as you know, the court has authorised the liquidation of your assets to pay off the creditors of Giller's Boatyard. The main asset, of course, is the yard itself and I'm calling to inform you that a buyer has now been found.'

'Oh…' Charlotte gripped the handset and with it, her emotions, ' … so soon.'

'Yes, I'm afraid so. Not having planning permission for further residential building, I rather thought the yard would take some moving but we now have a buyer wanting immediate purchase.'

'My goodness.' Charlotte knew of one local boatbuilder keen to buy this run-down yard nestling just off the main river. There was hope in her voice when she asked, 'Who is this buyer, Miss Fosdyke?'

Even a lawyer as experienced as Gwen Fosdyke seemed to have difficulty finding the right words. 'Charlotte, I know you're not going to like this but…'

'Miss Fosdyke…' Charlotte could hear her own voice rising, '… you're not going to tell me... it isn't…?'

'Yes, I'm afraid it's Professor Stack.'

'Oh God.' Charlotte tried, unsuccessfully, to stifle some tears. 'Miss Fosdyke, how could you… knowing the circumstances of all this?'

'Charlotte, try and pull yourself together.' Gwen Fosdyke felt for the young widow but her sympathy now was edged with authority. 'You must realise that Receivers have no option but to accept the highest bid. Professor Stack's offer wasn't particularly great but better than the others which were pretty derisory. Added to that, he's offering a cash deal which means we can clear the sale very quickly.'

'How quickly?'

'Exchanging contracts in about a week and finalising in ten days.'

Charlotte sighed. 'You seem to have it all worked out with me just an inconvenience in the middle. Miss Fosdyke, that man destroyed our lives. How can you expect me to live here and have daily contact with him?'

'Ah, that brings me to another point, I'm afraid.'

'Which is…?' Charlotte was back in control now.

'That Boatyard Cottage is an integral part of the assets and therefore to be sold with the rest of the estate.'

Charlotte could sense what was coming even though this whole conversation was tinged now with an aura of disbelief. 'Miss Fosdyke, when the bank foreclosed on the yard they allowed me to stay in the cottage. I pay my rent every month. Are you telling me I'm going to have to…?'

'… vacate? Yes, I'm afraid you are.' Gwen Fosdyke knew she was giving the knife an extra twist and hating herself for it but she pressed on, 'Professor Stack wants Boatyard Cottage for himself,

Charlotte, and is therefore giving you notice to leave.'

'But this is our… I mean *my* home.' Charlotte's words barely ascended her despair.

'I know, Charlotte, but that's how it is.' Gwen Fosdyke was keen now to wind up this painful conversation. 'The District Council helps anyone with housing difficulties, Charlotte. If you like I'll send you a form.'

'Playing the helpful councillor now, are we?' Charlotte's anguish was giving way to bitterness. 'I don't want your charity, Miss Fosdyke.'

'It isn't charity, it's what you're entitled to.' Gwen Fosdyke gave a genuine sigh. 'I'm only trying to help, Charlotte.'

'Yes, well I've had as much help as I can take these last few months.' Charlotte slammed down the phone, sat looking at the home she loved and was now about to lose, and collapsed into uncontrollable sobbing.

GWEN FOSDYKE REPLACED HER receiver. Many wondered why, as a woman qualified in both law and accountancy, she continued to practice in such a small Norfolk market town. The answer was her affinity with the Broads where, as a girl, she had grown up messing about in boats and walking the lonely marshes. Even in her teens, while friends were busy dating the local talent, Gwen preferred to be alone amongst the reedbeds, studying the ways of nature and forming an undying love for creation. Part of her would have loved to be a naturalist but her solicitor father had other plans for his only child, and so it was to Cambridge for a First in Law before Gwen returned to the family practice and her beloved Broadland.

As a country solicitor, Gwen could well have relaxed on her laurels as she conveyed properties and settled the seemingly endless list of divorce proceedings. Perhaps it was seeing first hand the pain and bitterness generated by the latter that drove her to shun personal relationships of her own. Instead, she poured all her considerable energy into her work and when the financial side of litigation assumed an ever more important part, studied accountancy and gained another degree. The result was a woman uniquely qualified, maturely handsome and desperately alone.

That sense of loneliness became all the more acute on the death of her beloved father. Gwen inherited the legal practice together with her father's integrity and sense of values, taking it to ever greater respect and prosperity. That alone would have been enough for most professional achievers but in her exposure to the day to day problems of others, Gwen recognised many social ills requiring urgent cure. To that end, and perhaps as a way of compensating for her empty private life, she secured election to the local council and was instrumental in expanding existing and even establishing new services to help the more vulnerable of her electorate. It won her the love and respect of many and brought a new sense of purpose to her life. It also brought emotions of which she was blissfully unaware when, in the course of her work, she had met a man and fallen hopelessly in love.

At an age when thoughts of romance and passion were as unexpected as they were exhilarating, Gwen chose to keep her romance a secret. That a special person should come into her life and bring a level of personal joy and happiness beyond her dreams, was something for which she was totally unprepared. Even more surprising was the uncomfortable realisation that for the first time ever, she was emotionally out of control. Suddenly, after a life of rigid adherence to principles, she found herself prepared to sacrifice anything, even her own integrity, for the man she loved. Rupert Stack was certainly a man well versed in using the love of a woman to his own advantage and Gwen's romance was only months old when he made his first demand.

She had never wanted the job of Receiver of Giller's Boatyard. Gwen knew and liked Alan and Charlotte Giller and liquidating the young couple's dreams seemed almost an act of vandalism. Then had come Alan's suicide adding an aura of personal tragedy to what was already a distasteful duty. It was when events were at their most distressing that Rupert Stack suggested she use her position and declare his offer for Giller's Yard as the highest bid. In reality, his bid was the lowest and faking the result would secure the property at rock-bottom price. Gwen could imagine her father turning in his grave at the hint of such corruption, but she had gone ahead and done it anyway. In her helpless infatuation, the love of her man overrode all ethical considerations. He needed her help and she gave it just as willingly as her body. Someday soon, they would marry and all this duplicity would be worthwhile, especially as yet another exciting dimension was surfacing in her already-convoluted life.

It was at a council reception that the local head of a political party selection committee had approached her. Would she like to be considered for parliamentary selection?

She would indeed. Gwen Fosdyke, Member of Parliament; how good that sounded but could she really achieve such a goal? The committee had no doubt she could: her standing locally was such that she was virtually assured of election. As new ambitions stirred within her, a sense of purpose took hold, a growing conviction that Westminster had always been her destiny. All the local projects she had pushed through had been models of their kind. She had achieved so much for those in need in her District; how much more could she do at a national level? Months ago she could have sat before the selection committee with a clear conscience, but in the interim a whole family of skeletons had settled in Gwen's professional cupboard. Would they ever see the light of day? The overall good demanded they never should.

JACK FELLOWS CAME ACROSS Peter Morecroft and his boats just a mile further upriver. The old wooden cruiser was moored to the river bank, looking very much the worse for wear, with the camouflaged dory that Peter used for his eel fishing, tied alongside. From the blackened stack on the cruiser's for'ard cabin, an oily column of smoke rose in the still air, its purpose explained by cheerful words from the stocky figure with a shaven head who'd just appeared in the cockpit.

'Mornin', Mr. Fellows. Just cookin' breakfast. Want some?'

The Ranger smiled as he climbed aboard. 'No thanks, already had some.' Jack knew what that breakfast would be and fried eels, even fresh ones caught just hours before, were a delicacy he found easy to forego. Pete would have been up since sunset, having baited and re-laid his long line of fyke nets, tended them through the night and then hauled and emptied his catch at dawn. It was a way of life that had been enacted in Broadland for ten centuries, a lonely unique life only followed by a hardy few. Jack gestured below. 'I'd like a chat though, Pete, if that's okay?'

'No problem, Mr Fellows. Come you on down.'

Peter Morecroft's accommodation could only be described as squalid, a floating tip where the odour of unwashed clothing and damp woodwork fought a constant battle for supremacy over the stench of raw bait and the aroma of fried eel. This morning, the latter seemed to be winning with a frying pan of the stuff lying half-eaten on the cabin table. Pete gestured Jack onto the couch opposite and nodded towards the kettle steaming on the stove. 'Coffee, Mr Fellows?'

Jack glanced at the chipped and stained mugs hanging overhead. 'Er, no thanks, Pete.' He nodded to the dory lying alongside and the black plastic dustbins containing live eels. 'How's trade these days?'

'Pretty good.' The fisherman dug back into his breakfast with enthusiasm. 'Had a good catch las' night with so little moon. I'll be takin' 'em in af'er breakfast to meet the chap from Hull who sells 'em to the Dutchies.' He tapped the small grubby cashbook beside him. 'Should be able to pay yer back some more at the end of the month, Mr. Fellows.'

'Don't worry about that, Pete. When you can.' Jack leaned closer to emphasise a change in subject. 'Pete, I've had a complaint from Professor Stack.'

Peter Morecroft's fork paused midway to his mouth. 'That bastard…' he laid the frying pan down on the table between them, '… wha's 'is problem now?'

'He says you're mooring close to him at night which he regards as intimidation.'

The eel-fisherman picked up the pan again and restarted his breakfast, avoiding Jack's eyes. 'Yeah, well if he feel threatened, so he should. I won't forgit what he done to me.'

Jack sighed. 'Pete, I told you to forget the past and keep well clear of Stack. You're right; the man is arrogant and got you into trouble, but promoting another confrontation with him will only see you come off second best, believe me. You've got your business here…' Jack swept his hand over the battered boats that were the young man's life, '… don't do something silly and lose it.'

Eels despatched, Peter tossed his greasy pan into the sink. 'Mr. Fellows, that bastard lied 'bout me in court and got me thirty days. Don't you think I'm 'titled to feel bitter?'

'Of course, Pete, but violence won't solve anything.'

'I didn't say nothin' 'bout violence.' The fisherman shook his head. 'I ain't sayin' I wouldn't like to re-arrange the bastard's face, but there's more than one way to skin an eel ain't there, Mr. Fellows?'

'Such as?'

'Such as gettin' somethin' on 'im that I can go to the coppers with.'

'Get something on Stack?' It was Jack's turn to smile. 'Pete, the man's a respected academic. His conduct and personality might leave something to be desired but that doesn't make him a villain. What on earth do you think you can "get" on him?'

Peter Morecroft shook his head again. 'I can't put me finger on it, Mr. Fellows, but somethin' tell me that man ain't up to no good. Tha's just a feelin' I 'ave. That museum business he run can't make many quid but now word is e's put in a bid for Giller's.'

'Giller's Boatyard?' Jack's worst thoughts had just been put into words. 'Pete, are you sure?'

'Tha's the word goin' round.' Peter Morecroft shrugged. 'That ain't right is it, Mr Fellows? He kill poor old Alan and then tries to git 'is yard.'

'Pete, you can't say that. Alan Giller took his own life when his yard went bankrupt.'

'Yeah, 'cause Stack din't pay him for that ol' galley … wha's it called? … *Raedwald*…' replied Peter, feelingly, '… 'ung back on coughin' up, he did, till the banks closed in an' we know what 'appened then… poor Alan went an' 'ung 'isself in 'is boatshed, an' all 'cos of Stack … bastard.'

Jack nodded. 'You're right Pete; if those rumours are only half-true, it would be a gross injustice if the Professor did get Giller's…' he nodded towards the unseen broad, '… but you think he's up to other shenanigans. Doing what, exactly?'

Peter Morecroft shook his head again. 'Like I says, Mr Fellows, I dunno…' he leaned forward conspiratorially, '… But what I do knows is, some strange bloke visit 'is boat every once an' a while at right odd hours.'

Once again, Jack felt his policeman's instincts surfacing. 'What sort of man, Pete; when and where?'

'Only when 'e's moored up at lonely places, by boat usually.'

Jack shrugged. 'Just a boating friend, probably, paying him a visit.'

'Wha', at two in the mornin'?' Peter tapped the table with his finger. 'An' 'e ain't the boatin' sort, Mr. Fellows. More like a suit type what don't like bein' out on the water one bit. And why do 'e only come when Stack's moored in some lonely spot? If 'e's legit', 'e could easier come when 'is nib's moored at some staithe.'

'So that's why you moor near Stack's boats at night: to try and suss what's happening?'

The fisherman nodded. 'Yep, and one night I'll git somethin' on 'im tha'll git 'im locked up.' He sat back, smiling. 'Then we'll see how 'e like doin' a bitta time.'

Jack got up to leave. 'Well, just make sure you stay within the law, Pete. No direct confrontation. I won't bail you out a second time.'

Peter followed him up the companionway onto the deck. 'Don't you worries, Mr. Fellows, I won't let you down.' He glanced around his boats. 'I owe all this to you, Mr Fellows, gettin' me licence back an' these boats, and I'll never forgit it.'

Jack slapped him on the back. 'You had a raw deal, Pete, and I was glad to help make amends. Don't throw it away.'

As he motored further upriver, the Ranger glanced back at the stocky figure preparing to move his boats. A good hard-worker was Peter Morecroft, though Jack had grave misgivings about the lad's new role as a sleuth.

PETER MORECROFT WASN'T THE only hard-worker that summer's morning, enjoying his breakfast as a reward for honest toil. Just a few miles downriver, in his marshman's cottage, Walter Giller pushed away his plate, stretched his legs under the heavy kitchen table and poured himself another cup of tea. Working these local marshes was something Walter had done since boyhood with his father before him. In those days a small army of marshmen had "drawn" dykes, mended walls, mowed marsh hay, shot wildfowl, fished the rivers and harvested reed and sedge. Now Walter was one of a dwindling breed of men who spent their working days in this singular trade. There had been attempts to train youngsters to follow on and most had enjoyed working the marshes in summer sunshine. Come the winter, however, wading knee-deep in icy water and cutting reed in a searing easterly, not one had stayed the course. Even his son Alan, had chosen an apprenticeship in boatbuilding rather than follow his dad onto the marshes, but in this Walter was pleased. Alan had become a first class boatbuilder and the owner of his own yard. With a lovely wife in Charlotte and plans to start a family, the future had looked so fair. And then…

A widower for three years, Walter never thought he would be glad his beloved wife was dead but, in these last few months, he had been only too thankful she was at peace in her grave rather than know the agony of losing an only son. As a lump formed in Walter's throat, he stood up from the table, grabbed his wax jacket from its hook behind the door and strode out towards the only antidote he knew to the emotional pain that so often welled inside him.

Out on his beloved marshes, the morning sun was slowly rising, dissipating the thin layer of mist that hung like a gossamer veil in the first light of dawn. From somewhere deep in the reed beds came the boom of a bittern, whilst in the dyke a line of small bubbles showed the progress of an otter returning to its secret holt. Here, alone, Walter swallowed hard, trying to contain his grief and knowing he must stay strong for Charlotte.

She had been the perfect wife for Alan, a girl who combined prettiness with loyalty and a determination to make their little business work. And it had been working until… Walter felt his sadness being replaced by the ever more corrosive emotion of bitterness. He tried to shake it away and as he did so, his mobile phone rang.

'Pops…. Is that you?' The words were forced out between half-suppressed sobs but he recognised her voice immediately.

'Charlotte, darlin'; wha's wrong. You sound right upset?'

She gulped hard. 'Pops, it's the cottage…they're going to throw me out.'

'Who is? What you talkin' 'bout, gal?'

'Professor Stack, Pops…' a heartfelt sob broke from Charlotte's throat, '…he's bought the yard.'

Walter Giller stood in shocked silence, his voice stilled and the hand holding his mobile shaking uncontrollably. Charlotte's voice came again, startling him back into consciousness.

'Pops…Pops... are you still there?'

He shook himself and blinked hard, his eyes staring into the middle distance. 'Yeah, still here, Charlotte.' His voice was quiet, steady and seemingly without emotion. 'Jus' you stay calm, gal, and don't you worry; tha's time this were sorted once and for all.'

Before Charlotte could reply he switched off the phone, took another look out over his beloved marshes and walked slowly back to the cottage.

CRUISING THE RIVER BURE towards Potter Heigham, Rupert Stack rang a named number on his mobile phone. It was answered by a familiar female voice.

'Gwen Fosdyke.'

'Gwen my dear, how's my favourite solicitor?… good…good… So the whole deal will be completed in just over a week?… excellent…and you've given that Giller girl notice to quit at the same time?'

On the other end, Gwen closed her eyes. 'I'm just not happy with evicting that poor girl. She's been through hell already and…'

But Stack cut her off in mid-sentence with a laugh. 'My dear Gwen, you really must do something about that soft spot of yours. Instead of worrying about some insignificant little widow, you need to be applying that intellect of yours to the question of planning permission.'

'What planning permission?'

'Permission for me to develop Giller's Boatyard.'

The background rumble of *Aethelberht's* diesel seemed almost the toll of doom to Gwen as she listened to Stack's words.

'But there can never be development of Giller's Boatyard. You knew that when you made your bid.'

'Of course I did, Gwendoline, but you are a respected District Councillor; you are in the unique position to make these things happen.'

'I've compromised my professional reputation and my own self-respect to get you Giller's Yard...' Gwen felt despair creeping over her like an insidious cloud, '...now you want me to betray my trust with the council. I can't. I...'

'Yes you can, dear Gwen, and you will.' Without further discussion, Stack switched off his mobile.

For the second time that morning, Gwen realised she'd been cut off. Was there anything, she wondered as she lowered her head into her hands, that a woman wouldn't do for the man she loved.

IT WAS NEARING MIDDAY when Jack's patrol took him past The Hall. The morning had been reasonably uneventful since his encounter with Professor Stack and chat with Peter Morecroft. Two speeding cruisers had needed attention after logging more than the stipulated five mph limit on the radar gun. Excessive speed on these narrow rivers meant increased wash which in turn led to bank erosion. A friendly chat with the speeding skippers had been enough to show them the error of their ways. If caught again they would get written warnings which they would do well to heed: a third meant court and a hefty fine. Apart from them and a day-boat on the wrong side of the river, the morning had given him plenty of time for contemplation on the problem of Professor Stack.

In all honesty, Jack had been hoping he wouldn't have time to think about the arrogant historian. Stack's exhibition and replica boat were certainly a fascinating attraction for visitors but the man himself seemed to go out of his way to hurt and offend others. His purchase of

Giller's Yard was bound to cause extreme ill will amongst locals and the on-going feud with Peter Morecroft wouldn't help. Deep down, Jack's instinct warned him that things would surely get worse before they got better. He felt the need to talk it over and so, as he approached The Hall, he was pleased to see Colonel Etherington just mooring his launch. Turning into the stream, he came alongside and leaned out of the wheelhouse window.

'Morning, Colonel.'

Colonel William Etherington looked up from tying *Goosewatcher's* stern-line. Long retired from the army where he had commanded the jungle warfare school, his tall slim frame still retained a regimental bearing and the smile below his clipped moustache was all the more sincere for its sparing use. 'Oh, morning Fellows…' he nodded to the quay just astern, '… tie up old chap and have a chat.'

Jack willingly complied: it was good to stretch his legs, especially in the company of this urbane, if slightly buffoonish, man. The old soldier had bought The Hall ten years previously and spent a small fortune with local tradesmen restoring the Tudor building. That and many other good works endeared him to the parish and established him, in everything but heredity, as the squire. After securing his own launch, Jack nodded down at the shining varnish and gleaming brasswork of the colonel's. 'She looks good, Colonel.'

Goosewatcher was Colonel Etherington's pride and joy, a vintage wooden slipper that had been bought in total disrepair off the Thames some years previous and lovingly restored by Alan Giller. Jack had never dared ask what that restoration had cost but the result was certainly a joy to behold. Colonel Etherington smoothed back his hair and nodded.

'Yes, young Giller did a fine job of restoring her.' He glanced back downriver in the direction of the yard. 'Damn shame that lad had to go top himself.'

'A shame indeed.' The colonel's remarks gave Jack an opening and he took it. 'I expect you've heard that Professor Stack has put in a bid for his yard.'

'I've heard rumours,' said Colonel Etherington, scathingly. 'Let's hope the blackguard doesn't get it. Of all the people who shouldn't benefit from poor young Giller's demise it's that ass, Stack.'

'You're not the first person to say that this morning.' Jack liked Colonel Etherington. In spite of his almost-eighty years and accompanying vagueness, there was not a lot happening in the parish that the old soldier didn't know about. Perhaps he even knew the answer to Jack's next question. 'Where has the man suddenly found the money to bid for boatyards, Colonel? If he hadn't enough to pay Alan Giller for his galley, how come he's so flush now?'

'But that's the point, Fellows: the damned man did have the money to pay young Giller.' The Colonel shook his head sadly. 'When a year back he decided to have that replica galley thing built to add to his exhibition, he got a fortune for the project from some regional development grant scheme.' Colonel Etherington's neck reddened visibly. 'Don't go much for all these grants misself, Fellows. Too many chappies taking advantage of them at the taxpayer's expense, if you ask me. Time was when a man had to earn…'

'So, Stack had the funding, reneged on poor Alan, and instead will use the money…'

'... to buy the yard he wanted in the first place.' The Colonel paused just long enough to fix Jack with narrowed eyes, 'Let's hope someone outbids the scheming blighter, heh, Fellows.'

Amen to that, thought Jack but didn't say. Instead he nodded upriver. 'Still a few miles to go so I'd better away.' He paused in climbing back aboard the patrol launch.

'If all this annoys us, Colonel, it must be sheer horror to Mrs. Giller. She still lives in the cottage doesn't she?'

'Indeed she does.' The Colonel cast off Jack's lines and handed them across. 'Poor girl, she must be in despair.'

Bringing despair to people's lives seemed almost a fetish for Rupert Stack, thought Jack as he motored away and headed further upriver.

Chapter Three

AT POTTER HEIGHAM, the man himself was putting up a *CLOSED FOR LUNCH* sign and easing his irritation with a glass of claret. The busy riverside village was full of visitors this sunny day and most, at some stage, had come to see the two strange boats moored at the staithe. *Raedwald,* with her ancient Anglo-Saxon lines and sense of living history, had attracted casual onlookers but it was *Aethelberht* and her golden brooches that had drawn the more serious observers.

A steady accumulation of three pound entrance fees should have put Professor Stack in a more amenable frame of mind. Instead, the endless repetition of, to him, inane questions had long since stretched his ever-vaporous patience to its already-inadequate limit. After unceremoniously ejecting a little girl for bringing her ice-cream onboard and having a confrontation with her incensed father, he'd shooed out his remaining punters, locked the doors and poured himself a glass of Margaux. He was about to treat himself to a second when Lisa Thornton's Range Rover appeared on the quay alongside.

Lisa was Stack's secretary and general assistant. Her base was the Professor's apartment in the town but most days she had to visit the boats with anything needing her boss's attention. This could be a variety of general admin but mainly it was Lisa herself. As she stepped onboard *Aethelbehrt* with an armful of folders and mail, her appearance was businesslike indeed, unlike her behaviour which was anything but.

'Hi, Darling…' she threw most of the files onto the saloon couch, holding onto just one letter as she put her arms around the neck of the historian, who had paused in filling his wine glass, '… how are things in the Anglo-Saxon world?'

Stack continued filling his glass with one free arm.

'Barely endurable, having to face, as I do, the mediocrity of the tedious British Public. You know how it is.'

Indeed she did, for Lisa shared Stack's pretentious outlook on life, a fact which may have influenced her employment, though an ill-disguised sexuality was the more likely. Never married himself, Stack's predilection had always been for women who were, and Lisa's employee relationship had quickly been subjugated into one far more intimate. For her part, a twenty-year age gap could be ignored as easily as her marriage vows, especially with a self-assured man whose expectations carried the sparkle of gold.

Lisa smiled and waved a letter in front of Stack's face, 'Never mind, darling, here's something that will cheer you up: confirmation that they are about to exchange contracts on Giller's Boatyard.' She tossed it onto the saloon table. 'It's almost ours.'

'Yes, I know; Gwen Fosdyke has already told me.' Stack never liked his secretary to feel she was ahead of him in knowledge and even less, her phraseology. 'I trust you use the word "ours" corporately rather than personally.'

Lisa drew back slightly, suspicion clouding features that had taken a full half-hour to make up that morning. 'I mean *ours* as in *us*, Rupert.' She ran a distracted hand through blonde hair faintly betraying darker roots beneath. 'I assumed you were having that Charlotte Giller ejected from Boatyard Cottage so we could live there together.'

'Well, my dear girl, you assumed wrong.' Stack poured a glass of the Margaux for his secretary and handed it to her. 'We've had some fun together, dearest, but not for one instant was there ever any intention on my part that it should be anything other than that.'

'But you told me… I thought we…' Lisa wiped away a tear and with it a good smear of eye-shadow as she ignored the offered wine and slumped onto the saloon couch.

'Rupert, you don't understand…' the eyes now fixing Stack's were at their most appealing, '… I had the most dreadful row with Stuart last night. He challenged me about us and … well, it just all came out. Darling…' she stood up again and edging close to the Professor, took the glass of wine and flicked her long lashes, '… I've moved out, Rupert; I've left him.' She pressed her body close against Stack's. 'Don't you understand, darling, I want to be with you.'

'You told him about us?' Stack stepped back a pace and gave a disgusted snort. 'That idiot husband of yours might waste his life painting silly little pictures in that dump of a mill, but this could seriously jeopardise the little business arrangement we have going.' The Professor slammed his glass down so hard on the saloon table that the stem broke, 'You stupid girl. Have you no idea of the vindictiveness of a jealous husband. It would only need him to start shooting his mouth off to have us both in gaol.'

Lisa jumped, startled at her boss's flash of temper but it served to knock her out of self-pity. She shook her head. 'Is that all you can think of, Rupert? How my leaving Stuart might upset the neat little scam that I…' she pointed to her own breast with a shaking finger, '…made possible for you.' The finger now pointed straight at Stack. 'You think more of money than you do of me.'

The Professor gave a short laugh. 'How right you are, dear girl.' He took out a spotted handkerchief and wiped away some wine that had splashed his designer shirt. 'You're bloody good at sex, Mrs Thornton, but that's all.' He stuffed the handkerchief foppishly into his breast pocket. 'I have big plans and I don't intend the ire of a scorned husband to complicate them. I think it best that our relationship terminates right now. Put more bluntly, Mrs Thornton, I want you out of my life.'

'Out… out of your life…' Lisa felt a mixture of anger and panic colliding in her throat. 'Are you telling me that, homeless and penniless, I'm now fired from my job as well as emotionally dumped?'

Stack nodded. "Fraid so, old girl.' He shrugged and picked up the formal letter from Gwen Fosdyke relating to Giller's Yard and scanned it absently. 'Future developments are very promising…' he tossed the letter back onto the table, '… but they don't include you.'

'It's her, dammit.' Lisa pointed distractedly at the letter in Stack's hand. 'It's that solicitor woman, Fosdyke, isn't it?' Lisa's trembling voice and narrowing eyes betrayed the struggle to find words rather than tears. 'I know you two have worked some shenanigans over that yard purchase. She's of more use than me now so I'm dumped, am I? Damn you!'

Stack shrugged. 'I couldn't have put it better myself.'

'But… but…' Lisa stumbled for words, '... we have a business arrangement.'

'My dear girl...' Stack laughed in his secretary's face, '... I know the source of your little merchandise and the time is well nigh for me to eliminate the middle man… or woman… from the whole equation.' He waved dismissively. It's all been very profitable to me but without you it will be more lucrative yet.'

Lisa visibly bristled. 'So that's it is it? Finished. Out.' Again, she pointed a shaking finger at Stack's face. 'Well, you won't get rid of me that easily, Professor-o-so-clever-Stack. I'm sure the police would love to know all the details of the little game we've been playing.'

'Would they indeed.' Stack smiled a mirthless smile. 'Well, in that regard, I rather think my tracks are covered somewhat better than yours, Mrs Thornton.' It was his turn to point a finger. 'Believe me, dear girl, any evidence of our transactions go no further than Wyford's Mill. That dim husband of yours might not realise what's going on with his wife or his paintings, but that won't save him if you so much as breathe a word to the authorities. Unless you're both partial to prison food, I suggest you keep your mouth shut.'

'Bastard!' Lisa spat the word out with almost the same velocity as the wine she threw in Stack's face. She searched for other words but none came. Instead she followed the wine with the glass itself but Stack ducked in time, allowing it to fly past into the aft bulkhead where it shattered like so many of Lisa's dreams. In a final burst of sobbing she turned on her heel, stormed off the boat and, with wheels spinning quayside gravel into *Aethelberht's* side, roared off in her Range Rover to she-knew-not-where.

Stack watched her go. The only regret he felt was that he'd said she was good at sex. Actually, he was as indifferent to that as he was her feelings. He went aft into the exhibition area and picked up one of the gold brooches. Things were going even better than he'd planned.

AS THE PATROL LAUNCH turned within the shadow of Wyford's Mill, Stuart Thornton returned Jack's friendly wave. His studio atop the old drainage mill provided a wonderful vista over marsh and river and usually, whenever Stuart saw the patrol launch approaching, he would run three floors down and be out waiting on his quayside by the time it arrived. Escaping the confines of his studio for a chat with Jack Fellows was always a high point in Stuart Thornton's day. The genial Ranger invariably had a story from his varied past and always a sincere interest in progress on the artist's latest painting. But today Stuart Thornton stayed up in his studio and wanted conversation with no-one at all.

Last night had seen a blazing row with his wife, Lisa. For months he had suspected she was having an affair with Professor Stack but Lisa had always denied it in that brazen, rather hard way of hers. But yesterday, over supper, a small disagreement had turned to altercation and that to anger. Finally, all had given way to bitterness fuelled by his own suppressed jealousy for a wife he both loved and despised.

He and Lisa had been married fifteen years and he tried to recall at what stage love and passion had turned to contempt and derision. They had met when he was a struggling young artist trying to establish his style and a living. He was experimenting between landscapes and human form and she had answered his advertisement for a model. Perhaps a willingness to remove clothes for money wasn't the best qualification for a future wife but he had fallen head over heels in love with the voluptuous brunette with a penchant for the more physical side of life.

Had she ever loved him? She had said she did, but in the back of Stuart's mind was always the suspicion that it was his semi-bohemian lifestyle that had attracted her rather than he as a person. Whatever; they had married and enjoyed several blissful years of shared endeavour as he established himself as a landscape painter of Broadland and enjoyed the rewards his talent brought. Lisa had no artistic ability of her own but he had always been the first to admit that much of his success was due to her. Whereas he was a shy, perhaps even brooding creative artist who never self-promoted, Lisa had been the one at exhibitions who, with persuasion and not a little flirting, had got the gallery owners to look at his work and give him a chance. The result had been paintings selling for quite healthy prices; not enough to make them rich but at least sufficient to sustain a modest living.

That was probably where the rot had set into their marriage. While he had been content to walk the rivers and marshes with his sketchpad, feeling his next work gradually forming within, Lisa had wanted the big-time and a break into the London market. The more he resisted, the more she accused him of lack of ambition. On the pretext of visiting galleries throughout the country, she started spending more and more time away. Certainly paintings were selling and she was driving him to more work than he wanted, but he also suspected that many of these absent nights were not spent alone and only began when she got this job with Professor Stack.

Lisa had said she needed a new challenge, to establish a career and income of her own. Becoming a part-time personal assistant to a renowned historian had seemed the perfect opportunity, but soon Stuart had become aware of disturbing changes in his wife's behaviour. Lisa had always been opinionated but within weeks of starting with Stack, she had turned downright bigoted. At the same time, she had spent longer and longer periods away from Wyford's

Mill. She blamed this on an ever-increasing workload and gave the same excuse for a corresponding reduction in their sex life. At first, Stuart had chosen … wanted… to believe her but eventually, in spite of her denials, he was certain she was having an affair. He had met Professor Stack early on in her employment and disliked the man on sight. Inevitably, dislike had turned to hatred. Just the thought of that arrogant academic's hands on Lisa, had been enough to drive Stuart into paroxysms of jealousy and despair. Now the worst had happened and she'd left him and he knew it was for Stack. With agonies of bitterness and betrayal welling from within, Stuart struggled to keep control. Shaking his head, he dragged himself away from this precipice of misery with the only antidote he knew: his work.

In the centre of the studio, a half-complete work in oils faced him. It was a standard Broadland scene of the style that had made his reputation: tranquil waters, big skies, a trading wherry with its huge black sail gliding into a glorious sunset. He picked up his brush and pallet, tried a few strokes and just as quickly put them down again.

There had been a time when his every painting had been a creation, an extension of his soul. Now his work seemed more like a factory production line. Lisa had somehow negotiated deals that demanded a constant flow of his landscapes and he had to provide. Inevitably he felt trapped into just the way of life he had always dreaded. With constant demands to increase output he started to feel even his love of art diminishing, but the money had to keep flowing if only to pay for the mill.

Ah! the mill. It was Lisa who had talked him into buying Wyford's Mill several years ago. It was the perfect image, she had convincingly argued, for a man destined to become a master. There was no doubting that the old mill, lying as it did on a bend in the river with stunning views over the marshes, was an idyllic setting for creation. Unfortunately, Lisa's penchant for luxury had driven plans for its conversion into the realms of fantasy and the cost ever-skywards. His studio, here at the very top, had been the most ambitious part of all, the whole of the old wooden cap being removed and replaced by this all-glass structure that gave the renovated Wyford's Mill more the look of a lighthouse than a traditional Broadland drainage mill. There had been outcries from many locals at first but over the years, helped by Stuart's friendly nature and the interest he brought to the locality, it had become an accepted part of the scene. Even Stuart, in spite of the millstone it metaphorically hung around his neck, had grown to love the old structure and the charm it seemingly oozed. Now, in these last few months, he had grown to hate it as the setting for so much anguish. He pulled a cover over the painting and slowly made his way down the stairs into their bedroom.

He gazed absently around the circular room with its bare brick walls and small windows, the pine bed and colourful duvet. Much of the wall-space was taken up by Lisa's ample wardrobe. Stuart took down one of her dresses, a favourite of his that had shown off his wife's curving figure to perfection. From its silken folds, the aroma of Lisa's perfume flowed out to tease his senses and with it came the far deeper, unutterably desolate sense of her loss. Still gripping the dress with fingers white with anger, Stuart Thornton rolled onto the matrimonial bed and sobbed his broken heart out.

'MMMMM, SOMETHING SMELLS GOOD,' said Jack, following the tantalising aroma of home-baking into the kitchen and reaching for one of the scones his wife was just removing from the oven.

'No you don't,' said Audrey, just as quickly removing them from arm's reach, 'these are for the church coffee morning; they're Reverend Jamieson's favourites.'

Audrey Fellows was warden of St Cuthbert's Church in the village, a demanding duty that her husband tried to help with in any way he could. In all honesty, Jack couldn't be described as a "pillar of the church" but he was definitely a "buttress" who regularly supported it from the outside. Audrey accepted this of a man far more Christian than many a regular worshipper. Placing the tray on the large kitchen table, she smiled impishly. 'All right, just one and not too much butter.'

'Cruel woman; I don't know why I love you,' declared Jack, settling into his chair, feigning hardship but secretly pleased his wife was keeping better tabs on his waistline than he was. 'How about some jam?'

'Just a little.' After thirty-seven years of marriage, Audrey had lost none of the prettiness that had first caught the eye of the young copper all those years before and still managed to balance common-sense with an infinite fund of tender care. 'And I'll make you a nice cup of tea to go with it.'

'Thanks, love...' Jack swallowed his last mouthful of scone, '... I need it.'

'Oh dear,' Audrey poured tea into Jack's favourite cup and handed it across before sitting down opposite her husband, 'bad day?'

'Not really... ' Jack spooned a heap of sugar into his tea and was reaching for a second before Audrey's raised eyebrows decided him against, '... it's just that pompous ass, Professor Stack.'

'Him?' Audrey knew only too well her husband's dislike of the historian, 'What's he been up to now?'

'Plenty.' Jack explained about the gold brooches and Stack's complaint against Peter Morecroft.

'Poor Pete,' said Audrey after listening to the tale, 'such a shame because he really does seem to be making a go of things since his time in prison.' Like her husband, she had a soft spot for the tough village boy who'd been in so many scrapes but been penalised so harshly for his last. It had been a joint decision of theirs to loan Peter the money for a new boat and gear when he was released. She shook her head. 'I do hope that dreadful Stack doesn't drive him to do something silly.'

'So do I.' Jack sipped his tea. 'Trouble is, Pete's got it in for Stack even more now he's heard our good Professor has put in a bid for Giller's Yard.' Jack stretched his legs under the table. 'The infernal man gloated to me himself this morning that he was buying a boatyard. He sounded pretty sure so I just hope someone outbids him.'

Audrey shook her head sadly. 'Then I'm afraid it's a forlorn hope, Jack. I met Reverend Jamieson this morning. He'd just been talking to a distressed Charlotte. Apparently, not only has Stack's bid been accepted, he's made it clear Charlotte herself will be evicted just as soon as the sale goes through.'

'Damn the man.' Jack sat staring into his teacup for a full minute before he looked up and said, 'Colonel Etherington told me that Stack's bid for the yard was based on money the development board had awarded him for *Raedwald*, money that should have gone to Alan Giller and didn't.' Downing the last of his tea, Jack turned back to Audrey and shook his head. 'Some day Professor Stack is going to get what's coming to him.'

'It's what's coming to poor Charlotte that worries me,' said Audrey, placing a tender hand over her husband's. 'Boatyard Cottage is the home she built with Alan and all her memories are there.' Audrey shook her head sadly, remembering the shock to their whole community when Alan Giller had hanged himself in his boatshed just a few months previous. Charlotte had been such a supporter of all local causes and made no secret of the fact that she and Alan hoped to start a family as soon as they could. Now all her dreams lay in tatters. 'And all because of that horrid man,' Audrey found herself saying aloud.

Jack nodded again. 'And don't forget poor old Walter Giller. Alan was the apple of his eye. To lose an only son just a few years after your wife is bad enough, but the old boy had put all his life's savings into Alan's yard too.'

Audrey sat, thinking of the elderly marshman facing old-age without financial security or the promise of grandchildren. Making an effort to brighten and find a more cheerful subject, she asked, 'Did you have your usual chat with Stuart Thornton today?'

'No, he waved to me from the studio but, for some reason, he didn't come down like he usually does.' Jack shook his head. 'Even at that distance I got the feeling the poor chap was weighed down by some great problem.'

'Probably that flirty wife of his,' huffed Audrey, trying not to sound too catty. 'We've all heard the rumours of her goings-on with Professor Stack.'

Indeed they had, but Jack had had enough of local troubles and needed diversion. It came in the form of a black and white dog crashing through the garden door, face full of joy and tail wagging at the sight of its master. Jack stroked the head nuzzling his leg.

'Hello, Spike, old chap. Time for your walk, is it?'

Audrey smiled at seeing how quickly their border collie could transform her husband's mood. They'd got Spike from a nearby dog refuge in their first week of moving to Norfolk. Jack loved walking but liked to have a reason and Spike was a perfect one. As Jack went off to get the lead and Spike darted about the kitchen with excited anticipation, Audrey started preparing their evening meal. How happy they were here in their little thatched cottage in the village. They had each other, good health and two fine daughters with families and careers of their own in London. Personal contentment though, inevitably leads to thoughts of others not so blessed. As she peeled the vegetables, Audrey couldn't help thinking about Charlotte Giller and her father-in-law, Walter. What would those poor souls do now?

WALKING SPIKE BESIDE THE river before supper was always a special time for Jack Fellows. As boats found evening moorings and sun and breezes slowly died, so a peace and stillness descended over river, marsh and wildlife. Many would say it was the perfect way to unwind, but Jack's working day rarely produced stress in need of alleviation. Rather, it was a time for quiet contemplation, a time when he could evaluate his day and weigh the plusses against the minuses. Usually the former far outweighed the latter but this glorious evening, as Spike trotted ahead investigating every new smell, Jack's thoughts were troubled. In spite of a lifetime handling other people's dilemmas, he was still sensitive to the anguish of others and he put his despondency down to the problems of the Gillers still praying on his mind. In his subconscious, he knew there was something else, some indefinable factor causing that prickly sensation of unease to creep insidiously up and down his backbone. Was it a policeman's instinct for incipient trouble or just a cynical nature honed by years of seeing the worst in every situation? Whichever, this was too beautiful an evening to wallow in pessimism. Mentally shaking such thoughts away, Jack paused to soak in the gifts of creation.

Beside him, the river flowed as it had from the dawn of time. On either side, the grazing marshes stretched, seemingly endlessly, from horizon to horizon, a flatness broken only by the stumps of sailless windpumps, pointing fingers of dereliction at the big Norfolk sky. Overhead, a marsh harrier hovered, lenticular wingspan working the thermals of the earth's dying warmth and its predatory eyes searching for the slightest movement below. Suddenly the effortless hover changed into a near-vertical dive into the marshes where another small life surely came to an inevitable and violent end.

It's a hard world for little things, thought Jack as he resumed his walk, thinking of how the harrier had killed with no thought for the life it was destroying. How often did humans acquire wealth purely for the sake of greed without thought for the pain caused to others? How often was that pain almost a cause for satisfaction rather than conscience? Perhaps he was misjudging the man, but instinct told him that Professor Rupert Stack enjoyed ruining lives. For all his intellect and learning, some predatory instinct caused a streak of sadism to run through this academic's relationship with others. It was while musing on this unattractive aspect of human nature that Jack heard the sound of an approaching marine diesel and, turning around, saw *Aethelberht*, with *Raedwald* alongside, making her way upriver. It was the Professor himself heading back to his evening mooring on the broad.

How lovely the Anglo-Saxon replica looked in this evening light. Anachronism that she was, the sail furled to crossed yard, wooden hull with its perfect sheer and the high curving bow, somehow looked just right. What wasn't right was the curling wave that that bow was now producing: Stack was driving his boats well in excess of the four miles-per-hour limit for this stretch of the river. Jack paused and, as the boats came level, gave a "Slow Down" signal with his hand.

It's an easy thing to not recognise someone outside familiar circumstances. Out of uniform, away from his patrol launch, it was perhaps understandable that Rupert Stack failed to recognise the Ranger whose job it was to enforce the river rules. What Jack couldn't understand was the insulting gesture of dismissal that the historian obviously felt the need to give in return. As boats ancient and modern churned past with quarter-waves rolling against the fragile river bank, Jack made a mental note of his first job on the morrow. Whether up or still in bed, Professor Stack could expect an interview on the subject of river speeds at very first light.

Perhaps we all take some pleasure in making life awkward for others at times, thought Jack smugly, as he whistled Spike and turned for home.

Chapter Four

IN THE KITCHEN OF Wyford's Mill, Stuart Thornton poured himself another stiff scotch. The kitchen was open-plan and also served as dining area and living room; occupying as it did, the whole of the first floor. Like all mills, Wyford's tapered upwards. With the ground floor left as a workshop-cum-utility room, the first was the largest living space. In winter, the woodburning stove brought a special cosiness to this snug den with its wooden units and natural brick walls. On this summer's day, the small-paned windows were open, allowing gentle zephyrs to waft in off the marshes and naturally cool its circular confines.

Stuart had come down from his studio with the intention of forcing some food into his system. He'd eaten nothing all day and wanted none now, but self-care demanded some sustenance and he'd broken two eggs and fried an omelette. However, just the sight of the oily concoction sliding onto his plate had been enough and he'd just as quickly emptied the lot into the wastebin. It was unfortunate that the whisky bottle was standing on the work-surface nearby. The good three fingers he'd poured had been downed in almost one gulp and the anaesthetising of his emotions for the first time that day had produced a welcome, if false, respite from reality.

Having poured a second tumblerful, Stuart forced himself to sip it more steadily and as he did so, he considered his way ahead. Finding solace in work had been singularly ineffectual; the very talent that had brought meaning to his life seemed to have gone the way of Lisa, and after a frustrating hour of negative creation he'd taken this latest canvas and impaled it over the easel. Attempts to find comfort in favourite music had been equally unsuccessful and only confirmed his suspicion that mental trauma deadens all senses except anguish and loathing.

The latter, he reserved for Professor Rupert Stack who, in Stuart's inebriated reasoning, now became the sole villain in this debilitating drama. As the whisky level fell, so Lisa became a dedicated wife enticed from him by the machinations of the evil academic. Why had he ever allowed her to work for Stack and why had she allowed herself to become financially embroiled with her employer? Stuart had no idea of what that dubious arrangement might be and had always shied from asking, but that the two had more going on than pure sex was evidenced by the considerable cash inputs Lisa had brought to the Thornton coffers.

Well, none of that mattered any more. In fact, Stuart realised, *nothing* mattered any more except a levelling of scores. He glanced up and realised darkness had fallen. How long had he been sitting here in his cups? He didn't know and didn't care. All he did know now was that he had to do something and the sooner, the better. He got up, knocking the whisky bottle over as he did so, stumbled down the stairs to the ground floor and opened the door.

The cool evening air hit him with sobering impact but didn't stay his resolve. Lisa had taken their Range Rover but that was of no consequence because where he was going needed conveyance of a different medium. In the small cut by the mill lay the dinghy. It rocked alarmingly as he jumped into its leaf-strewn bottom and let go the line. The outboard motor took a couple of pulls before it started with a jolt and the dinghy surged forward. Opening the throttle to full, Stuart Thornton disappeared into the night.

THE SUN WAS WELL below the western horizon as Charlotte Giller hard-pedalled her way up the shallow incline of the river valley. Often on a summer's evening, she and Alan had pulled their bikes from the shed at Boatyard Cottage and cycled the country lanes together, savouring the fragrance of field and hedgerow while chatting away as only a couple in love with life and each other could do.

Blessed sweet memories, but now as of another world, for Charlotte's ride tonight was no gentle melancholic journey of nostalgia recapturing moments of lost happiness with Alan. Tonight she was cycling with a purpose, a fraught trek through the darkness with thoughts that were darker still. Charlotte had a mission and all her energy was directed towards its execution.

This was the culmination of a dreadful day at Boatyard Cottage, the worst since Alan's suicide. Memories of that appalling day were painful enough but she remembered how her initial anguish had been tempered by other emotions. Entwined in her all-consuming anguish had been the sense of failure of a wife whose husband felt so degraded as to take that final, desperate step. All their married life she had supported Alan in his every endeavour. In the good times she had run the office, painted boats, swept and cleaned and done all the other hundred things it took to run a boatyard. In the bad she had tried to renegotiate loans, called creditors and pleaded with banks while all the time giving love and assurance to a husband steadily descending into the pit of despair.

In the end, even her capacity for love hadn't been enough. She would never forget their last night together, how she had finally fallen asleep with Alan cradled in her arms but woken in the early morning to find him gone. She had gone straightway to the boatshed where he so often retreated to find solace amongst his beloved wooden boats. She had grown used to finding Alan there, sitting forlornly with his head in his hands, but this morning it was to discover her beloved husband turning slowly at the end of a length of hemp from the shed's main beam. Amongst the maelstrom of Charlotte's other emotions, she could still recall the sliver of anger that she'd felt at the time. After all she'd done and fought for, how could Alan have just "copped out" and left her to face the desolation of their shattered lives alone?

The months following had been a nightmare of inquests, receivers and hearings, but, thankfully, in that time, her feelings had mellowed. Alan's father, Walter, battling his own sense of unquenchable loss, had still found time to be a pillar of support to a daughter-in-law he genuinely loved. The old marshman had quietly nourished Charlotte's slow realisation that, far from failing Alan in her love, it was his feelings of being unworthy of that love that had finally driven him to that dire ultimate act. That understanding alone had driven out the anger and self-recrimination, to leave just a deep sorrow for such a waste of a good life and unbelievable hatred for the man who'd caused it all.

Professor Rupert Stack stood alone amongst Charlotte's list of men she wished dead. This arrogant intellectual had surely not failed to realise the extremes of despair to which his non-payment was driving poor Alan. Even if he had, Charlotte could not have made things clearer in her pleadings with him to pay for *Raedwald*. But her entreaties had fallen on deaf ears, creditors had foreclosed and Giller's Boatyard had gone to the wall. And now, the man she held responsible for the death of her husband had bought the very yard he'd driven into bankruptcy and, to add further pain to despair, was about to have her thrown from her home.

In her desperation she'd called Walter Giller, Alan's dad, and just as quickly regretted it. Pops had enough baggage of his own to carry without her adding to his burden. He'd told her "not to worry", but the detached icy coldness in his voice had caused her do just the opposite. She had spent the day wondering what her father-in-law meant by "sorting it", and alternating between extremes of intense anger and bitter frustration at the plain unfairness of the whole situation. It was bad enough to be evicted by the very man who'd ruined your life, but something told Charlotte that even this transaction was not as straightforward as it seemed. Giller's Boatyard might be run down but she knew of at least one other yard-owner in Broadland keen to acquire it. That Stack was the highest bidder seemed altogether unrealistic and Charlotte was convinced that somewhere down the line there had been some unethical dealing. But where?

She'd once had a high regard for Gwen Fosdyke, but her experience of the last months had made her cynical of everyone. Stack's evil hands, she knew, were capable of insidiously worming their way into the most upright of institutions, and she was sure now that even Gwen Fosdyke had somehow fallen under his evil spell. Doubtless, all involved would have covered their tracks and anyway, who would take the word of a sad deranged widow against those of a respected District Councillor and intellectual academic? Inevitably, Rupert Stack and his cohorts would have the last profitable laugh.

It was late afternoon before Charlotte finally decided on her course of action. From being continually on the defensive it was time to take attack to the enemy camp and give Professor Stack some of his own medicine. Just making that simple decision made her feel better and formulating a plan of attack dispelled instantly the sense of impotence that had clouded her life for months. With new-found resolve and the thought that she had nothing left to lose anyway, Charlotte went to the boatshed and rummaged amongst the sad remains of Alan's tools. Finding the ones she needed, she dropped them into a rucksack, shouldered the load and wheeled out her bike. Sometime in the future she would doubtless have to pay a price for tonight's events but in her own conscience, Charlotte knew that what she was doing was right.

This sometimes-cruel world was in its last minutes of twilight as she cycled on into the ever-darkening countryside.

CHARLOTTE WOULD HAVE HAD even more reason to worry about her father-in-law if she had seen Walter at this time. The icy hatred that had almost overwhelmed the old marshman when he heard that Charlotte was to be evicted from Boatyard Cottage, had stayed with him all day. He had promised his daughter-in-law that the problem would "be sorted"; the rest of his day had been spent working out how.

Not easy for a man whose whole world, for most of his life, had been a few hundred acres of marshland. Stack, on the other hand was a "brainy type" with a seemingly infinite capacity for callous cunning. As Walter wrestled with the problem, only one thing was clear: Professor Rupert Stack's tyranny must come to an end. The man had brought untold grief to the Gillers and been the cause of young Peter Morecroft going to gaol. On top of that, there were dark rumours of his "messing about" with that artist Stuart Thornton's missus. Whether Stuart knew of the liaison, Walter had no idea. He'd never had much time for the flighty Lisa but he liked her husband, a young Broadsman with abundant talent and a kind heart to match.

Walter hadn't achieved much work this summer's day as he grappled for a solution. Fighting Stack in the courts would cost money and all Walter's had gone down with his son's boatyard. Besides, the man was so cleverly canny, he'd win every time anyway. Just as futile would be to appeal to his compassion: the man didn't have any. In the end, of course, the answer was so obviously simple.

That night, after finishing his tea, Walter made his way down to the old boatshed. It lay next to a skeleton drainage mill that for a hundred years had surely and steadily pumped water from the grazing marshes back into the river. The old boat inside the shed was almost of the same vintage. It was a marsh punt, an open, long, low, clinker built double-ended craft that for centuries had been the working boat of the marshes. Walter still used this one in his everyday marshman's life, working the river and dykes, but spurning always the use of an outboard motor. In spite of his age, he was still strong and fit and everywhere he needed to go, he either rowed or poled. From the rafters above the punt, he took down the set of oars. Then he loaded his knapsack containing a flask of cocoa, a beef sandwich wrapped in newspaper and an aged flashlight. Finally and gently, he placed on the for'ard thwart, his double-barrel shotgun and six twelve-bore cartridges.

Walter Giller was off to "sort it".

ALREADY "SORTING IT", WAS Lisa Thornton. After leaving Stack on *Aethelberht*, she had driven her Range Rover blindly at speed along country lanes, her state of shock and anger combining to produce a lethal combination that was only neutralised when she pulled into a convenient farm track and, with shaking fingers, lit a cigarette.

Control returned, but with it reality and the picture it painted wasn't good. In the space of twelve hours she seemed to have effectively lost her husband, home, lover, job and lucrative sideline. Lisa banged the steering wheel in a futile effort to vent frustration before running the same hand distractedly through her bleached hair. What to do? An obvious course was to return to Wyford's Mill and make her peace with Stuart, but even Lisa's opportunist nature shied away from such immediate contrition. Tears started to well in her eyes and she reached into her pocket for a tissue and in so doing, felt the keys.

They were the keys to Rupert Stack's apartment in town. Lisa had her own set because the apartment was where she administered Stack's business as well as sharing his bed on not a few riotous rainy afternoons. Well, that bed could serve another purpose tonight, perhaps not with the permanency she had visualised at the start of this day, but a stopgap at least until its owner returned. Besides, she had personal things in her office desk that now needed clearing.

As Lisa drove slowly away and headed for town, she struggled to come to terms with her new situation. 'God,' she thought, 'how could I make such a mess of everything?' Having asked herself the question, Lisa made no attempt to answer it. As was her nature, she instead immediately sought others on which to release the anger now reboiling within her. Husband Stuart, with his lack of ambition and charisma came in for some mental abuse, but there was no doubting the man to whom Lisa now directed her abundant capacity to hate: Professor Rupert Stack.

Like Stuart, Lisa now managed to mentally rewrite her life prior to Stack. In her mind, she had been a happily married woman until woefully seduced by her debauched employer. Now, after a year's gruelling effort to establish that stupid floating exhibition and succumbing to his every desire, he had cast her out like so much garbage. In any normal working relationship she could have taken him to the cleaners, but Lisa's fury was fuelled by the knowledge that she would never dare and Stack knew it.

Early on in her employment, when talk with her boss had become easier between the bedsheets, Lisa had asked Stack's advice. The result was a mutually convenient and extremely profitable arrangement. Only now did she recognise the danger of dealing with such a manipulative man. Stack had used her professionally and sexually, even professed to want a permanent relationship, while all the time bringing her into his power and control. This hold meant she would never see another penny out of Professor Stack. More worrying still, she knew his venom was quite capable of shopping her just for spite. Little by little, Lisa felt some of her anger being brushed aside by the cold hand of fear. What could she do? She lit another cigarette and as she did so the expression "fight fire with fire" seemed to burn its way into her bitterness.

Of course, the solution was obvious: if Stack could control her with threatening knowledge, she could do the same. She had a fair idea of his goings-on and how he made huge lumps of cash. She'd been part of it and even hoped to share the ultimate spoils. Well, now she would use it to other advantage. All she needed was hard evidence and that doubtless lay at the very place she was heading. Here was a way in which she could secure immunity from his control, extract a satisfying dollop of revenge and perhaps get her hands on more money than she had ever imagined.

Lisa allowed herself the first smile in hours as she sped ever-faster towards town.

IT WAS NOT MONEY that prayed on Gwen Fosdyke's mind as she burned her office lights in the same town. With District Council work to transact in addition to her own legal casework, Gwen had ample reason to stay late. However, she believed in regular hours and her solicitor's office usually closed on the dot of five-thirty. But this summer's evening, as staff in the outer office shut down computers, locked filing cabinets and put on coats, Gwen stayed at her desk.

'Some late stuff to sort before court on Thursday, Rose,' Gwen explained wearily to her secretary when she popped her head around the boss's door. 'Just leave the keys here and I'll lock up when I go.' The secretary and clerks headed homeward leaving their boss in the peace she'd craved all day.

That peace though, failed to reach Gwen's heart as her legal mind struggled to find a compromise in the cauldron of emotions that seemed to be competing for her very integrity. She'd built her reputation on an ability to think fast under pressure but now, with so many anxieties and misgivings all juggling for solution, even her normally-imperturbable judgement and intellect felt stretched to breaking.

How long was it, she wondered, since she'd even known the meaning of contentment? The answer to that was easy: all her present woes had come with Professor Rupert Stack. This morning's telephone conversation had been the last straw. For the rest of the day Gwen had been wrestling continuously with the seemingly insoluble conflict of love versus professional principles. How cruel that the love she had kept so secret now threatened to destroy her life and work. She thought of the cliché that love always comes at a price and realised grimly that her own forfeit had come cruelly soon.

Love for the man had driven her to do everything Stack had asked. It had been a simple exercise to manipulate the bids in his favour. She'd had to dupe people who trusted her and abandon the professional ethics she'd always cherished but, in the end, Stack was getting his yard. Now he wanted more. Having Charlotte Giller evicted from her cottage had been his next demand and Gwen had done that knowing she was hammering the last bitter nail into that poor girl's coffin. But even that hadn't been enough; now he demanded development permission for the yard. For that she would have to fight the District Council and Broads Authority, neither of whom would want this old boatyard turned into housing. Gwen didn't either but many would be swung over just on the strength of her own reputation.

As the hours passed and twilight turned to darkness, Gwen sat at her desk reflecting on how much good had happened before so much bad. This road to iniquity had begun with love and romance but was now lined with degradation. It was also, she realised only too well, very much one-way, without even the option of a u-turn back to probity. For the first time in her life, Gwen felt despair in a situation almost irresolvable.

Almost, but not quite. From somewhere beyond, Gwen sensed the strength of her beloved father touching her beleaguered soul. There and then she decided she would not let this corrupt man ruin her life's work and the lives of so many others. Gwen picked up her telephone and dialled a number from memory. When it answered she said simply, 'We need to talk… right now.'

There was agreement, discussion of time and place and then, with the strength of decisive action banishing despondency, Gwen grabbed coat and briefcase and switched off her office lights. She was about to open her door to the outer general office when she heard the faintest movement on the other side. Even as Gwen froze into immobility, there came the sound of the main office door closing quietly too. Someone had been out there listening the whole time. Who? None of her staff would linger any longer than necessary. Or had she, with her nerves stretched to the limit, only imagined it? Nothing in the outer office was disturbed and there was no-one in sight beyond. Gwen shrugged her troubled shoulders, switched off the remaining lights, locked the door firmly behind her and walked out to her car.

Phantom visitors, she thought whimsically, would be the least of happenings before this fraught night was through.

FURTHER DOWN THE HIGH STREET in Rupert Stack's first floor office-cum-apartment, Lisa Thornton sank down behind her desk. Her work here had mainly involved liasing with museums for the loan of artefacts, applying for grants, preparing the many academic papers Stack was continually submitting to international bodies and handling the day-to-day accounts of the floating museum. That was the ethical face of Professor Rupert Stack's academic life; below, she knew all too well, lay an underworld of villainy and corruption.

That she was the instigator of at least some of that corruption, bothered Lisa not at all. What did was her suspicion that she had creamed off such a derisory percentage of it. And now, Stack had discovered her source and planned to cut her out altogether. Well, if there was cutting to be done, Lisa Thornton could wield a pretty sharp knife herself and make a bundle more money into the bargain.

The trouble was, to do that she needed Stack's contact and that was a secret known only to the professor himself. To maintain that secrecy, he'd been resolutely thorough in keeping his meetings with that shadowy individual utterly secret, and just as assiduous that no record of his details reached her prying eyes. In reality, until now she'd made no great effort to discover them, begrudgingly accepting the Professor's clandestine expertise and her own pitiful share. Well, if Stack could go it completely alone, so could she. All she needed was the contact data. Lisa sat down behind her desk and considered where it might be.

The obvious answer was in the computer before her but she knew that Stack, like so many classical academics, had difficulty using a cash machine, let alone programming software. Or did he? Was his declaration of being a techno-phobe just pure smokescreen? With a man as devious as Stack, anything was possible and more than once, on coming to work in the morning, she had suspected he had been using the computer. If so, where were the files? Not contained on the hard-drive; she would have come across them very easily. If he had the information, it was either on floppy disc or CD but where were these? She went to the Professor's own desk across the room, knowing that every drawer would be locked. They were.

'In for a penny, in for a pound,' said Lisa to herself and went out into the kitchen, pulled a heavy screwdriver from a drawerful of tools and returned to Stack's desk. It took a fair amount of work and not a few foul words, but eventually she had levered open three of the drawers and found nothing more valuable than some chequebooks and bank statements. The latter were enough to confirm that the academic could well afford to lose a few thousand but she needed data to make that happen.

Lisa was well aware that the splintered wood of the desk represented very much the burning of her own boats. Stack would have no doubt as to the perpetrator but it was a calculated gamble on her part: if she obtained what she sought, it would be reason enough to prevent Stack ever going to the police, but only if she found it. She took a deep breath, attacked the fourth drawer and, even as it sprung open, she saw the metallic glint of a CD. Hardly daring to hope, Lisa sprang back to the computer and slipped in the disc.

"ENTER PASSWORD", said the infernal response; Stack obviously did understand computers and he'd set his files up to ensure they were for his eyes only. Lisa fought back tears and strove to keep her focus on reality. What password would her boss use?

It could be one of a million but gambling had brought her this far and she had nothing to lose with more. With a shaking hand, she typed "RAEDWALD" onto the keyboard and clicked "ENTER".

"WRONG PASSWORD" came back the instant response followed by the warning that one more would lock down the file. 'It's now-or-never time,' thought Lisa and typed in "AETHELBERHT".

Like the raising of some magic veil, a screen-full of data materialised before Lisa's euphoric eyes.

THE BOATS THEMSELVES LAY at anchor just off the main fairway of the broad. Relaxed on a couch in *Aethelberht's* saloon, Rupert Stack poured himself another glass of vintage brandy. Arriving here just before sunset, he had cooked a fulsome supper accompanied by a fine wine in celebration of what, to him, had been a most rewarding day. Not only had the purchase of Giller's Boatyard got a completion date and the eviction of the stupid girl in the cottage been put in place, he had even instigated the process of obtaining development permission. All achieved he ruminated, by gaining knowledge which enabled him to manipulate others. As icing on his narcissistic cake, he could even congratulate himself on dumping his useless secretary and her boring amatory ways. He had endured them as a way of maintaining their lucrative business arrangement but, now he knew her source, Lisa Thornton and her share of the profits could be effectively sidelined.

Content in the afterglow of his food and wine, Stack poured another Napoleon, stretched his legs and thought gleefully of his future. With the money he'd accumulated, the development of Giller's Yard could go ahead just as soon as that efficient and persuasive Councillor Fosdyke inveigled her fellow members into granting permission. Stack allowed his thoughts to drift whimsically over development possibilities.

He glanced at the golden brooches, removed from their display case and lying now in front of him on the saloon table. As on most nights, he delayed securing them in the safe until he went to his bed, savouring instead, the sheer magnificence of the artefacts until the last possible moment. He knew himself to be ruthless and cruel in his dealings with others, but the historian in his soul could still delight in the beauty and symmetry of creations from another millennia. It pained him to think that in less than a month, he would have to return them to the British Museum ... unless...

Helped by the brandy, Stack's mind began turning over possibilities and again his thoughts turned to Giller's Yard. What if, instead of building houses, he built a permanent museum devoted, like this floating one, to the Anglo Saxon period? On the face of it, there would be more money in housing but, if he could secure artefacts like these brooches, then his museum could be a veritable treasure house. But how? Established museums clung to their treasures tenaciously and though prepared to loan for short periods, would never surrender them indefinitely. The British Museum had vaulted storerooms filled with such treasures that never saw the light of day. What a coup if he could obtain some for his own museum right here in Broadland, but that would need the intervention of someone with far greater influence than Professor Rupert Stack. Who?

Gwen Fosdyke, he knew, was in line for parliamentary election and equally surely, once seated in Westminster, this veritable powerhouse of a woman would soon be heading for even higher office. And Gwen Fosdyke would do as he asked. He was thinking years ahead, but with a potential Secretary of State in his power indefinitely, what limits could there be on his manipulation?

Stack glanced at his watch: it was past midnight. Time for bed but ah, what dreams he would be dreaming this night. Downing the last of his brandy, Stack rose unsteadily to his feet. Before him, the gold and stones of the brooches glinted enticingly in the subdued cabin lights. He picked them up, took them to the safe and reverently placed them inside below the coins. With the heavy door closed and locked, he spun the combination dial but with it his thoughts were spinning also, to times far ahead when these beautiful creations and others would be in his permanent care.

Before taking to his bed, Stack took one final look outside. On the port side *Raedwald* lay, her ancient rigging stark against the weak moonlit sky. To starboard, those same ethereal beams were reflecting off small wavelets as a stiffening breeze stirred the waters of the broad. A parting in the clouds allowed more moonlight to flood the broad and, as it did so, Stack saw something. Switching off the cabin lights to recover his night vision, he looked again and saw a shape materialising from the darkness.

It was a small boat and it was coming alongside.

THE LAST QUARTER OF an old moon was sliding eerily behind a thin veil of stratus as Peter Morecroft entered the broad. A weather front was obviously passing through, the now-gusting wind carrying horizontal rain and kicking up small whitecaps on the broad's black surface. In spite of the elements, however, the outboard motor clamped to the transom of his open dory stayed silent. For this work he needed silence and so, steadily and carefully, he rowed.

Hours previous he had checked his line of fyke nets on the river's edge and now he was on his second mission of the night, the task he set himself whenever Professor Stack was moored nearby.

Once again he was keeping watch on the historian's every movement.

Peter was well aware that his presence was taking a toll on Stack's nerves. He knew the Professor to be a physical and moral coward, but he had no intention of punching his lights out, satisfying as that would be. Thirty days in Norwich Prison had seemed like a life sentence to a boy raised under the wide skies of the marshes, and certainly enough to cement a resolve never to return. Stack's lies had sent him to gaol once and would do so again unless he played his cards right. Peter was determined to extract retribution but that revenge would be by legitimate means and not physical violence. He had brought from prison only one asset and that was an enhanced awareness of the criminal mind. After many incarcerated hours thinking about Professor Rupert Stack, he had come to the conclusion that, for all his learning and hoity-toity manner, the academic was, at heart, a villain.

He had talked it over with Mr. Fellows, the Navigation Ranger. Jack Fellows was the man Peter respected most in this world, a hard-nosed ex-copper who had taken a liking to the tough lad struggling to make his way as an eel-catcher. When others had placed obstacles in his path, it was Mr Fellows who had been there to offer help and advice. He was the only one to believe and speak up for him when Stack had made his false accusation. It was thanks to Mr. Fellows' good words in court that his sentence had been as light as it had.

Nevertheless, they'd still found him guilty and not only sent him to gaol, but also confiscated his boat and gear. He came out of prison to freedom and little else. Then Mr. Fellows had loaned him the money to buy another boat and got him back his eeling licence. Peter would never forget that. He'd never known a real father but Jack Fellows was the nearest thing he could imagine to such a figure. He'd told the Ranger of all his suspicions of Professor Stack but, as Mr. Fellows pointed out, suspicion was one thing and hard evidence another. Well, if proof was what was needed, Peter decided, proof was what he would get and then Professor High-and-Mighty Stack would get a dose of his own medicine.

Keeping an eye on the academic hadn't been difficult. Eel-catching was night work and even before his arrest and imprisonment, Peter had perceived the other strange world of Professor Stack.

Raedwald and *Aethelberht,* he'd noticed, often moored overnight in isolated locations. As such, there was nothing strange about this;

many boat people chose the solitude of broad and marsh in preference to a congested staithe. What was odd was that it was these nights in remote locations that Stack chose to entertain a guest. Stack would collect this lone man in darkness and the stranger would depart under the same cover. At first, Peter had been faintly amused by these comings and goings and open-minded enough to accept them. If the Professor was gay, that was his business. There were rumours, of course, concerning Stack and Mrs Thornton but the Professor wouldn't be the first man to enjoy a variety of sexual pleasures.

Unfortunately, eel-fishing's unsocial hours meant Peter was invariably the sole witness to Stack's night-time liaisons. Was this the reason the historian had lied under oath and had him put away? Quite possibly, but if it was meant to drive Peter from his area, it failed. As soon as he had a boat and licence again, he'd returned to his old patch and this time with an acquired knowledge of the criminal mind. Much as he would have liked to start spreading unsavoury rumours about a man for whom he held nothing but contempt, something told Peter these nefarious visits were of an altogether more sinister nature.

And so he kept watch on Stack and waited for his moment. Just what the man was up to, Peter had no idea, but he knew he wouldn't rest until he'd found out. How? Getting a closer look into the Professor's boat could be one answer and tonight, with so little moon, might be the night if Stack was there. Peter continued rowing into the broad, looking over his shoulder as he pulled at the oars. There were just two boats at this north end, well apart and lying to their mudweights. Only one was still showing lights and that boat had an old galley moored alongside. Peter turned towards *Raedwald* and *Aethelberht*, easing his stroke and the splash of his oars as he did so.

How ghostly the old boat looked in the pale streaks of moonlight, just like one of the Viking ships that Peter had read so much about as a boy. Apparently, this replica was of a vessel far older than the Norsemen's, but just the symbolism of that high prow and stern, the stacked oars, the mast and yard and furled sail, somehow radiated an aura of sinister malevolence that Peter found hard to ignore. He glanced at his watch: three a.m. Death's midnight. Shaking away dark thoughts, Peter took a firmer grip of his oars and, in the gusting wind, rowed ever closer.

That wind was blowing even stronger now, creating a healthy chop on the water that slapped against his bows. Hopefully, those same wavelets would be slapping against the hulls of Stack's boats, effectively covering the sound of his approach. *Aethelberht's* saloon curtains were closed but a streak of light showed an opening big enough to see through. He would never get a better chance than this. Possibly Stack wasn't even onboard but unlikely; the man never left his boat. Perhaps though, in these squally conditions, he could still nose inside. It was a risk worth taking if it produced the evidence he sought. The wind had veered westerly now, blowing him beam-on towards the cruiser. He shipped his oars and silently drifted alongside. A few pulls at *Aethelberht's* gunwale and he was right beside the gap in the curtains. Fighting instincts that told him to get out now while he could, Peter raised his head above the level of the deck and peered inside.

He'd been longing for this moment for months. He hadn't known what to expect. Now he was looking into Professor Stack's saloon and what Peter Morecroft saw this night was beyond anything he could have ever imagined.

'WHAT IS IT JACK?' Audrey Fellows felt her husband turn over again for what must be the hundredth time that night.

'Sorry, love; what with that storm passing through and everything else, I just can't sleep.'

Which meant that she hadn't either. It was the "everything else" that worried Audrey. During her husband's days with the C.I.D., this was a dilemma faced on many a night when the current case stubbornly refused to crack. Since retiring to Norfolk and his new job, their sleep had been blissfully tranquil. Whatever was causing a return to those troubled symptoms now, Audrey's solution was the same.

'Right, let me make us some tea and then we can chat.'

Ten minutes later, leaning towards each other with steaming mugs between, Jack admitted what his wife half-guessed.

'It's all this trouble that suddenly seems to have infected the community, Audrey. Here we are living in an idyll but with enough strife and aggravation to fuel the U.N. There's Charlotte Giller about to be evicted, Stuart Thornton in despair over his wife's affair and Peter Morecroft heading for big trouble again unless he winds his neck in. And all owing to one man.'

'Professor Stack?'

'Exactly. He's like a cancer spreading through the area.'

Audrey cradled her mug as if its warmth could neutralise the coldness she always felt at that wretched man's name. 'Is there anything you can do about it?'

'That's the trouble: nothing...' Jack took a sip of his own tea, '... or at least about the cause. All we *can* do is help ease the effect.'

'Which won't be easy. So much pain and anguish for so many people.' Audrey finished off her tea. 'But you won't be of much help to anyone, Jack, if you're tired before you start.' She rubbed his shoulder affectionately. 'Come on, skipper, try and get some sleep.'

Jack looked at the clock beside him and the lightening of the sky through the curtains. During his sleepless hours, an overhanging branch had been banging the roof as a line squall passed through the parish. He shook his head. 'Dawn breaking, love. That was a good blow last night. I need to check if any boats dragged anchors on the broad. I'll get up and make an early start. That way at least you'll get a bit more shuteye.' He swung out of bed and slipped on his dressing gown. 'Besides, I have to explain the penalties of exceeding river speed limits to our good Professor Stack.' He allowed himself just the faintest of chuckles. 'I'll enjoy *that*.'

Or so he hoped. As he headed for the shower, Jack felt again that same ominous sensation of incipient trouble.

ANOTHER DAWN, ANOTHER DAY, but this one slightly more overcast and with the overnight breeze still causing a slight overfall on the river's ebb. On the broad, it was fresh enough to provide good sailing for all those yachts becalmed the day before, though neither of the two sailing cruisers anchored at the south end were yet hoisting canvas. At least no boats had dragged and ended up on the lee-shore overnight. Already figures were mopping decks and Jack caught just the whiff of frying bacon as he cruised past, his launch's lean bow cutting cleanly through the foot-high wavelets rolling down the broad. Normally he would have stopped to exchange some banter with the sailors, but this morning he stayed resolutely on course for the replica galley and museum-motherboat anchored at the north end.

It was still only six-thirty when Jack drew abeam Stack's boats. *Aethelberht's* curtains were still closed and there was no sign of life on her deck. 'Still sleeping,' he thought, chuckling inwardly as he came alongside, not sparing diesel power or noise as he went astern to stop level with the larger boat's bow, 'Well, that should wake our dear Professor from his slumbers.'

But, apparently, it didn't. No tall stooped figure appeared, to expound caustic comment on being woken so early. Jack climbed on board *Aethelberht* and secured his bow and stern lines to the cruiser's cleats before knocking on the curtained bow doors. But no-one responded. Over all hung a sinister and deathly silence.

'PROFESSOR STACK!'

There was no reply. Surely, Stack must be onboard, having vowed never to leave his boats unattended with the treasures below. Jack tried the doors but they were locked. He edged carefully astern along the narrow side decks and down into the well which led to the double doors of the museum space. Surprisingly one of these doors was open, its curtains blowing in the breeze. Jack went through into the exhibition area where only yesterday, he'd admired the order and professionalism of the displays. This morning he stood in silent horror as he faced a scene of cruel devastation.

Where there had been a classified and comprehensive depiction of Anglo-Saxon life, there now lay only the results of total vandalism. Display cases had been ripped from their fittings and smashed across the floor. Underfoot, broken glass lay strewn amongst shattered artefacts and splintered woodwork. Picking his way through the debris of broken pottery, scattered coinage and discarded ancient weaponry, Jack headed for the saloon. There'd been a feeling to this boat the second he set foot on board. Now, as he worked his way for'ard, it deepened with every step. He'd attended enough crime scenes to recognise it immediately. It was the smell of death.

In the saloon the devastation was, if anything, worse. Every cupboard had been opened and the contents emptied across the floor. The heavy safe door lay wide open to reveal an empty interior. Disturbing as these immediate impressions were on Jack's forensic mind, he was viewing them at this stage as just a backdrop to the scene. At the for'ard end of the saloon was the main object of this whole tableau. There, full length, face down, lay the body of Professor Stack.

The stillness of his form and the pool of blood in which it lay were indication enough but, just for form, Jack bent down and tried for a pulse. Stone dead and for quite some time, judging by the coolness of that wrist. The cause wasn't difficult to see. Perhaps the historian in Stack might have gained some comfort from the fact that he'd been done to death by an ancient dagger that still lay buried to the hilt in his back.

Almost subconsciously, Jack reached into the pocket of his waterproof, brought out his mobile phone and dialled 999.

Chapter Five

'WELL, DOC; HOW LONG?'

Detective Chief Inspector Phil Hengrove of the Norfolk Constabulary leaned his broad back against the saloon bulkhead, as the grey-haired man bending over Professor Stack's body thoughtfully wiped his thermometer.

'About five hours…' the pathologist glanced at his watch, '… which makes time of death about two this morning, give or take a half-hour. There's considerable bruising about the face and body consistent with him having a good beating but they're not the cause of death. That's pretty obvious: fatal damage to vital organs caused by a knife wound between the scapulae… the shoulder blades.'

'I know what scapulae are, thank you, Doc.' Hengrove nodded towards the bronze dagger protruding morbidly from the encircling blood-drenched shirt. 'How deep is that thing in?'

'I'll need to have a better look back at the lab but I estimate...' the pathologist once again leaned over the body, '… at least five inches.'

'Which would take a pretty strong man… person?'

'That or an enraged one. As I said, he was pretty badly beaten prior to his death ... lots of bruising as you can see.'

'Right… Bailey…' Hengrove turned to the young Detective Constable beside him, '… get the forensic lads to work. Both boats are crime scenes so we'll leave them here for now, well away from Johnny Public.' He turned to the uniformed figure standing silently at the aft end of the saloon. 'That won't be a problem will it, Jack?'

'None at all.' Jack Fellows was conscious of his unique situation. Normally, only police would have been present at this initial examination but Phil Hengrove was well aware of Jack's CID background. They'd met during regular liaison between Police and Authority and it was a measure of their mutual respect that the DCI was regarding the Ranger on almost equal terms. Jack nodded towards his launch. 'Just let me know when you want them towed in.'

'Thanks.' Hengrove led Jack back on deck where white-overalled Crime Scene Investigators were just climbing onboard from the Broads Beat RIB now lying alongside. Its crew, two fit-looking constables with close-cropped hair and black T-shirts, listened as Hengrove gave his orders. 'Right, you two, get round to every boat anchored here last night. Find out if anyone saw or heard anything. We'll need full statements later so make sure you get their details and intentions.' As the RIB, blue light flashing, sped away in an arrowhead of foam, the DCI turned back to the man who'd seen this procedure all too often and hoped he'd never have to again. 'So what do you know about the victim, Jack?'

'Professor Rupert Stack; academic and historian of repute, pompous with it, not universally loved.'

Hengrove's eyebrows rose enquiringly. 'Enemies?'

Jack gave a mirthless laugh. 'Only everyone he ever came into contact with.'

'Like that, was it.' Hengrove shivered slightly. 'This is too much fresh air for me first thing in the morning, Jack.' He nodded down into the saloon where the C.S.I. team were already painstakingly peering into every nook and cranny. 'There might be the stench of death down there but at least it's warm.'

The DCI led the way back down to where Stack's body still lay just as Jack had found it: face down, one leg bent at the knee, head on one arm, the other arm stretching forward. Between Stack's protruding shoulder blades, the ornate dagger glinted in the rising sun, a beautiful piece of artistic creation from the sixth century but just as deadly in the twenty-first. Unmoved by such notions, the police surgeon was just closing his bag. Hengrove turned to him. 'Would death have been instantaneous, Doc?'

The grey head nodded. 'Virtually. He might have lingered a few seconds; thirty at the most.'

'But long enough to do that?' The flash of a forensic photographer's camera illuminated what Hengrove was pointing to, something Jack had seen the instant he found the body. Stack's stretched arm was lying in a pool of his own blood, the hand clenched except for one extended finger. With the tip of that digit he had scrawled just two letters: PM. Jack guessed the DCI's next question. 'Know anyone with those initials, Jack?'

Jack hesitated and in those seconds the young DC's mobile phone blessedly rang. 'DC Bailey… okay, go ahead…' The young officer scribbled notes into his pocket notebook, '… copied… thanks.' He switched off and turned back to Hengrove. 'HQ, guv'nor. They've run a check on Professor Stack. Only data they can find is that he appeared as principal witness at Norwich assizes about a year ago. Some local lad called Peter Morecroft threatened him with a gun.'

Hengrove looked up at the deckhead in deep thought. 'Morecroft... Morecroft... I remember... young eel-catcher... got thirty days.' He turned back to the Ranger. 'In your manor, Jack.'

From the second he'd seen those initials, Jack had dreaded this moment, but he nodded and gestured to Hengrove to follow him back on deck. As they walked back through the boat Jack pointed to damp patches on the carpet that covered both saloon and museum space. 'I wonder what made those?'

The DCI shrugged. 'Who knows; perhaps young Morecroft trying to cover his tracks. We'll ask him when we get him.'

Outside, in the weak sunshine, both men leaned over *Aethelberht's* after guardrail. Jack spoke quietly. 'Phil, Peter Morecroft didn't do this. I know it.'

'How do you know it?' Hengrove wasn't even facing him but looking out straight across the broad.

'Because since being released, he's worked hard and kept out of trouble. I know this lad and I'd swear for him like I did at his trial.'

Hengrove took out a packet of cigarettes and lit up. 'Jack, you and I know that villains are the world's best actors. They'd swear devotion to Mother Theresa while planning their next job.'

Jack shook his head. 'Phil, that's the point; Peter Morecroft isn't a villain. A few boyhood scrapes maybe, but Stack's account of him threatening with a firearm was pure fiction. Okay, he and the Professor were a clash of cultures if ever there was one. Stack had been on Peter Morecroft's case for months, accusing him of setting his nets too close to the surface and exceeding speed limits in his dory. In the end, Morecroft went to have it out with him...'

'... and threatened him with an unlicensed firearm,' Hengrove completed, taking a long drag at his cigarette.

'Wrong...' Jack shook his head again, '... a shotgun, Phil, not a firearm, and it wasn't his but a friend's who'd loaned it to him to go ratting.'

'That's not what he said in court.'

'No, because he didn't want to get his friend in trouble.' Jack made a conscious effort to lower his voice. 'Pete swore that gun stayed in the bottom of the boat the whole time he was arguing with Stack. The Professor must have noticed it because when he reported the incident to the police, he told them Morecroft had threatened him with it. The whole thing was a fabrication on Stack's part.'

Hengrove smiled condescendingly. 'The magistrates thought otherwise.'

'Of course.' Jack turned to look his friend straight in the eye. 'Phil, they had the word of a renowned academic against that of a tearaway village lad. Who would you believe?'

'Okay…' Hengrove tossed his cigarette end into the broad, '… so the lad served a month for something he didn't do. That would make anyone bitter. Men have killed for less motive Jack, but we know there was another, don't we? You told me yourself that the safe held priceless gold artefacts. Well it doesn't now. Clearly, Morecroft arranged his own little compensation package.' There was a touch of exasperation creeping into Hengrove's voice. 'Jack, face the facts, Peter Morecroft had a grudge against the victim who scrawled his assailant's initials - PM - in the last of his life-blood. How plain can it be?'

Jack held up his hands in supplication. 'I know Phil, but look at it another way: if Morecroft did it, why would he be so stupid as to leave such a clue against himself?'

The DCI shrugged. 'Perhaps because Stack didn't scrawl those letters until after his assailant had gone. The Doc says the Professor could have lived thirty seconds: plenty of time for Morecroft to be off and away without realising his victim was pointing a dying finger.'

'But what about the trashing of the boat; that level of destruction wasn't done in seconds.'

'Perhaps that was done before the killing.'

'While the Professor just looked on smiling!' Jack exclaimed sarcastically before consciously moderating his tone. 'And then there's the safe. Phil, that piece of ironmongery had a multi-combination lock. Morecroft's an eel-fisherman, not a locksmith.'

'Jack, let me just run this scenario by you.' The DCI was clearly drawing on his last dregs of patience. 'Peter Morecroft visits Stack in the night, realising the man he hates has a fortune in gold on his boat. Morecroft is young and strong, knocks the Professor around a bit and coerces him into opening his safe. That done, he knocks out Stack and trashes his boat just to vent some bitterness. When he finally gets control of himself, he realises this time he faces life. He has no other option but to eliminate the living witness and sends the historian to that big museum in the sky with his own ancient weaponry. What he doesn't realise is that Stack has a bit of life left in him yet, enough to scrawl Morecroft's initials while the lad himself is making his getaway.' Hengrove lit another cigarette. 'Well, how does that all sound, Jack?' Before the Ranger could answer, there was a crackling from the DCI's pocket.

'Charlie Quebec three-three, Charlie X-ray seven-nine.'

Hengrove pulled out a handheld VHF. 'Yeah, seven-nine, go ahead.'

'Sir; we're on a hire cruiser, the *Polar Star*. Skipper heard some banging around midnight and saw the eel-catcher's boat alongside *Aethelberht*.'

'Right. Get his home details and a statement.' Hengrove turned back to the Ranger. 'That's good enough for me, Jack. Where is he?'

Further argument was futile; Hengrove had his job to do. Jack nodded to where the river left the north end of the broad. 'About a mile upriver. He lives on an old wooden cruiser.'

'Right.' The DCI re-called the RIB and gave Jack's directions, '... get up there, find him and call me back when you have.'

The RIB surged away, its quarter-wave curling back to where *Aethelberht*, *Raedwald* and the patrol launch all lay rafted together. It was strong enough to rock the boats before rolling on its way to the edge of the broad. Somehow it seemed to symbolise the turbulence now infecting these normally placid waters. Jack thought of young Peter Morecroft, a lad certainly possessing motive, means and opportunity. Could he really have misjudged the young eel-fisherman so completely?

IT WAS JUST FIFTEEN minutes before the RIB radioed back to Hengrove.

'We've got Morecroft, sir. Sitting here on his boat mending his nets. What now?'

The DCI stubbed another cigarette. 'Any aggro?'

'No, sir. Just a bit nervous if anything.'

Hengrove seemed almost disappointed. 'Okay, one of you bring him here; the other have a good look round his boat.'

'Roger; will do, sir.'

Hengrove turned to Jack standing beside him on deck. 'I'm looking forward to a chat with that young man. In the meantime, what else can you tell me, Jack? I understand you got a look inside that safe only yesterday.'

'Not much of one. Stack seemed more than anxious that I

didn't, but what I did see was interesting enough.'

'Such as…?'

'Well, apart from the gold brooches, there were some coins.'

Hengrove's eyebrows rose enquiringly. 'Coins? What sort? How many?'

'Silver and very old by the look of them. There must have been dozens, all stacked in columns like they'd been counted.'

Hengrove nodded towards the empty safe. 'But gone now with the gold. Not a bad night's work for Mister Morecroft.' Further discussion was ended by the roar of the returning RIB's engine. Both Jack and the DCI returned on deck as it came surging alongside with Peter Morecroft sitting rather dejectedly in the bows. Hengrove wasted no time with formalities. 'Right, young man, up here to answer some questions.'

Peter climbed up onto *Aethelberht's* deck, his worried look breaking into a brief smile at the sight of his friend, the Ranger. 'Mr. Fellows, wha's all this about. I ain't done nothin'.'

Jack slapped him on the shoulder. 'Just answer the questions truthfully Pete, and everything will be okay.'

The DCI's manner wasn't quite so avuncular: 'Morecroft, where were you last night?'

'Workin' me eel nets.'

'Any witnesses to corroborate that?'

'No, only the eels wha' I caught.'

'So how come you were working at night anyway?'

'Eels only swim at night…' Peter paused to roll his eyes, '… so tha's when we catch 'em.'

Hengrove gave a short sniff. 'Okay, smart Alec, so let's be more specific: where were you between midnight and two o'clock?'

'Back at me boat.'

'So you were nowhere near this boat last night?'

'… No.'

'You don't sound so sure, Morecroft.'

'I said, "no", din't I?'

Hengrove stood for a few seconds, studying the young eel-catcher and letting him reconsider his words. 'That's your final answer?'

Peter turned towards the one man he trusted. 'Mr. Fellows…'

Before he could continue, Hengrove said, 'I have a witness, Morecroft, who puts your boat alongside this one last night.'

'Not at them times, I weren't.'

'Ah, but you admit you were here then.' There was a glimmer of triumph in Hengrove's voice now. 'What time, Morecroft?'

'Later: three in the mornin'.' Once again, Peter turned towards his friend, the Ranger. 'Mr. Fellows, I just come to have a shufty at what Stack were up to like I always done. But I din't kill 'im.'

'Kill him…' Hengrove jumped on the point immediately, '… who said anything about a killing, Morecroft?'

The young eel-fisherman shook his head and sat down dejectedly. 'Like I said, I come here to spy on the Professor. He's … were… up to no good; I'm sure of it. Anyway, last night I sees his lights on but no Professor. I decides to have a closer look at wha's goin' on like, but when I sneaks a look through the window I sees the whole boat trashed and 'is body lyin' in a pool of blood. Din't take no Sherlock Holmes to tell he'd bin murdered.'

'And having discovered this serious crime…' Hengrove crossed his arms, '… it didn't occur to you to call the police?'

Peter looked at his feet. 'Less I have to do with the law, the better.'

'I bet.' The DCI was looking down at staining on the young eelman's fishing smock.

'Is that blood on your front, Morecroft?'

'Yeah, from guttin' rabbits for bait.'

Hengrove looked enquiringly at Jack. The Ranger nodded back.

'It's true, Phil, rabbit entrails are one of the baits used in eel pods.'

'Hmmm, well we can easily check that.' Further discussion was suspended as, once again, Hengrove's VHF crackled to life.

'Charlie Quebec three-three, Charlie X-ray eight-two.'

'Yeah; go ahead, eight-two.'

'Simpson here, sir, on the eel-catcher's boat. I've found something you might be interested in.'

'What?'

'A couple of old coins, sir. Look like silver to me.'

'Good work, Simpson. I'll send the RIB back to pick you up. Bag the coins and bring them with you.' The DCI turned back to his suspect. 'Well, that settles it as far as I'm concerned. Peter Morecroft, I'm arresting you on suspicion of murdering Professor Rupert Stack. You don't have to say anything but it may harm your defence if you do not mention, when questioned, something which you later rely on in Court. Anything you do say may be given in evidence.'

'But, I din't do it.' There was desperation now in the young lad's voice as he turned pleading eyes to the Ranger. 'Mr. Fellows, you gotta believe me… I don't know nothin' 'bout no coins an' I din't kill no-one.'

'Take it easy, Pete.' As Hengrove went for'ard to talk to headquarters on his mobile phone, Jack had just minutes to speak. 'Pete, be straight with me and I'll help you. Is what you've just said the truth?'

Peter nodded. 'Every word, Mr Fellows. I know I were wrong to say first I ain't bin here but I were scared stiff they'd think I done it… an' they do. But believe me, that Stack were already dead when I found 'im at three.'

'And you didn't enter this boat?'

'No, Mr Fellows. As soon as I seen that body I revved me engine and scarpered quick.'

'Where?'

'Straight back to me cruiser for a stiff rum. It'd shak'n me, Mr. Fellows, I tell ya.'

'I can believe it…' Jack put a friendly hand on the eel-fisherman's shoulder. A lifetime of listening to liars made the truth all the more real when he heard it, '… and I believe all the rest too, Pete. It won't be easy but I'll do all I can to help you.'

The relief on the young man's weathered face was soon wiped out by Hengrove's return.

'There's a car waiting at the staithe. Bailey!…' The young DC appeared from below, '… I'm going in with Morecroft. You stay here with the C.S.I.' He turned to Jack. 'Where's the most secure place near here to stick these boats, bearing in mind they're still a crime scene?'

Jack nodded to the western outlet of the broad. 'Giller's Boatyard. It's closed now and reasonably remote.'

'Good. Can you tow them in with that launch of yours?'

'No problem.'

'Right, let's get going then. Morecroft…' Peter almost jumped at the DCI's bark, '… down you go.'

As Peter climbed into the waiting RIB, Jack edged Hengrove confidentially to one side. 'Phil, I see how bad things look for young Morecroft but, believe me, you're making a mistake. I'd stake my pension that he didn't do it.'

Hengrove shook his head. 'I work with facts Jack and, until I know otherwise, this case looks open and shut.'

Jack leaned closer to the DCI. 'I know how stretched your resources are Phil, but there's more than one person out there with motive to kill Stack. How about if I make my own enquiries and see what else I can dig up?'

'A bit of private sleuthing, you mean.' The DCI shook his head. 'No way, Jack. Stick to your own job and leave investigation to those of us still paid to do it.'

Hengrove went to climb in the RIB but Jack blocked his way. 'Phil, you said yourself this is my patch, and you know my past experience. What happens on these waters is my job. If I promise to keep you informed at every point along the way and keep the arrangement strictly between us, what harm can it do?'

The DCI took a few seconds to thoughtfully digest the offer. Almost reluctantly, he nodded. 'Okay Jack, but on the strict condition that it's purely informal. I can't stop you asking questions and, if you want to offer yourself as a police informant, that's up to you. You know the drill.'

Jack shook Hengrove's hand. 'Thanks, Phil.'

The DCI climbed over the side and in seconds he and his prisoner were speeding away, Peter with the look of a man twice struck by lightning and Hengrove, the satisfaction of a case as good as solved. Jack watched them go and then climbed aboard his own launch and started the engine. Proving Pete Morecroft innocent wasn't going to be easy and the sooner he got on with it the better.

Chapter Six

GILLER'S BOATYARD LAY WELL away from the village, its two wooden sheds, quay-heading and slipway devoid of boats or movement. Alan had always taken pride in keeping his yard smart and tidy, but now, over all there hung an air of sad neglect. Only the cottage showed any sign of life as Jack and his small flotilla approached.

Boatyard Cottage lay at one end of the yard, a light still burning behind its kitchen's small-paned window. Very soon the stable door beside it opened and Charlotte Giller came out to meet them. Even in the early-morning light, Jack could see her slender figure weighed by a mountain of recent anguish, and her pretty face wearing an expression of near-loathing at the sight of *Aethelberht* and *Raedwald* gliding into the yard. It changed to confusion as Jack went astern and swung the boats beam onto the quay and she could see, for the first time, it was the Ranger's launch towing them in. She stepped forward to greet Jack as he jumped ashore.

'Problems, Mr. Fellows?'

'Yes, big ones.' Jack took her briefly to one side. 'Mrs. Giller, Professor Stack was murdered last night.'

'Oh God…' Charlotte Giller's hand went to her mouth as if to stifle more words, but there was no doubting her shock, '… what time did this happen, Mr. Fellows?'

'About two this morning, the experts think.'

'But… but I never heard a shot or anything.'

Even allowing for the shock of his news, Jack was surprised that this young widow's reaction was more of panic than satisfaction at the death of the man who had so blighted her life. 'He wasn't shot Mrs. Giller; he was stabbed to death.'

'Oh…' a wave of relief seemed to visibly pass over Charlotte's pretty features as she sought to express reactions she didn't feel, '… how terrible.'

'Yes.' Jack nodded back towards the boats from where uniformed police and white-overalled officers were already emerging. 'Mrs. Giller, we need to put these boats somewhere secure until all the forensic work is complete. Can we use the yard?'

Charlotte didn't answer immediately but seemed transfixed by *Aethelberht* and what she contained.

'Is … is he still in there, Mr. Fellows?'

'Yes…' Jack put his arm around the slim girl's shoulders and turned her away, back towards Boatyard Cottage, '… but don't concern yourself with that, Mrs. Giller. How about if we put the boats in the wetshed? There'll be a police guard left here to keep an eye on things.'

Charlotte nodded. 'Yes, of course.' She shrugged her narrow shoulders. 'I suppose, in reality, you don't even have to ask because legally this is almost Professor Stack's boatyard now anyway.'

Amidst the rest of the morning's happenings, Jack hadn't even considered this final irony: that Stack's first visit to his newly acquired boatyard should be as a contorted corpse. Macabre as this was, Charlotte Giller's feelings were still Jack's main concern.

'I'd still understand if you didn't want him near, Mrs. Giller.'

She shook her head. 'No, it's okay. I wouldn't want him in the boatshed where Alan… Alan died, but you can use the wetshed.'

'Thanks Mrs Giller; I'll go and get them warped in straight away.' He nodded over towards the cottage. 'Why don't you go and put the kettle on and I'll join you for a cuppa just as soon as I'm done?'

She brightened into a smile. 'That would be nice, Mr. Fellows.'

She scuttled off, a girl with many problems to cope with but a big one now effectively neutralised. She'd shown genuine shock at Stack's murder but walking back to the boats, Jack was troubled by two thoughts. Why had Charlotte Giller assumed that Stack had been shot and why had she not asked the one question everyone usually did: "Who did it?" Perhaps she already knew.

IT WAS THIRTY MINUTES before Jack knocked on Boatyard Cottage's open back door and ducked through the low frame onto the quarry-tiled floor. The kitchen was large, an appealing mixture of rustic pine units and modern appliances. There had been no attempt to clear the clutter that lay atop most surfaces, but the sense of homeliness this produced was only heightened by the enticing aroma of percolated coffee wafting over all. Charlotte smiled, took the pot from the brightly coloured range and motioned to the large pine table that filled the centre floorspace. 'Come in, Mr. Fellows, and rest yourself. I guess you've been going non-stop since the crack of dawn.'

'Just about...' Jack pulled up a chair and glanced at his watch: nine-fifteen, '... and call me Jack if you don't mind me calling you Charlotte.'

'No, of course not.' She sat down opposite, poured coffee into two large mugs and pushed one across to her guest. 'Well... Jack... did you get the boats in okay?'

He nodded over the rim of his mug. The coffee was strong, just as he liked it. 'Yep, both of them. You'll find the whole shed taped off as a crime scene now. The forensic team will be working for a few days yet but hopefully, today...' Jack paused, sensing the delicacy of the situation, '... the coroner's men will come and take away the body.'

Charlotte smiled understandingly. 'It's alright, Jack. I'm afraid the thought of Professor Stack's body affects me far less than the prospect of his living presence. I loathed the man and there's no point in denying it.'

'I can quite believe it.' Jack took a sip of his coffee, realising he was about to tread on sensitive ground but needing facts rather than rumour. 'If what I've heard is correct, Professor Stack was the man who actually drove you and Alan to bankruptcy.'

'He did indeed...' Charlotte sipped her own coffee, '... and nothing will ever convince me he didn't plan the whole thing. He needed a base and Giller's suited him very nicely. You probably know the story of how he held back payment until we went under.'

'I know the basic details,' said Jack, 'but I'm still amazed he found any grounds to complain about such a beautiful boat as *Raedwald*.'

Charlotte put down her mug. 'By constantly upgrading the specifications. Our original contract was to build a replica Anglo-Saxon galley.' Her eyes were looking out through the kitchen window now towards the boatshed, and Jack guessed her thoughts were with her late husband, toiling away there on that beautiful boat. 'Alan put his heart and soul into *Raedwald*, but how far can you take authenticity? Stack started making more and more impossible demands: special wood, hand-made nails, hemp rope. We tried to accommodate them but these things cost the earth and when it became obvious that the whole job was going to be a horrendous financial loss for us, the bank refused further loans and we couldn't buy the materials anyway. Stack then refusing to pay was the last straw. The bank foreclosed on us, called in the Receivers and you know the rest.' She shook her head. 'I think it was the loss of pride at having his work called into question, as much as the stigma of bankruptcy, that drove Alan to do what he did.' She shook her head wearily. 'The really hurtful thing was that Professor Stack already had the money from a development grant.'

'So I heard…' Jack looked up from his coffee, '… and instead used it for...?'

'I can guess.' Charlotte didn't voice her suspicions but instead looked back to her guest and forced a brave smile. 'All history now of course, so no point dwelling on it.'

'No,' Jack shook his head sadly, the poignancy to this whole tragic tale being all the greater in the victim's own words, 'but I can well imagine the prospect of Stack becoming your new landlord wasn't one you relished.'

Charlotte nodded. 'It certainly wasn't, but it wouldn't have happened anyway because, only yesterday, I got notice to quit the cottage.'

'Yes, I heard he was evicting you.' Jack's eyes took in the life-weary look of the girl opposite. 'But not anymore.'

'I suppose not.' Charlotte's own eyes showed only a momentary flash of hope. 'Or at least not immediately, though whoever owns the yard now could still have me evicted.' She held up the coffee-pot and Jack nodded for a second mug.

'I wonder who that is, Charlotte? Any idea who might be Stack's beneficiary?'

She shook her head again. 'I've no idea. He certainly wasn't married and I'm not aware of any immediate family.'

Jack nodded. 'Just how did he manage to buy the yard anyway?'

'By submitting a bid to the Receiver.' Charlotte poured herself another mug. 'Presumably his was the highest, though I find it hard to believe. I know of at least one boatbuilder around here who would have paid reasonable money for the yard and allowed me to stay on in the cottage.'

'Who was the Receiver?'

'Gwen Fosdyke.'

Jack took a sip of his coffee, more to give himself thinking space than refreshment, before looking again at the cosiness that was Charlotte's home. 'Well, nothing is going to happen immediately, Charlotte, but it would be good for you to know how the land now lies.' He swigged back the last of his coffee and stood up. 'I guess the only way to find out for sure is to talk to Stack's solicitor. Who was acting for him?'

'Gwen Fosdyke,' Charlotte repeated, her voice carrying just the faintest tinge of suspicion.

Jack's eyebrows rose. 'She was your Receiver and his solicitor?'

Charlotte gave a short scoff. 'More than just his solicitor, if you ask me.'

'How do you mean?'

But already Charlotte was regretting her momentary outburst. 'Nothing. Just forget I said that, Jack.'

Jack wouldn't, but temporarily placed it in his mental "check later" file. 'Didn't you even query the conflict of interest, Charlotte?'

She just shrugged. 'I only found out Stack was the new owner of the yard yesterday. Perhaps I should have kept a better track of things but I'd got to the point where I just didn't care anymore. There's a limit to how much fighting you can do when you're coping with grief.'

'I can believe that.' Jack went to the sink, rinsed his mug and then ducked his way out through the low doorway and back into the fitful sunlight. He glanced across to the wetshed; a policeman now stood guard at the door. Jack nodded towards him. 'Any problems with the media, talk to the copper.'

'Okay.' She nodded towards the standing police car. 'Have they any idea who did it, Jack?' The question was asked with a catch in her voice as though she feared the answer.

'They arrested Peter Morecroft this morning on suspicion.'

'Oh...'

Jack scanned the young woman's face. She'd obviously picked up the doubt in his answer but was her reaction relief, confusion or sadness? Hard to decide and perhaps he shouldn't try; Charlotte Giller had been thrown quite enough shocks this deathly morning without instant judgements on her demeanour. Instead Jack gave her arm a reassuring squeeze. 'I'd like to talk more, Charlotte, but…' he nodded towards his launch, '… work to do.'

'I'll be okay.' Charlotte slipped on the coat she'd grabbed as they went out. 'I'll see you off.'

'And then what?' Jack was concerned she shouldn't be alone with her thoughts and Stack's body in the yard.

'Work. I help out at Starcraft.'

'Colin Newell's yard ... doing what?'

'Boatbuilding.' She smiled, recalling happy memories. 'I learned a lot from Alan over the years and became pretty handy with the tools myself. Starcraft were short-handed so...'

Already, Jack was slotting pieces of this jigsaw into place. 'Were they the yard who wanted to buy yours?'

Charlotte nodded. 'Yep, but now I'm just grateful for the job. It works in well after my early-morning paper-round.'

Jack laughed. 'I can see you're a girl who won't spend too much time with your head in your hands.' They'd reached the launch now. As he climbed on board Jack turned, the smile gone, his eyes searching. 'Charlotte, one final question. Have *you* any idea who else might have killed Stack?'

Her eyes met his. 'So you don't think Pete Morecroft is the killer?'

'No.'

Charlotte shook her head. 'I can think of many who'd like that man dead, myself included.'

Motoring away from Giller's Yard, Jack looked back at the slim girl, deep in thought, wheeling her bike out of the boatshed. A gutsy girl was Charlotte Giller, a girl he respected, even if he wasn't sure she was telling the whole truth.

As he headed out into the broad, Jack glanced back a final time to see Charlotte peddling out of the yard on her way to work. There indeed was a girl with enough spirit to have killed Stack herself.

JACK'S INTENTION WAS TO visit *Polar Star*, the anchored cruiser whose skipper had stated seeing the eel-catcher's boat alongside *Aethelberht* during the fatal hours. He always regarded interviewing witnesses as something akin to picking fruit: no matter how thoroughly you did it, there was always more there for the gathering. He was glad to see the cruiser still at anchor off the fairway and was heading towards it when the glint of sunshine reflecting off polished brass caused him to change direction towards the familiar boat just entering the broad.

It was *Goosewatcher*, Colonel Etherington's slipper-launch. As the classic boat came abeam and slowed, Jack swung his patrol launch around, dropped some fenders and came gingerly alongside. He was well aware of the Colonel's concern for the well-being of his craft, but this forenoon the old soldier obviously had other concerns.

'Morning, Colonel.'

'Morning, Fellows; what the devil's been happening? Police buzzing about in those infernal blow-up things and talk of some murder or something.'

'Yes, true I'm afraid…' the boats were stopped now and Jack slipped a warp around *Goosewatcher*'s midships cleat to hold them rafted together, '… Professor Stack was murdered on his boat last night.'

Colonel Etherington listened intently as Jack told of his finding the body.

'Good Lord, what's the place coming to.' The Colonel shook his fine head. 'Mind you, doesn't surprise me. Chap was a bounder and no mistake. Had it coming to him if you ask me. Have they got anyone yet?'

'Peter Morecroft. The police arrested him this morning.'

'The eel-catcher chappie?' Colonel Etherington gave a knowing grunt. 'Well, that doesn't surprise me either. Didn't he do time not so long ago for threatening Stack with a shotgun?'

'Yes, but in my opinion he was unjustly convicted on false evidence and I'm just as sure he didn't do this murder either.'

'Hmmm.' The Colonel seemed unconvinced. 'You're the policeman, Fellows, but I think you might be putting your money on the wrong horse there. Morecroft's a bad egg in my opinion. Caught him poaching at The Hall once, you know. What do the police reckon his motive was?'

'Robbery. The gold brooches and some coinage are gone...' Jack had heard of Peter's encounter with Colonel Etherington's gamekeeper years previous. In his opinion it was just another case of boyish mischief but it had contributed to young Morecroft's local reputation as a "wrong un", '… but poaching's a long way from gold robbery, Colonel, and even further from murder. Morecroft didn't do this and I intend to prove it.'

'Well, I think you have your work cut out, Fellows…' Colonel Etherington was looking the Ranger up and down as though doubting his sanity but knowing better than to try and dissuade him. Instead he managed a quick smile of reluctant approval, '… but good luck anyway, old chap.'

'Thanks, Colonel. Tell me, did you see anything unusual on the river last night?'

'Good question.' The colonel scratched his grey close-cropped hair. 'Can't think of anything, Fellows, except I did see a chap rowing.'

'Rowing; where and what time?'

'Pretty late. I'd gone down to the boathouse in me dressing gown. Left me mobile phone in the boat and needed to charge it.' Colonel Etherington rolled his eyes in exasperation. 'Sometimes wonder if these modern gadgets are worth it. Time was when you could go boating in peace. Now the blessed phone rings all the time and...'

'The rowing boat, Colonel. You were telling me about the late-night rower.'

'Ah yes...' Etherington scratched his head again, '... where was I. Oh yes, the rower. Yes, went down to the shed 'bout oneish and there's this boat rowing by. Some of these fishing chappies have been using my dock at night so thought I'd caught one of the blighters. Damn cheek! Some of them, you know, sit there with their lamps and sandwiches and...'

'Which way was the boat going, Colonel?'

'Upriver I think. Yes... upriver.'

'Away from the broad?'

'Yes.'

'Did you recognise who it was?'

The old soldier shook his head. 'Not as such. Not much moon last night. Pretty dark actually but I think I knew the boat.'

If Colonel Etherington had ever suffered capture and interrogation in his army career his captors would have got precious little information thought Jack, with not a little exasperation of his own. 'What boat was it, Colonel?'

'That artist chappie's... what's his name... Thornton.'

'Stuart Thornton from Wyford's Mill?'

The Colonel nodded. 'Yes, that's the one. Pretty sure it was his boat. Even said "Night, Thornton" but he didn't answer. Typical moody arty type if you ask me. All the same, them arty types; too busy trying to "capture the feel on canvas" or some such to give the rest of the world...'

'But you think it was definitely Stuart Thornton's boat. Why are you so sure, Colonel, if it was as dark as you say?'

'Old memory isn't too good these days, Fellows, but I still remember details,' replied the Colonel, tapping the side of his nose knowingly. 'Easy to spot Thornton's boat because he built that extra height on the gunwale just by the bow. Told me it kept the spray off when he was motoring hard.'

'But he wasn't motoring last night?'

'No, old boy; as I said, rowing. Strange, 'cause the chap seemed to be in a dashed hurry, pulling away on his oars like there was no tomorrow.'

And for Rupert Stack there wasn't, thought Jack, before saying, 'Thank you, Colonel. I appreciate your time,' letting go the warp and allowing the two boats to idle apart.

'Only hope it's of help.' Colonel Etherington nodded towards where *Raedwald* and *Aethelberht* had lain that night and where Stack had died. 'Bad business, Fellows. Hope you find what you're looking for. It'll take a hundred per cent effort on your part but keep me advised of progress if you can.' He gave a little laugh. 'Stack was a blighter in life but at least he's given us a bit of excitement in death. What?'

Goosewatcher motored away, a vestige of another age but with a period charm all of her own. Not unlike her owner thought Jack, smiling to himself and swinging the patrol launch onto a heading back to the broad's eastern side and the still-anchored *Polar Star*. Last night's witness could still throw fresh light on the mystery but Stuart Thornton, aggrieved husband of the victim's mistress, was a man Jack wanted to speak to very, very soon.

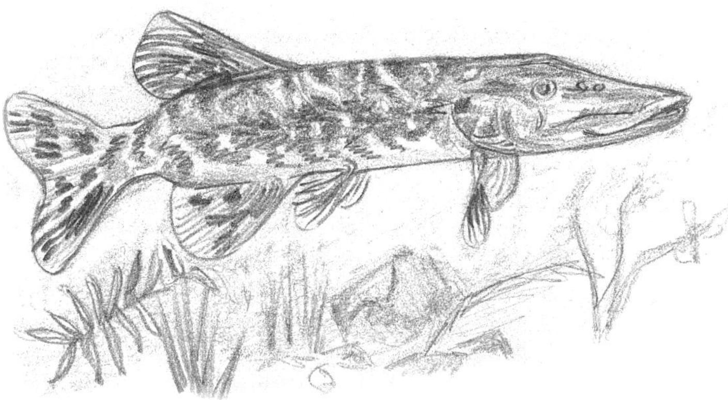

Chapter Seven

THE SKIPPER OF THE *Polar Star* was a bluff Yorkshireman, whose physical size matched his northern hospitality. As Jack came alongside and introduced himself, the north country accent in reply was as pronounced as it was warm.

'Ah told copper all I knew but come aboard lad, if I can help thee more,' he responded, obviously accepting the Ranger's uniform as authority enough. 'Been holidaying on't Broads for twenty-odd years now but first time we've known a crime, let alone murder,' he explained with grim humour, leading Jack below, easing his considerable bulk behind the saloon table and introducing himself as Tom Ledger.

'Well, it's good of you to give me more of your holiday time,' said Jack taking the couch opposite as Mrs. Ledger joined them. 'What time did you anchor here last night, Mr. Ledger?'

The big Yorkshireman scratched his balding head. ''Bout five it was. We picked boat up earlier an' was headin' for Yarmouth but knew we'd never make it on't tide so decided to spend night in this lovely spot.'

'So, the victim's boats, *Raedwald* and *Aethelberht*, arrived after you?'

'Aye, they did.' Mr. Ledger gave a good-hearted chuckle. 'Gave us a reet funny turn, ah can tell you, lad, when we sees that old boat comin' into'd broad. Thought we'd gone through a timewarp or summat.'

Jack nodded and smiled. 'And then you heard some banging coming from *Aethelberht*, the motor cruiser, during the night?'

'That's reet, lad. Crashing and banging like they was fightin' World War Three out there.'

'What time was this, Mr. Ledger?'

'Ten past midnight. I remember checkint' clock in't wheelhouse as I went topsides, thinkin', "Whose makin' all this racket at this time a neet?"'

'And what did you see when you went on deck?'

'Not a lot really, lad. There were lights on't cruiser and figures movin' behind curtains like they were fightin'.'

'How many figures?'

'Two as far as't I could see.' Mr. Ledger leaned forward shaking his head. 'I suppose, lookin' back, I should have done summat but it would have meant up-anchorin' and motorin' over and, anyway, you don't like to interfere, do you?'

'Especially when you're on 'oliday,' added Mrs. Ledger, obviously keen to support her husband. 'I says to him, "leave 'em be, Tom. No sense you getting mixed up in others' troubles".'

'Understandable,' reassured Jack, instinctively taking a notebook and pen from his top pocket and recording the times and details already mentioned. 'Now, I understand you actually saw the eel-fisherman's boat alongside?'

'Aye, I did.'

'How did you know it was the eel-fisherman's boat?'

'Because I'd seen it day before and chatted to lad hi'self. Nice lad he seemed too. I wasn't sure of't tide times at Yarmouth and he seemed sort who'd know, so I stops and asks him. Couldn't have been more helpful, could lad, and we chatted on ag'in. I like a bit of fishin' misself so he tells me all about his eel-catchin', settin' his nets an' the like. Fascinating stuff, it were too.'

'I'm sure.' Jack paused to select a fresh page in his notebook and also take time to think. 'Mr. Ledger, which way were the boats pointing when you got up to check the noise?'

'This way, like we are now,' said the skipper, pointing towards the west.

'And where were the victim's boats?'

'Over there, over to starboard,' answered Mr. Ledger pointing north to where *Aethelberht* and *Raedwald* had lain when Jack found them.

Glancing at the notes he had just made, Jack took time to digest their significance. 'That's what puzzles me, Mr. Ledger. You see, we know the victim always towed *Raedwald,* the old galley, on the port side of his cruiser and that's where she was when I found them this morning. So, if all the boats were lying on westerly headings last night, any boat on *Aethelberht's* starboard side would be out of sight.' Jack smiled again to reassure his witness that this was still a friendly chat and not interrogation. 'I'm not sure how you could have seen the eel-boat in those circumstances, Mr. Ledger.'

The Yorkshireman smiled back. 'But I didn't; not then anyways.'

'But you just said you did.' Jack frowned. 'I'm not sure what you're saying, Mr. Ledger.'

'I'm sayin', I didn't see t'eel-boat when I got up to check noise. I sees it later when I got up again to check anchor.'

'You got up twice?'

Tom Ledger nodded, smiling with the good-natured satisfaction of one who knows he's misled authority. 'That's reet, lad. When I goes on deck to check noise, the boats were pointin' like you said. I couldn't say whether there was any boat on't other side or not, but guess there must have been 'cos of fightin'. Anyways, I goes back to bed after that, an' goes to sleep until wind wakes me again later on. Blowin' a good un, it was and I'm worried anchor might be draggin' isself. So, I goes up on deck to find wind has gone reet round an' so hast boat. Other boats has gone round too so's their other side is facin' us now. Can't 'ear much above noise oft wind but what I sees now is eel-catching lad and 'is boat alongside the big cruiser.'

'So you saw Peter Morecroft in his boat then, Mr. Ledger?' Jack leaned a little closer across the table. 'At any point did he board the cruiser, the *Aethelberht*?'

'Not when I was lookin' which wasn't for long,' said Tom Ledger, shaking his head.

'What time was this now, Mr. Ledger?'

The Yorkshireman shook his head again. 'Now there you got me lad, 'cos this occasion I didn't check time. Jus' wanted to make sure boat were safe and get back down here to wife and warmth.' He smiled and gave Mrs. Ledger a playful nudge and she made a face back before turning to Jack.

'Will you have a coffee, Mr. Fellows?'

Jack closed his notebook and stood up, shaking his head. 'No thanks, Mrs. Ledger, I must be off.' He turned back to her husband. 'Did you tell the police officer this: that you went on deck twice and didn't see the eel-boat until the second time?'

'Aye, but 'e didn't seem to think it that important.' Mr. Ledger followed Jack on deck. 'Is it?'

'It could be.' Jack shook the big Yorkshireman's hand. 'I'm very grateful for your time, both of you.' It was only when he was climbing down into the launch that he paused for no other reason than old-copper's instinct. 'Before I go, is there anything else you can tell me; anything else either of you saw last night that might have seemed strange?'

The pair looked at each other and shrugged before Mrs. Ledger spoke up. 'Well I saw something, but I don't know if it's important.'

'What?' Jack paused in casting off. 'What did you see?'

Mrs. Ledger smiled. 'Well, it were while Tom were up on deck the first time checking that noise. I looked out of window on my side and saw a boat.'

'What sort of boat, Mrs. Ledger?'

She smiled, seemingly self-conscious at her lack of nautical knowledge. 'I couldn't see it too well 'cos it were dark and the cloud were covering what little moon there were.'

'Tell me exactly what you saw.' Jack tried to keep the impatience out of his voice, knowing that getting this homely woman flustered wouldn't help at all. With effort, he eased his tone. 'Anything will be helpful, Mrs. Ledger.'

'Well, it were a small boat which seemed odd at that time of neet. It were a rowing boat, with just one man working the... the...'

'... oars,' Tom Ledger finished for her with just a little exasperation in his voice. 'I didn't see it misself, Mr. Fellows, 'cos I were distracted by all that commotion on t'other boats. Missus only tells me 'bout it when I comes back to bed an' by that time 'e's gone.'

Jack turned back to the worried-looking wife. 'Can you describe this boat... this rowing boat... at all, Mrs. Ledger?'

She gave a pained expression. 'Well, as I say, it were a small boat but it were bigger than a normal rowing boat. About half the length of this boat,' she nodded at their own cruiser, 'an' pointed at both ends an' reet low down in the water too. It just seemed very odd that a man should be out rowing a boat like that at midnight.'

'Quite a few fishermen do,' said Jack, smiling. 'Did he look like a fisherman, Mrs. Ledger? Can you describe him at all?'

Mrs. Ledger shook her head. 'No, 'fraid not, Mr. Fellows. As I said, it were dark. He did seem to be wearing a cap though, typical Yorkshire flatcap it looked, which you don't see much down here, and he had some sort of jacket with a hood. Couldn't see his face though 'cos he were bendin' over the... the oars all the time.'

'Understood,' said Jack, nodding. 'Did either of you see this boat again, the second time you got up to check the anchor?'

Both shook their heads. 'Sorry we can't be more helpful,' said Mr. Ledger with genuine regret, handing down Jack's stern line.

'You've both been incredibly helpful.' Jack allowed his launch to glide clear of *Polar Star*. On deck, the Ledgers waved him goodbye, their beaming faces showing satisfaction at his words.

Jack himself was well pleased with his findings, even if they raised more questions than answers. Cruising across the broad he mulled over Mrs. Ledger's description of the rowing boat. Approximately fifteen feet, double-ended and with low freeboard. There was really only one boat that fitted that description. The marsh punt was the traditional working boat of the Broads marshmen and Jack knew of only one used locally. Walter Giller still rowed a marsh punt and he certainly had motive enough to kill the man who'd destroyed his only son.

WALTER GILLER WAS FRYING his breakfast and listening to the local radio station when the breaking news came through of Professor Rupert Stack's death on the Norfolk Broads. No specific details were released by Norfolk Constabulary at this time save the stark fact that they were treating this as a murder enquiry. A telephone number was given for anyone with information to help the police.

Walter paused in turning his bacon to listen to the bulletin. Then he forked the bacon together with the two eggs, onto his plate and made a large mug of coffee. He was about to sit down when he paused, grabbed the rum bottle from the sideboard and poured a generous splash into his coffee. On the same sideboard was a framed photo of Alan, tanned and smiling as he looked up from replanking one of his beloved boats. Walter raised his mug to the image, said, 'God rest you Alan,' and then tucked into his breakfast with more appetite than he'd known for a long time.

THAT SAME BULLETIN CAME through as Gwen Fosdyke was driving to work. In happier days she had always enjoyed the five miles between village cottage and town office. On the country roads she could let her mind slowly mull over the workload for the day ahead and on the evening run home, unwind from whatever stresses they had generated. These last months though, her journeying thoughts had become increasingly troubled, culminating in this most awful of climaxes. Now, betwixt home and office, she pulled into the roadside and listened to the dreaded words. Her reaction to the announcement surprised her. She was free now of all the dreadful obligations Professor Rupert Stack had put her under and from the torment of continually compromising her professional ethics and personal good name. She should have been experiencing a great sense of release with this heartless man's death, but instead was suffering paroxysms of guilt and regret. Gwen thought again of her dear father and what anguish this would have caused him; she sensed him watching over her now and shivered at what his feelings would be.

The radio bulletin had given a number for any person with information. Had anyone witnessed this crime? Could she still end up on the wrong side of her own court?

THE BROADS BEAT WERE just securing Peter Morecroft's boats either side of their RIB as Jack came abeam. He glanced at his watch: just short of noon but already it felt like a full day.

After interviewing the Ledgers on *Polar Star*, he'd radioed in a full report on the morning's events to his superiors at the Broads Authority. At the same time, he'd requested their permission to pursue his own enquiries. Serious as murder was, his primary job was enforcing river by-laws and assisting boaters and the Authority might take a dim view of extra-curricular sleuthing. His immediate supervisor had promised to pass on the facts to higher control and get back to him. Just minutes ago had come the Authority's decision: any investigations on the river could be accepted as falling within his work remit; any beyond it would have to be conducted in his own time. Well, tomorrow was a day off for Jack with an auxillary manning his launch. He had a shrewd idea now how it might be spent.

At the same time as radioing back this permission, the Authority had ordered the Ranger back to Peter Morecroft's boats where police were standing by. The eel-catcher's little fleet was also now a crime scene and the plan was to tow the boats to another secure yard for forensic examination. Jack's launch would escort them. As he came alongside, he was hailed by the Broads Beat Officer on the bow of the cruiser.

'We'll tow them; you go ahead and keep the fairway clear.'

'Okay.' Jack had come out of his wheelhouse into the launch's open well. 'Where are you taking them?'

'Starcraft's yard. They've been advised and given the okay.'

That was where Charlotte Giller worked, a boatyard two miles upriver on the edge of town. Jack took up station just ahead of the three boats and led the way as Peter Morecroft's home and livelihood moved slowly towards its new berth. There, the C.S.I. team would be painstakingly combing both cruiser and dory. Knowing the squalid state of the eel-catcher's existence, Jack didn't envy them, but the thought still touched him with sadness. Was it only yesterday that he'd sat there with the young eel-fisherman in his tip of a saloon and told him to keep clear of Stack? How he wished now that he'd been more forceful in his warning and that Peter Morecroft had taken greater heed.

LISA THORNTON SWITCHED ON the ten o'clock news and learned about the death of her boss. She'd overslept and, considering the traumatic nature of the previous days, it was miraculous that she'd slept at all. But Lisa had snuggled down on the apartment sofa that night with all the contentment of one who had scored over the most devious man in the county.

The data now downloaded from Stack's personal files was all she would need to establish her own little nefarious deals. Or perhaps not so little if the figures listed together with contact details were anything to go by. Obviously certain people were prepared to pay way beyond anything she had ever thought. For the first time, she realised how exploited she'd been by her late boss.

The revelation, when she heard the headline news item that Stack was now "late" in every sense, did at least allow Lisa to relax. Having woken late, her fear had been the Professor appearing any minute to discover her squatting and his desk forced open. After leaping off the sofa, throwing on her clothes and frantically collecting her things, she'd automatically switched on local radio. Within minutes, the headlines had told her there was no rush at all and that no-one would ever have to fear Professor Rupert Stack again.

Although possessed of an undeniable ruthless streak, Lisa's immediate natural reactions were ones of shock and disbelief. These, however, quickly mellowed into undeniable satisfaction diluted only slightly by the question of who had actually done the dastardly deed. She realised it could be any of the innumerable enemies the man had generated over the years, but one candidate who did spring to mind was her own husband, Stuart.

Stuart, although seriously wimpish, had undeniable love for her that frequently manifested itself into bursts of almost insane possessive rage. In such a jealousy-triggered confrontation, her husband would have been quite capable of killing Rupert Stack.

Lisa lit her first cigarette of the day and contemplated the ramifications of possibly being married to a murderer. They weren't altogether unpalatable. If Stuart really had killed Stack and eventually got banged away for life, Wyford's Mill might well be hers for good. With that scenario satisfactorily accepted, Lisa then applied her scheming mind to the more immediate effect that Stack's death would have on her plans.

It took only seconds to decide that it would only make things simpler. No-one knew that both their working and personal relationship had ended yesterday. As far as the rest of the world was concerned, she would now be just the distraught secretary tragically robbed of her employer. This was still her office and she would remain here on the payroll for many weeks yet while Stack's estate was wound up. Lisa threw her coat into a cupboard, went into the kitchen and percolated some coffee.

And how would that estate be distributed? Back in the lounge-cum-office, Lisa sipped her Colombian and considered the wealth now up for grabs. As far as she knew, Rupert Stack had no family and had never mentioned any beneficiaries to his considerable pile. Had he even made a will? If he had, it crossed Lisa's mind that she might even be mentioned. Any will would doubtless have been written with that infernal solicitor-woman Fosdyke who might well have engineered her own little inheritance. Who was to say Gwen Fosdyke hadn't brought forward the glad day by killing Stack herself? The thought of the solicitor being the actual murderer then raised the unappealing spectre of an innocent Stuart not destined for life in prison. Lisa could find herself estranged and homeless yet.

It was a disturbing thought. If a will did exist, then there would be a copy but where? She'd already been through the desk drawers and found no such document. There was no safe in the apartment. What Stack did have were books, hundreds of them lining the walls in floor-to-ceiling cases and between their pages it would be the easiest thing in the world to conceal copies of vital documents. Could a copy be there? Lisa went to the bookcases.

The problem was where to start with hundreds of books and tens of thousands of pages. It was time for more deduction. Legal documents, even if folded, would still require a fair-sized book to hold them. The largest books were on the bottom rows, some leather bound and all relating to the Anglo-Saxon period. She fingered her way along volumes covering studies in agriculture, warfare, seafaring, architecture, fashion, religion, customs, monarchy, science. She stopped at the last one: science; surely there was little science in what were always termed the Dark Ages? She pulled the volume and noticed its lack of weight even before it was half out.

It wasn't a book at all. In reality it was more like a box file but bound just like its neighbouring volumes. Gulping with excitement, Lisa laid the leather tome on the floor and pulled open its cover.

Initially she felt disappointment: there were no legal documents here, just a couple of large envelopes. She pulled out their contents. In the first were some photo prints taken with a digital camera. Their subject was wonderfully revealing. In the second envelope were copies of newspaper cuttings. They were from newspaper articles eleven years previous which included other photos. A quick read and a closer study of the photos and Lisa knew how Rupert Stack had achieved so much of late. Now she could use them likewise. Perhaps he never had made a will and it mattered little now whether he had or not; the contents of those envelopes would bring his small fortune all to her.

'Yes,' she shouted to herself as she punched a fist of triumph into the air. Within minutes, her fertile, scheming mind had worked a plan. She went straight to the phone, rang Gwen Fosdyke's office and made an appointment for that very afternoon.

Chapter Eight

IF LISA THORNTON thought there had been no witnesses to her and Stack's altercation of the previous afternoon, she was wrong. As Jack guided the little police flotilla towards Starcraft's yard, he finally got through to the busy number he'd been calling for the last half-hour.

'Information Centre, Potter Heigham', answered the cheerful female voice. The Broads Authority ran information centres at many of the Broadland staithes and the Potter Heigham one was very close to where Professor Stack had invariably moored his boats.

'Hi Gemma, Jack Fellows here.'

'Morning Jack, what can I do for you?' Gemma Honeywell was a bubbly efficient young woman whose friendly manner never wavered regardless of the queue of visitors and their questions.

'Gemma, I expect you've heard the news regarding Professor Stack?'

'Yes…' Jack sensed rather than heard the young assistant take a nervous swallow, '… bit creepy really seeing as he spent most of yesterday moored right outside my window.'

That answered one of Jack's questions: Stack had said he was heading for Potter Heigham but until now there had been no confirmation he actually had.

'Anything odd happen while he was there, Gemma; anything out of the ordinary?'

'Not really; we had one family come in and complain that Professor Stack had been very rude to them but that was nothing new. Lots of people looked over *Raedwald* and the museum boat and by twelve-thirty the professor had shut up shop for lunch. His secretary visited him shortly after. Not too happy a visit though, judging by the way she left.'

'Lisa Thornton…?' Starcraft's yard was in sight now but this last snippet of information had got Jack's attention, '… why, what happened?'

'Oh, you know, usual sort of thing: stomped off the boat looking seriously pissed off and sped off the staithe.I was actually going to get you to have a word with her, Jack. She shouldn't drive on the staithe anyway and she only just missed a couple of pensioners and managed to wheel-spin shingle over some kids.'

'Okay, I'll talk to her,' said Jack, glad of an operational excuse to interview the bolshie Lisa. 'Thanks, Gemma; you've been a great help.'

He rang off and concentrated on leading the police into the small dyke that served as Starcraft's main mooring. From the boatshed, the familiar figure of Colin Newell and a couple of yardhands came out to take their lines.

'Tie them over there, Jack.' Colin pointed to the empty quay beside the main workshop. Starcraft was a traditional Broads boatyard where Colin Newell ran a small hire fleet while, at the same time, restoring and repairing more traditional craft. The latter was work very much akin to Alan Giller's old business and there was more than a passing similarity in the two men. Alan had been in his early thirties when he died and Colin's fresh complexion and flowing hair had all the vitality of a healthy, vibrant man of the same age. Perhaps his nature was rather more relaxed than Alan's intensity but he took his work seriously just the same and had built up a good reputation over the years as a skilled boatbuilder and a fair businessman. As he took Jack's line, he nodded towards the police RIB and Peter Morecroft's boats gliding in astern. 'Strange business.'

'It certainly is.' Jack climbed ashore and helped secure his launch. 'Thanks for your co-operation, Colin.'

The boatbuilder shook his head. 'I'm doing it for Pete Morecroft, Jack. He might be a bit wild but he's a good lad all the same and I want his boats to be looked after until he sorts things out.'

'You know the story then.'

Colin Newell nodded sadly. 'Yeah, Charlotte told me when she came in.'

As if on cue, the girl herself appeared at her boss's shoulder. 'Morning again Mr… Jack.' Glancing down at the chisel she still held in her hand, she quickly said, 'Fitting new bottom planks … are you ready for another coffee, Jack?'

'No thanks, Charlotte…' Jack nodded towards the Broads Beat Officers who had just secured the old cruiser and eel-boat alongside, 'but I bet those coppers are… if it's no trouble.'

She smiled. 'Of course it's not; I'll go and put the kettle on.'

'A great girl, that,' said Jack, not failing to notice the admiration in Colin Newell's eyes as Charlotte returned to the boatshed.

'What… Charlotte…?' The young boatbuilder was doing a lousy imitation of indifference, '… yeah, and a good little worker too. I'm certainly glad of her skills here with the workload as it is.'

'Things busy then?' asked Jack as he followed Colin back into the shed.

The boatbuilder nodded. 'Very much so. There aren't too many craftsmen left who can work on the old wooden boats and even fewer since poor old Alan went. This is what boatbuilding is all about.' Colin gestured into the main workshop where a traditional thirty foot wooden sailing cruiser lay propped on cradles. Shavings lay spiralled on the floor while over all hung the evocative aroma of well-seasoned timber, glue and varnish. No gelcoats, alloy spars or stainless fittings here; just solid wood and shining bronze. 'Wooden boats take a lot of work and we turn away more than we can handle. What we need…' he paused to take a large mug of steaming coffee from the tray brought over by Charlotte, '… is more yard space.'

'Like Giller's.' Jack felt he was saying bluntly what Colin wanted to but somehow felt he shouldn't. Perhaps it was Rupert Stack's death but more likely Charlotte Giller herself standing beside them.

She too seemed to sense the awkwardness of the moment. Nodding towards the refitting cruiser she said, 'Work to be done Jack, if you'll excuse me.'

'Of course.' Jack watched Charlotte slide back under the expanse of the sailboat's hull where she quickly took chisel and mallet to some exposed frames. Well understanding Colin Newell's attraction to such a capable girl, he turned back to the lad himself. 'You actually put in a bid for Giller's Yard, I believe?'

The boatbuilder nodded. 'Yep, a fair one too and I wouldn't have evicted Charlotte like Stack…' he glanced in the direction of the unseen broad, '… the mean scheming bastard.'

'Well, he's a dead bastard now.' Jack wanted some of Colin Newell's obvious bitterness dissipated before the police joined them. 'I'm not sure how his death leaves the legal situation with regard to Giller's Yard, Colin. The sale hadn't reached completion so perhaps you can make another bid.'

'You really think so?' The boatbuilder's whole demeanour had suddenly brightened. 'That would be great, Jack. I wouldn't let it slip through my fingers a second time.'

'Heh, hold it, I'm no lawyer…' said Jack, seeing the young man's premature excitement, '… but I should be seeing one in the next day or so. I'll try and find out.'

Further discussion ended with the entrance of the police into the shed. Charlotte came back out from under the boat where she'd obviously been keeping her ear to the conversation, and took the Ranger's hand. 'Thanks for all you're doing Jack.' She glanced towards the police. 'I'll go and get their coffee now.'

Back outside, Colin Newell looked sadly at Peter Morecroft's dilapidated boats. 'Who do you think did it, Jack?'

'I don't know, but I'd stake my pension it wasn't him.' In the bottom of the open dory were the plastic dustbins still containing live eels. Jack pointed them out. 'Pete's catch of last night; a pity if they go to waste.'

Colin smiled. 'Don't worry Jack, I'll get them sold and save the cash for when he comes out.' He nodded back to the boatshed where the police were enjoying their coffee. 'Meantime, I'll make the Broads Beat earn their break by reporting a problem of my own.'

'Not serious, I hope?'

The boatbuilder shook his head. 'No, just the same as we've had many times before: local kids pinching my dinghies and going for a nightime jaunt.'

Jack's official interest was aroused. 'When did this happen?'

'Last night was the last time. Just one dinghy and no damage done, but I could tell it'd been out as soon as I came in the yard this morning.'

Motoring away, Jack thought of so many young men on the Broads earning their livelihood by skill and sheer hard work. Colin Newell was an example of the best.

With his desperate desire to have Giller's Yard, he was also a suspect.

IT WAS AFTERNOON BEFORE Jack came in sight of Wyford's Mill. Somehow its ancient structure now seemed rather more desolate. That saddened him because, although many locals had opposed the old mill's conversion to part-studio, he personally had always admired the result. The glass structure atop the tower had been tastefully designed and not altogether out of sync with its surroundings. History and heritage were a big part of Jack's love for this area but he was not a man to dwell in the past. The Broads themselves had been formed by the flooding of peat diggings in the fifteenth century and were not natural features in the strict sense of the word. It wasn't inappropriate, then, that man should still impose his influence over them. Besides, whether people or things, Jack felt there was always room for some eccentricity in this world and Wyford's Mill had more than its share.

The same couldn't be said of its owner. For an artist, Stuart Thornton was surprisingly normal and unassuming. An honest man, he had no pretensions save a sincere love of his art, his subject and the joy its combination gave others. If anything, he was a little unworldly, but that deficiency was more than counterbalanced by his wife.

How a simple soul like Stuart Thornton had ever bonded with the likes of brassy pseudo-blonde Lisa, had always been a mystery to Jack. He'd met her only a few times during his visits, spoken to her even less and worked very hard at avoiding instant dislike. It hadn't been easy. Stroppy to the point of rudeness, Lisa had made it very obvious that Stuart's time was far too valuable to be squandered on idle chat with passing Rangers, but that made Jack all the more determined to continue his visits. The artist obviously liked and benefited from these occasional short doses of male company and Jack too enjoyed talking to a man with such undeniable talent, but always the more so if Lisa were absent.

That seemed to be quite often of late. That she was pushy, flirtatious and ambitious was obvious, but more disturbing was Jack's conviction that underneath her fake tan lay a streak of downright nastiness. Stuart had never spoken of her relationship with Stack but the signs of latent distress were obvious to see and he felt for the man in his anguish. Well, that third party was dead now, but did the artist know? Or did he, perhaps, know more than he should? Jack eased alongside the mill's quay heading and jumped ashore to find out.

In normal times Stuart Thornton would have already been down to meet him with steaming mugs of coffee. Yesterday, Jack had sensed he was in the mill but Stuart had not appeared. This morning again, the only movement at Wyford's Mill was the sway and hiss of the surrounding reedbeds in the freshening wind. The Thornton Range Rover was also absent which invariably meant Lisa was happily likewise. Stuart's dinghy was there though, moored in the narrow cut, dug beside the mill's towering structure.

It was quite a small boat, about twelve feet, clinker built of wood with its outboard motor still clamped to the transom. Although only two horsepower, the outboard could shift the little dinghy along at quite a fair speed, so much so that Stuart had increased the height of the gunwale in the bow to cut down spray during choppy crossings of the broad. In the boat's bottom, amongst assorted leaves and junk, lay discarded oars and a plastic fuel can. Jack eased himself on board and gave the can a shake: empty. Next he checked the motor's integral tank: dry.

'Looking for something, Jack?'

The Ranger spun around, startled by the voice behind him and realising he'd been caught snooping on a friend.

'Stuart. I didn't think you were here.'

'Obviously.'

There was more than a little asperity in the artist's voice. Jack climbed out of the boat and came straight to the point.

'Professor Rupert Stack was murdered on the broad last night.'

Stuart Thornton nodded. 'Yes, I know, I heard it on the morning news.'

If the news had caused him any reaction, he betrayed none in voice or manner. Jack pressed on.

'Stuart, Peter Morecroft has been arrested on suspicion. All my old copper's instinct says he's innocent and, in my capacity as Ranger, I'm conducting my own enquiries to prove it.'

'And you think I did it?'

'I'm thinking nothing at this stage.' It was time to bring the tone of this interview down to a more amenable level and Jack took his friend's arm. 'Stuart, I just want to have a chat with you. Any chance of coming inside?'

The artist blinked and then smiled, sheepishly. 'Of course, Jack ... and I'm sorry for my abruptness but I'm a bit uptight right now. I've had a few problems lately and this murder thing has capped it all.' He turned and led Jack into the mill. 'Let's get the kettle on.'

They walked into the ground floor and up the stairs to the kitchen-cum-living-room. Jack never failed to admire the snugness and sheer functionality of this circular room. Fitted cleverly to one half of its circumference were pine units peppered by the latest in kitchen technology. The other half was the living space comprising just a couple of cushioned rocking chairs and a comfy sofa. Jack eased into one of the rockers while Stuart poured the coffees. In spite of its modern conversion, a period charm still seemed to ooze from the mill's redbrick walls.

'How did Lisa take the news of Stack's death?' The question was a cutting one but Jack needed to open this painful subject as quickly as possible.

Stuart placed two steaming mugs on the small pine table and sat down in the opposite rocker. 'I don't know, Jack. She left me yesterday.'

'I'm very sorry to hear that, Stuart.' Jack reached for his mug, at the same time allowing his eyes to fix on the artist's. 'Stack?'

Stuart only nodded, his eyes closed to hold back welling emotion. Jack, sensing that a complete breakdown was only a wrong word away, tried to keep his own voice avuncular.

'That's a terrible thing to happen to any man, Stuart, and I know how much you loved her.' Once again he fixed his friend with questioning eyes. 'Enough to drive you to desperate measures?'

Stuart Thornton looked up, shaking his head as though to clear away incipient tears. 'I was mad with jealousy, Jack. All I could think of was that arrogant bastard with his hands on my wife. I'm not a violent man by nature, Jack, but… but…' His voice trailed off, as though swallowed by dreadful recall.

'But what, Stuart?'

The artist swallowed hard. '… but, I guess I killed him, Jack.'

THE REVELATION CAME AS no surprise to Jack but two words did. 'What do you mean, "I guess", Stuart?'

The artist shook his weary head again. 'I mean that I didn't intend to kill him and didn't think I had until I heard this morning's news.'

Jack pulled his chair closer and gave his friend a reassuring smile. 'From the beginning, Stuart. Tell me what happened, right from the beginning.'

'Okay, I want to tell someone. I've been to hell and back, Jack.' Stuart took a nervous swallow of his coffee before running a shaking hand through his long thick hair. 'Like I said, Lisa and I had a blazing row the night before last and yesterday morning she walked out. I've suspected for months that she and Stack were having an affair and… and…'

Jack stopped him. 'I think we've all known about the affair, Stuart. Tell me what you did about it.'

'Nothing at first except spend the day in emotional despair. By the evening, though, I was well into my cups, a little bit crazy and knowing I had to do something. Stack invariably anchored on the broad for the night, so I finally just jumped in the dinghy and motored off to have it out with him.'

'Without even checking you'd got enough fuel,' added Jack. 'A witness saw you rowing home.'

'Really,' The artist didn't seem unduly perturbed that he'd been spotted, 'but, yes, I ran out of gas as I reached the broad and had to row the rest of the way and then home afterwards. After what happened on the broad, it was the minutest of problems.'

'So you rowed up to Stack's boat; what happened then?' questioned Jack, keeping the story on track.

'Well, Stack must have seen me because he came out on deck and asked what I wanted. I said "my wife", and you can imagine how things went from there. He said she wasn't with him so I climbed onboard and stormed below to find her. He was telling the truth, actually; she wasn't there. He followed me down, of course, and ordered me off his boat. I accused him point blank of seducing my wife and that's when he became more and more abusive with that condescending arrogance that only Stack can muster. He said it was Lisa who'd seduced him and he could understand why with a husband like me. I think that's when I hit him.'

Jack shook his head. 'I think I would have too, Stuart. What then...?'

Stuart shrugged and gave a short chuckle. 'A full blown punchup, really. Stack's not much of a fighter but neither am I and so we just punched and dragged away at each other in the museum area of the boat, knocking over most of his display cases and smashing the place up pretty badly. As I said, I'm no Tyson but I had jealous rage on my side and eventually Stack was on the floor and out for the count.'

'But not dead?'

'No, alive; I'm sure of it.'

'Did you check: pulse, breathing?'

'No, but he was giving the odd moan so I was sure he was semi-conscious.'

'What did you do then?'

Stuart smiled slightly and shook his head. 'My blood was well up by that time, Jack. I felt such hatred for this man and his stupid museum business that had lured away my wife. Just to get some more venom out of my system, I finished the destruction of the display area that we'd started in the fight: smashed the rest of the cases, emptied the artefacts over the floor. Pretty vandal-like really but it made me feel better.'

'And then you rowed home?'

'Yes, straight here and feeling more and more stupid with every stroke.'

'What time did all this happen?'

The artist thought for a second, scratching his head. ' I can't say exactly but I reached his boats just before midnight and got back to the mill about an hour and a half later.'

'Yes, you were seen rowing about one a.m.' Jack paused to think. 'Stuart, did you go in the saloon area of the boat at any time?'

'No.'

'Or remove anything from the boat?'

Stuart shook his head again. 'Absolutely nothing, Jack. I was there for revenge, not theft.'

Jack nodded. 'Okay. What did you do once you got back here?'

Stuart gave a mirthless laugh. 'Had myself a good stiff drink and tried to get some sleep, which was pretty difficult, considering. I finally dozed off fitfully and woke sometime after sunrise. Later, I switched on local radio, heard the news and realised I must have hit the bastard harder than I'd thought and he'd died of some internal injuries or something.'

Jack didn't enlighten him but said, 'Two more questions, Stuart...'

'Go ahead.'

'Did you see Peter Morecroft on the river last night?'

Stuart shook his head again. ' Not the lad himself, only his boats. When I went past his eel-set there was light in his cabin and smoke from his chimney. I guessed his nets were down so I stayed well clear of the banks. When I rowed back, things were just the same.'

'And you didn't see any other boats either?'

'None.'

'Right.' Jack stroked his chin, thinking. 'Stuart, you're going to have to answer to the police for what you've just told me and can probably expect an assault charge.'

The artist nodded. 'And manslaughter... or will it be murder?'

'Neither, I hope, if what you've told me is true.' Jack smiled confidentially. 'I can't say too much, Stuart, except that Stack died at a different time and in a different way to what you've described.'

Stuart Thornton buried his head in his hands. 'Thank God. And all morning I've been thinking I'm a murderer.'

Jack gave him a friendly slap on the back. 'Well, you haven't done yourself any favours and you're not out of the woods yet, old friend, but just answer the police like you've answered me and you should be okay.'

'Right...' there was undeniable relief now flooding the artist's drawn features, '... thanks Jack... for everything.'

'Don't mention it. You've helped me too, Stuart. What you say confirms to me that Peter Morecroft wasn't near Stack's boats either, at the time he was murdered.' Jack nodded towards his mug. 'Now, how about another coffee?'

While Stuart gladly reboiled the kettle, Jack stretched his legs and scanned the room. Leaning against the brick wall was one of Stuart's paintings, a beautiful oil on canvas depicting a moonrise over the marshes.

'Lovely work, Stuart. What lucky person is getting this one?'

'Thanks, Jack.' He paused from pouring the mugs. 'Actually, I don't know who buys my paintings anymore. I just churn them out and they go to galleries all over the country and are sold on from there.'

'Really...' Jack took the offered mug, '... which galleries?'

Stuart shook his head. 'I think there's one in Elm Hill, Norwich, but other than that, I have no idea...' Momentarily his expression saddened, '... Lisa used to look after the marketing side of things.'

'Where is Lisa now, Stuart?'

Once again Stuart Thornton shook his head. 'I have no idea of that either.'

IN FACT, AT THAT very moment his wife was being ushered into the office of Gwen Fosdyke. The solicitor stood up as Lisa Thornton strode in. She had met the artist's wife at a council reception for local businesses and spoken to her on just a few occasions regarding the purchase of Giller's Yard. She couldn't say she liked the woman. Nevertheless, she offered her a civil hand and the seat opposite.

'I'm sorry to hear about your boss's death, Mrs Thornton.'

'Yeah, tragic.'

Gwen noted the sarcasm but kept her tone even.

'So, how can I help you, Mrs Thornton?'

Lisa placed her leather briefcase beside her, leaned back in the comfortable chair and crossed her legs. Gwen Fosdyke's office was on the first floor and, being at the end of the High Street, had good views over fields and marshes. Even the top of Wyford's Mill was just visible on the skyline. Lisa's thoughts, however, were far from her old home.

'As you know, *Miss* Fosdyke, I was Professor Stack's personal assistant. Until I'm directed otherwise, I shall still be running his office. No doubt some of my work now will include winding up his estate. I therefore need some questions answered by you.'

Already Gwen was feeling uncomfortable with this meeting.

'Of course, I'll help you in every way I can but I'm not sure…'

'You were his solicitor, weren't you,' Lisa interrupted.

'Yes, but…'

'Then I know you'll be able to help me.'

Gwen Fosdyke paused for a second, more to control her irritation than to think. When she did speak again, it was through slightly closed lips. 'What are your questions?'

Lisa's manner was unabashed. 'Just one for starters.'

'Go on.'

'Did he make a will?'

Gwen Fosdyke sat back, making no effort to disguise her exasperation.'Mrs Thornton, you might well be the late Professor Stack's "personal assistant", but that does not give you the right to come marching in here demanding confidential information. Rupert Stack's estate will be dealt with by due process and that really needn't concern you.'

'Oh, really.' Lisa paused to light a cigarette and noticed with satisfaction the disdain on Gwen Fosdyke's face. 'Well, perhaps it is my business; perhaps the old boy had left me something.'

The solicitor shook her head, smiling with amused bewilderment. 'You really do take the biscuit for nerve, Mrs Thornton. If Professor Stack had made a will you would still not be party to its contents at this stage. Traditionally, wills are read after the funeral but, in point of fact, Rupert Stack did not leave a will with me and so the question as to whether you are a beneficiary is irrelevant.'

'So, as far as you know, he died int… int…?'

'... intestate. I can't say on that. He may have lodged a will elsewhere but certainly not with me.'

'But are you his executor?'

Gwen rolled her eyes in exasperation.

'Acting as someone's solicitor does not automatically mean they are that person's executor. Executors are appointed by the testator - the person making their will - and, I can assure you, I never received any such instruction from Professor Stack.'

Lisa smiled. 'Good. Then I'm appointing you as Professor Stack's executor.'

Gwen Fosdyke slowly but audibly exhaled.'You weren't listening, Mrs Thornton. Only the testator can do that and only before their death unless they leave a will stating such. As I say, I know of no such testament.'

Lisa leaned across the desk, smile gone, eyes piercing. 'No Miss Fosdyke, it's you that wasn't listening. I'll say again. You are now Professor Stack's executor and, what's more, you are going to write his will.'

Gwen Fosdyke stood up and pointed to the door.

'Mrs Thornton, I think it's time for you to leave. Go now and I might not report this conversation to the authorities. Come up with any more such ridiculous suggestions and I won't be so lenient.'

Lisa didn't move except to take a long draw at her cigarette before blowing its blue smoke towards the ceiling. 'Sit down, Miss Fosdyke.'

Gwen had never been spoken to in such a way before but there was something so latently threatening in Lisa Thornton's words that she found herself unbelievably obeying.

'That's better.' Lisa sat back. 'Now, as I said, Miss Fosdyke, you are going to become the executor of Professor Stack's estate, you are going to write his will and ... guess what? ... I am going to be the only beneficiary.'

Gwen fought to control her anger and feign a tolerance that she certainly didn't feel for this stupid young woman. 'Mrs Thornton ... Lisa ... do you have any idea what you are asking? Even if I agreed to such a patently deceitful plan, it would be impossible. The will itself could appoint me as executor but that would require Professor Stack's signature plus two witnesses, all of which would obviously be impossible.'

Lisa stubbed her cigarette on her chair-arm before flicking it into the waste-bin. 'Forge them.'

'Forge them?'

'Yes, it shouldn't be too hard. You must have many examples of Stack's signature and others you can use for the witnesses.' Lisa ran her hand through her hair with the manner of one growing bored. 'Just do a bit of ... what do they call it?... "creative writing".'

Gwen held up her hand.

'Lisa, stop, this has gone far enough. If you think I would even consider jeopardising my integrity and professional reputation for such an appalling fraud, then you seriously misjudge me.'

'Actually, I think I have you judged spot on, Miss Fosdyke.' Lisa brought the briefcase onto her lap, flicked the combination locks and brought out a buff envelope. From this she produced copies of the two photos and newspaper clippings. One by one she laid them neatly on the solicitor's desk. First she pointed to the photos. 'Have you seen these before?'

Gwen Fosdyke looked down at the full-page digital computer-printouts. There was a throat-tightening gasp of despair in her voice as she quietly uttered, 'How did you get these?'

'Never you mind. Bit raunchy, aren't they?' Lisa giggled. 'Who'd ever think a respectable District Councillor could do things like that?' She looked Gwen straight in the eye. Presumably, you didn't know our good Professor was doing a touch of the David Bailey's when he took these?'

Gwen was still looking down at the graphic incriminating images. 'No.'

'Ah.' Lisa shook her head as though to indicate her sympathy was purely sarcastic. 'So you see, Miss Fosdyke, when you talk about your "integrity and professional reputation" I really can't take you too seriously can I?'

'No.'

'And, I think I'm right in saying, if these little gems ever found their way into the wrong hands, then your legal business, political career and ambitions would all be pretty well shot to hell?'

'Yes.'

Lisa sat back. 'How lucky for you then, Miss Fosdyke, that it was me who found them. And to think that all I want to keep them our little secret, is a bit of legal shenanigans that won't cost you a penny.'

Gwen rubbed her forehead as though to rid herself of this nightmare, but when she returned her eyes to Lisa's, her voice carried just a whisper of its old authority.

'Blackmail is a very serious offence, Lisa, and the courts usually manage to protect the victim's reputation. How do you know that when you walk out of here I won't just pick up the phone and call the police?'

'How do I know...?' Lisa was doing a bad imitation of Gwen's refined accent. 'I know because I also have these.' She tapped the illustrated newspaper cuttings. She didn't even wait for Gwen's response this time but asked simply, 'When will you have the will ready?'

Gwen paused only seconds before answering quietly, 'Two days.'

'Great, all ready for the reading then, whenever that will be.' Lisa brushed the sheets of copy paper towards Gwen, some of them floating onto the solicitor's lap. 'You can keep these. Don't worry, the originals are very very safe.' She stood up and clicked shut her case. 'Right, I'll pop back in a couple of days to see the result. And if you should even consider calling the cops, remember...' Lisa's voice dropped to a confidential whisper as she paused in the doorway, '... I *know* who killed Professor Stack.'

Chapter Nine

IF LISA THORNTON FELT elation in doing wrong, then, by an antithesis of character, her estranged husband was experiencing grave doubts at doing right. He stood now in front of North Walsham Police Station, the taxi having just dropped him outside its unwelcoming doors.

Following Jack Fellows' advice, he was handing himself in but with orders not to mention his afternoon conversation with the Ranger. Neither had he made any preliminary phone call, preferring to keep his confession and police questioning in their domain rather than his. Nevertheless, sticking your head in the lion's mouth was never easy and all the more so if what you had to say implicated others you still loved.

For the truth was that Stuart harboured the dread thought that his own wife was Rupert Stack's murderer. Jack had told him that Lisa had left Stack's boats in distress, and Stuart knew only too well the physical violence that Lisa's wrath could trigger. That she could kill Stack in the bitterness of rejection was entirely possible. Added to that, as the Professor's assistant, she also knew the value of the artefacts onboard *Aethelberht* and possibly even the combination of the safe in which the brooches were stored. The gleam of gold would always be an irresistible enticement to the greedy likes of Lisa, a thought that introduced another frightening factor into this already disturbing equation: Lisa's dubious and secret business "arrangement" with Professor Stack.

Whatever that arrangement was, Stuart was convinced it was doubtless beyond the bounds of legality and possibly downright criminal. He had never wanted to know the details, a factor which only confirmed Lisa's impression of him as spineless. Now, with the police investigating the Professor's murder, would the truth of this whole scam come out? Had the Professor himself threatened Lisa with exposure? That alone might be enough for her to murder him.

These were tormenting thoughts as Stuart literally stood on the threshold of the law. That he had to confess his own attack on Stack was obvious. That he should implicate Lisa was out of the question. Most would think him mad for shielding a wife so unfaithful, but his love for her was like an addictive drug that could never be assuaged. No, he would admit his own misdoings but say nothing of anything else. Stuart took a deep breath and went inside.

'POOR STUART THORNTON.' Audrey Fellows took her husband's by-now cold tea. 'I'll get you a fresh one, Jack.'

The Ranger had been about to take his first sip of the cup he'd been dreaming of all day, when the telephone rang. It was Detective Chief Inspector Hengrove.

'Jack, Phil Hengrove.'

'Hi, Phil…' Jack took a quick gulp of his tea, '… how's the investigation going?'

There was a barely audible sigh from the other end.

'Progress, but not in the direction we thought.' Hengrove paused as though unwilling to admit some unpalatable fact. 'Would you believe that some artist called Thornton, came in the nick late this afternoon and admitted working Stack over himself? How's that for a slammer?'

'What, Stuart Thornton?' Jack was doing his best to sound incredulous, 'I can't believe it.'

'No, I thought that would shock you.' The thought that he had "scored one over" on the ex-Detective Superintendent had obviously restored the DCI's flagging confidence. 'Anyway, Jack, I thought you'd probably know him, seeing as he lives on the river.'

'We've chatted sometimes.' Jack was finding it hard not to smile at his own duplicity.

'Good. Any chance of you coming in tomorrow? Anything you can tell me about the man will be helpful: character, matrimonial background, that sort of thing.'

'Well, tomorrow's my day off, Phil, and I've got lots to do…' Jack could see some mutual advantage to this situation, '… is it important?'

'Yes it is, Jack.' The DCI sighed. 'I thought you wanted to help me in this enquiry?'

Jack put on his best strained voice. 'I do, Phil, and … okay, I'll come but I need to ask you a favour in return.'

'Which is?' There was suspicion now in Hengrove's voice.

'I'd like to talk to Peter Morecroft.'

'Impossible, Jack. Too irregular.'

'Yeah, I understand, Phil. Of course, us talking about Stuart

Thornton could be construed as falling within my Ranger work. Strictly speaking I'd better clear that with the Broads Authority. That might take some time so...'

'All right, all right, Jack...' Hengrove broke in. '... I'll give you twenty minutes with Morecroft but there'll be one of my lot with you the whole time.'

'Fair enough.' Jack hung up, well pleased except for his cold tea. He'd already told Audrey of his day's investigations and Stuart Thornton's revelation. Now he passed on this latest development.

While she busied herself brewing a fresh pot, Audrey asked: 'Does this mean poor Stuart is under arrest?'

'Probably.' The Ranger kicked off his shoes and stretched his legs under the kitchen table, stroking Spike with his toes as he did so. ' Stuart will be a prime suspect now and have a lot of explaining to do. Admitting fighting someone a couple of hours before they're murdered but saying it wasn't you does stretch the imagination, and Phil doesn't know him as well as I do. I'm afraid Stuart will be facing a battery of interrogation and, as he's already confessing to assault, the police will have no problem getting him remanded. If he's really lucky, he might get released on bail.'

'That flighty wife of his could drive a man to anything...' Audrey paused in pouring her husband's tea, '... are you really sure he didn't do the actual murder, Jack?'

'Yes, I am. Remember, Stuart himself thought he'd killed Stack. If a man will admit to beating someone to death, why would he lie about the method? And anyway, Colonel Etherington saw him rowing home before one a.m. The pathologist reckons death occurred an hour later which puts Stuart well clear.'

'Unless he went back to finish the job.'

Women's logic, thought Jack as he swigged his last gulp and went for Spike's lead. His every instinct told him Stuart Thornton was just as innocent as Peter Morecroft, but Audrey's remark was a valid one. He'd never thought gentle-souled Stuart capable of fighting, but the artist had proved the destructive power of jealousy. Perhaps that same jealousy had driven him to commit the ultimate crime after all. Perhaps he was wrong and Stuart Thornton really was the killer.

WHILST JACK FELLOWS WAS walking the marshes with Spike, agonising over a maelstrom of conflicting evidence, Lisa

Thornton was back in her late boss's apartment beginning phase two of her path to riches.

She had no doubts that coercing Gwen Fosdyke into making her the sole beneficiary of Stack's estate would eventually make her reasonably wealthy. But not immediately, what with probate, inheritance tax and the like to be settled. That might take weeks and, even then, the liquid assets would be limited to the late Professor's cash-in-bank, which was substantial but not a fortune. The bulk of the estate lay in assets such as the apartment, those wretched boats and Giller's yard. Lisa was sure she would use the apartment herself, the boats might well take a long time to dispose of and the purchase of the boatyard was incomplete and possibly void. On top of this, there was always the spectre of some unknown relative crawling out of the woodwork and contesting the will. No, Lisa told herself, she had to diversify and taking over Stack's end of the market in their illicit trade meant vastly improved profits.

Lisa switched on the computer and once more brought up details of Professor Stack's mysterious contact. Then she keyed in an e-mail and hoped she wouldn't have to wait long for a reply. Excitement, intrigue and money; this was what life was all about, thought Lisa as she switched off the laptop, went to her late boss's drinks cabinet and poured herself a generous Martini. 'Here's to wealth,' she toasted out loud, holding the glass up to her own personal god of greed.

'MORNING JACK. GOOD OF you to come in.' DCI Phil Hengrove stood up as the burly figure of the Ranger was shown into his office. 'You've met DC Bailey…' he indicated the young detective constable sitting to one side and a chair on the other, '… take a seat.'

Jack sat down and took in Phil Hengrove's office: the stacked files, the whiteboard with current investigations listed in blue felt-tip, the half-eaten sandwich and accumulated coffee cups. This could have been his old office at Scotland Yard or a senior officer's in any police HQ in the country. They and the atmosphere they generated were universally the same. Outsiders would probably find it intimidating but Jack felt immediately at home.

'So, Stuart Thornton beat up Professor Stack?'

'Yeah, reckons our good Professor was knocking off his wife and Thornton went to have it out with him.' Hengrove gave a full rundown of Stuart's account of the night which, of course, Jack had heard before, but to which he feigned total ignorance. 'The thing is,' continued the DCI, 'he admits to beating Stack but swears he didn't murder him.'

'Do you believe him?'

Hengrove sat back. 'I'm not sure; part of me wants to… he seems a nice enough bloke… but jealousy, especially when it's your wife, has always been a pretty good motive for murder. It's stretching coincidence a bit far to accept he goes and beats up Stack and then, hey presto, an hour later the Professor gets murdered. Can you believe that?'

'I can when the victim is Rupert Stack who could well have had assailants lining up to do him in. Added to that, Phil, I have a witness who saw Stuart Thornton rowing home an hour before the murder time.'

'Who?'

'The local squire.' Jack gave the account of Colonel Etherington's sighting of the artist.

Hengrove turned to his Detective Constable who had been noting the details in his pocket book. 'Check on that, Bailey.'

'Right, sir.' The young detective jumped up and was gone.

'Okay, Jack…' the DCI seemed to relax a bit now his friend and he were alone, '… tell me all about our Mr Thornton.'

Jack gave a full character rundown on the artist, making no secret of his liking for the man. 'He certainly had motive and opportunity, Phil, but somehow I feel he's telling the truth.'

'Why?'

'Because the safe was robbed of the coins and gold brooches. That doesn't fit in with the jealous husband scenario.'

'True, but having killed Stack he might just have taken those on impulse. Or…' Hengrove looked at Jack over the top of his half-moon glasses, '… your friend Morecroft is telling a part-truth. Perhaps he really did find Stack dead but, knowing there were gold artefacts on board, took advantage of the situation and got himself a little treasure.'

Jack shook his head. 'Unlikely; Pete's no safe-cracker.'

'Then, how come those two coins were found on his boat? Bailey took them to Norwich Castle Museum. Apparently they're Anglo-Saxon and worth a tidy sum to any private collector but their main value to me,' said the DCI, tapping his file, 'is that they link Morecroft to the crime scene.'

'But do they?' Jack held out his hands in supplication. 'They were all you found in his boats, Phil. If Morecroft did steal the gold brooches and the rest of the coins, where are they?'

'Anywhere along the river bank or even on the river bed,' countered Hengrove. 'He had plenty of time to dispose of them during his getaway back upriver. I've got the diving team combing the area right now. Don't worry, I'll find them.'

'I hope you do,' said Jack, sincerely. 'How about other evidence? Anything back from forensics?'

Hengrove shook his head. 'Not yet. It's not easy, seeing as half of Norfolk went through that boat on the day of the murder.'

'Through the museum part, yes…' Jack leaned forward, '… but not in Stack's living quarters. You've probably found out, like me, that Thornton's wife Lisa visited the boat at midday but, as far as we know, the only other person to enter the saloon was his murderer. If Stuart Thornton is telling the truth, you won't find his forensic footprint in there and, I'm willing to bet, you won't find Peter Morecroft's anywhere. How about that blood on his fishing smock, have you had that checked?'

'Yeah, rabbits' as he said,' admitted Hengrove begrudgingly, 'but we haven't finished with him yet.' The DCI noted the disapproving look on the Ranger's face. 'Still convinced of his innocence, aren't you, Jack?'

'Until you find stronger evidence, yes.'

It was Hengrove's turn to lean forward. 'Face the facts, mate; like Thornton, he had motive and opportunity but to cap it all, his initials were written in blood by the victim. What more do you want?'

Jack shrugged. 'It was no secret that Pete was out to get even with Stack. He was the perfect fall-guy. Those initials could have been scrawled by the real murderer just to put us off the scent.'

'And that "real murderer" could have been your other mate, Stuart Thornton,' countered Hengrove, sitting back in his chair.

'Not Stuart; he's not the sort to throw blame on another and the murder method doesn't fit anyway.' Jack nodded to what was obviously Stuart's statement in the already bulging case-file. 'If he was prepared to confess to manslaughter by beating up Stack, why not admit to stabbing him?'

'Because that might indicate some premeditation, downright murder and a life sentence,' answered Hengrove.

'Maybe, but remember, Colonel Etherington saw him rowing

home an hour before Stack's death and, talking of times...' said Jack, taking the cue, '... your Peter Morecroft theory doesn't gel with one of your other witnesses either.'

'Which witness?'

'Tom Ledger, the hirer of the *Polar Star*.'

'Who saw Morecroft's boat alongside Stack's and the two figures fighting,' said Hengrove, flicking open a file on his desk and obviously reading Ledger's statement.

'And, there's the discrepancy,' countered Jack. 'Peter Morecroft reckons he wasn't at Stack's boat until three in the morning, by which time our good Professor had been dead for an hour. He's telling the truth. Ledger remembered looking at his wheelhouse clock when he got up to check the racket raised by the fighting, but that wasn't when he saw Peter Morecroft's boat. It was when he got up a second time that he saw Pete's dory.'

'And he wasn't sure what time that was...' The DCI was still scanning the statement. '...but probably "shortly after".'

'But that's the point: it wasn't. Ledger might think it was shortly after but I know it wasn't.' Jack leaned back in his chair. 'In fact Phil, I can tell you exactly what time Ledger got up that second time.'

'How come?' There was suspicion now in Hengrove's eyes as they came out of the file.

'Because, as your statement will show, Ledger got up that second time to check his anchor. A sudden squall was coming through the broad and he needed to check the boat wasn't dragging. So the question is: what time did that happen?'

'And...?' Hengrove could see what was coming.

'That line squall was associated with a cold front moving through this area at the time.' Jack threw a small piece of notepaper onto the DCI's desk. 'There's the number for the met office at RAF Marham. If you ring them, like I did yesterday, you'll find they logged that front going through the station at one-twenty a.m. moving at twenty-one knots. The broad is just under thirty-five nautical miles east of Marham, which therefore puts the front going through the murder scene at...'

'... about three.' Hengrove completed for him, somewhat begrudgingly. 'Okay, Jack, so Morecroft was still there at three but that doesn't mean he hadn't murdered Stack at two and spent the next hour opening the safe and gathering his loot.'

'Come off it, Phil.' It was the Ranger's turn to give a derisive laugh. 'Like I said, Pete Morecroft's no locksmith and there was no evidence of the safe being forced either.'

'No, but he could have got the Professor to open it under duress.'

Jack shook his head again. 'In which case, he wouldn't have spent a full hour at the murder scene. After killing Stack he would have grabbed the loot and shot home like a bunny.'

'Which brings us back to two coins found on his boat,' countered Hengrove, wearily.

Jack nodded, stood up and turned to the DCI. 'You promised I could talk to him, Phil.'

Hengrove moved to the door and opened it for Jack.

'Be my guest. Perhaps he'll be able to give you the solution.'

Jack followed the DCI down the corridor, hoping against hope he was right.

IT WAS MIDDAY NOW and Charlotte Giller was using her lunchbreak from Starcraft to catch up on a bit of shopping. The events of the last two days had robbed most of her appetite but she hoped the delicatessen might offer something to tempt it back.

Starcraft's yard was only minutes from the town centre and just walking the High Street was an escape from her worries, uppermost of which was the failure of her father-in-law, Walter, to answer his phone. Added to this was the continuing uncertainty of her tenancy of Boatyard Cottage. Would the heir to Stack's estate inherit the property or would it go back on the market? As if to answer the question, it was at this worst possible moment that she ran into Lisa Thornton.

'Well, if it isn't our little boatyard girl,' said Lisa, coming out of the dress shop carrying two large carrier bags. 'Let you out for a bit have they?'

'Hello, Mrs Thornton.' Charlotte detested the brassy blonde and not just because she'd taken an active part in her proposed eviction. 'Getting over our grief with a bit of retail therapy are we?'

'Just keeping up with the latest fashions,' countered Lisa, seemingly ignoring the sarcasm. Instead, she nodded towards Charlotte's paint-stained jeans and tee-shirt. 'Something you wouldn't understand, dearest.'

'No, but what I do understand is that your late boss somehow manipulated our honourable Councillor Fosdyke,' Charlotte nodded down the High Street towards the solicitor's chambers, 'into securing Giller's Yard over the top of higher bids.'

'That's a very serious accusation.' Lisa was doing what she was very good at: looking down her nose at someone she regarded her inferior. 'I should be careful if I were you, Charlotte, bandying allegations of which you have not the slightest proof. Your time would be better spent packing your few belongings and finding somewhere else to live.'

'Who said I have no proof?' Charlotte was making a real effort to control the anger and bitterness welling within her. 'And, as for moving, perhaps I won't have to now Professor Stack is dead.'

'Ah, I'm afraid you're in for disappointment if that's your hope,' chuckled Lisa. 'It will be public knowledge soon enough so you may as well know now, Charlotte.' She looked up and down the High street as if to check no-one was listening and lowered her voice with mock confidentiality. 'The fact is, I am the sole beneficiary of Professor Stack's estate and as such, pending completion of the purchase, that makes me the new owner of Giller's Yard and Boatyard Cottage.'

'You… the new owner…?'

Charlotte was too taken aback to do other than splutter her incredulity, but the bully in Lisa wasn't finished yet.

'Afraid so, little girl.' She gave a patronising smile. 'Of course, I wouldn't dream of living in that damp little hovel but it won't be standing for much longer anyway. I plan to redevelop Giller's Yard at the first opportunity.'

'Redevelop…?' Charlotte couldn't believe what she was hearing. '… but you can't… the council will never let you.'

'Ah, there you're wrong again, deary.' It was Lisa's turn now to nod towards Gwen Fosdyke's chambers. 'Planning permission can and will be granted. Believe me, the diggers will be demolishing those old boathouses and that cottage of yours quicker than you can say "eviction".'

Charlotte fought to contain her tears. 'Over my dead body, Mrs Thornton.'

Lisa laughed. 'Well, you should know all about dead bodies, shouldn't you, Charlotte?'

'What do you mean by that?'

'I mean …' said Lisa, raising her head to look even further down her nose, '… where were you on the night Professor Stack was murdered?'

'I … I was at home in Boatyard Cottage,' spluttered Charlotte, suddenly feeling very unsure of herself.

'Is that so?' Again, Lisa glanced up and down the High Street. 'Do you know, dear girl, I could have sworn I saw you here in town that very night. You didn't borrow a boat from Starcraft and take a little trip to the broad, by any chance?'

'No, of course I didn't.' Charlotte gave a scoff that even she found unconvincing. 'What a ridiculous suggestion.'

'Is it? Until a few seconds ago you were convinced that Professor Stack's death would cancel out the sale of Giller's Yard.' Lisa forced a little smile of condescension. 'If I were you, deary, I'd start working on the story you're going to tell the police when they come knocking on your beloved cottage door.'

And with that, Lisa turned on her heels leaving Charlotte contemplating the sad fact that Professor Stack had bequeathed more than his estate to his erstwhile mistress: he'd endowed her with his penchant for causing pain as well. The only comfort that gave was the thought that Lisa Thornton might perhaps meet an equally sticky end.

Chapter Ten

'HELLO, PETE, HOW ARE THINGS?'

Peter Morecroft stood up as Jack Fellows entered the interview room with his smiling greeting.

'Sit down.' The police constable detailed by DCI Hengrove to monitor their meeting moved over to the recorder, switched it on and said, 'Interview between Ranger Jack Fellows and suspect Peter Morecroft at twelve thirty-five hours,' in as bland a monotone as he could manage.

Peter sat as ordered. 'Not too bad, Mr. Fellows, considering.'

'Considering what, Pete?'

'That I'm stuck in 'ere for somethin' I din't do … agin.'

'Right … well, let's try and do something about that, shall we?' Jack sat down opposite the young fisherman. 'We've got just twenty minutes, Pete, so tell me, right from the start, everything you did and saw the night of Professor Stack's murder.'

Peter shook his head. 'I've told 'em …' he nodded towards the constable, '… so many times, Mr. Fellows.'

'Tell *me* … again.'

'Well, I 'ad me tea at six o'clockish an' then had me nets up, checked all were okay an' put some rabbit innards in the pods for bait.'

'That's when you got the blood on your smock?'

'Yeah. Then, after I got the nets down agin I went for a row to pass the time 'til sunset. I row down to the broad and sees Stack's boats there.'

'This is important, Pete, and I want the truth,' Jack broke in. 'Did you just row to the broad and happen to see Stack's boats, or did you go there with the specific purpose of seeing if they were there so you could return later and spy on Stack?'

Peter Morecroft looked at his hand for a second before coming to a moral decision. 'You're right, Mr. Fellows: tha's why I went … but I weren't goin' back later with any idea of doing the bloke over or even goin' on 'is boats. All I wanted …'

'I know, Pete.' Jack held up a calming hand. 'So you saw Stack's boats on the broad. What then?'

'I jus' goes back to me boats and has a drink, keepin' the odd eye on me nets.'

'Your nets were in the same place as your boats: midway between The Hall and the broad?'

'Yep, strung out quite a few hundred yards along the riverbank, a course, but with me own boats midway.'

'And then what?'

' Well, all seem well with me nets early mornin' so I thinks I'll go back an' see if 'e's got 'is strange visitor like, an' I might see what 'e's up to. So, I jus' sets off in me dory for a scout at Stack on the broad.'

'What time did you set off on this "scout"?'

''Bout two thirtyish.'

'And in the time between midnight and setting off yourself, did you see or hear anyone else on the river?'

Peter shook his head. 'Nope, but I wouldn't anyways 'cos most of a time I were down below, curtains drawn an' radio an' lights on.'

'Okay; so what time did you reach Stack's boats?'

'Like I says, Mr. Fellows, it were jus' after three. I remember lookin' at me watch 'cos it suddenly start gettin' right stormy - lotsa wind an' rain - an' I'm wonderin' how long it'll take me to row home if it git any worse. The wind'd swung all the boats at their moorin's an' I were right glad to git alongside Stack's if only to be in its lee.'

'And that's when you looked into *Aethelberht* and saw the Professor's body?'

Peter nodded. 'Yeah, an' quite a turn it give me wiv that knife stickin' out from between 'is shoulders an' the aft end of the boat all smashed up like. No place for me, I thinks, an' 'eads 'ome like the devil hisself is behind me.'

'So you didn't as much as set foot on either *Raedwald* or *Aethelberht*?'

'No.'

'But you didn't try and call the police either, Pete. Why not?'

''Cos I knows how bad it look for me, what wiv my record an' like.' The young man shook his head regretfully. 'Wish now I had, Mr. Fellows, but I jus' did what seem best at the time.'

Jack nodded. 'So you headed straight back to your boat?'

'Yeah.'

'And you saw no other boat on the river either going to the broad or returning?'

'No ... nothin'.'

'When you got back to your boat, what did you do then?'

Peter Morecroft allowed himself a slight smile. 'Pour misself another stiff rum after what I'd sin. It were gettin' light by then an' time to haul me nets so I goes and busies misself wiv that an' it takes me mind off things.'

'How long did it take you to haul the nets?'

''Bout an hour. Good haul it were too but I'd lost some 'cos an otter or summat had chewed 'is way through me skirt net.'

'That's the net between the pods isn't it?'

'Yep, guides the eels inta the pods. Law makes us have an otter-guard on the pods now but this bugger 'ad 'ad a go at the skirt. Made one 'ellava mess,' said Pete, with feeling.

'And between then and the police arriving; did you go anywhere?'

Again, the young eel-catcher shook his head. 'Nowhere. I jus' goes back aboard me cruiser for some breakfast an' then goes up on deck an' starts sprokin' me net. Right mess it were, I tell ya. I were still workin' at that when the fuzz came an' got me.'

'Okay.' Jack sat back. 'Just two more questions, Pete: firstly, the police found two silver coins in your dory. Any idea how they got there?'

'No idea, Mr. Fellows. Never seen 'em afore. S'pose they could 'ave come up wiv the haul but it never 'appened afore …' he paused, '… worse luck.'

Jack smiled and nodded before continuing. 'Professor Stack's dying action was to scrawl your initials in his own blood. Do you know about this?'

Morecroft nodded. 'Yeah, Mr. Hengrove told me.'

'Why would Stack do that, Pete?'

'No idea, Mr. Fellows, an' tha's the truth on it. I swear I never set foot on tha' boat tha' night or any time. Stack lied once afore to git me in trouble wiv the law; p'raps this were his final dig at me.'

'Final being the operative word,' said Jack, with grim humour. 'Right, Pete, I'll keep digging until I find out who really killed our Professor Stack.'

'So you still think I'm innocent, Mr. Fellows?' There was a mixture of hope and desperation in Peter Morecroft's voice.

Jack nodded. 'Yes Pete, I do.'

Morecroft gave a relieved sigh. 'Tha's good enough for me.' He nodded towards the outside world that, at times, he must be wondering if he'd ever see again. 'What now then, Mr. Fellows?'

Jack didn't answer immediately but, after a minute's thought, he said, 'Neither you nor any of the other witnesses saw any unaccounted boats upriver of the broad. It seems pretty clear then that whoever did commit the crime came from downriver and the south.' He stood up and shook the fisherman's hand. 'Just bear up and co-operate in every way you can, Pete.'

'I'll try, Mr. Fellows.'

Walking out of police headquarters, Jack was convinced more than ever that Peter Morecroft was innocent. There were still questions needing answers and he was determined to find them. Walter Giller, the marshman, lived downriver and Mrs Ledger on the *Polar Star* had seen a marshpunt on the broad that very night. Jack climbed in his car and headed back to the marshes.

FOR THE THIRD TIME since sending her e-mail, Lisa brought up the server and checked for replies. There was just one, from the address she had mailed an hour before. She read the reply with increasing excitement. It was short, to the point but just the one she wanted. The contact would meet her tomorrow but he needed the same secrecy as he'd always demanded from Professor Stack. Where would they meet? Lisa replied confirming the meeting and promising to advise the location just as soon as she'd worked out the best place. Then she picked up the phone and dialled a local number.

IT WAS TO Walter Giller's boathouse that Jack first made his way on arriving at the marsh where the old man lived and worked. The walk from the track to the river was a long one that took him past the marshman's cottage where he stopped and knocked on Walter's door. There was no reply and Jack wasn't surprised, knowing that the seventy-five year old would be out on his beloved marshes as he was on every other day of the year. Moving on a few hundred yards brought him to the river and boathouse.

It was a traditional building of wooden lapboard construction and reed-thatched roof. From its open end, a flash of colour caught Jack's eye as a kingfisher skimmed back over the river, its electric blue plumage vivid against the colourless water inches below its wings. Alongside the boarded quay-heading, lay Walter's grey clinker-hulled marshpunt. In the old boat's wide bottom, a pair of well-used oars lay in a good few inches of water. Either the boat had become leaky or Walter had recently been rowing in heavy rain. There was nothing else to see here so Jack made his way back up the track and onto the marshes.

His ears led him to the marshman: the swish and crackle of metal striking vegetation. Walter was at the edge of the marsh, thrashing away with a small scythe.

'Morning, Walter.'

The old marshman looked up from his labours, blinked and then recognised his visitor. 'Oh, 'ello, Mr. Fellows, what bring you here?'

'Just to have a chat, Walter.' Jack nodded towards the pile of harvested undergrowth. 'Cutting saw-sedge for thatching, are we?'

'Yep,' Walter climbed up onto the track, 'sedge in summer; reed in winter.'

'The sedge is for the ridge, isn't it?' asked Jack, picking up one of the stalks but being careful not to cut his fingers on the leaf that gave the grass its name.

The old man nodded. 'Tha's right. Reed's bootiful stuff for the main roof but it in't pliable enough for the ridge. They use sedge for that. Does a good job, though it only last 'bout half the life of the reed.'

Jack glanced again at the small scythe in the marshman's hand. 'Hard way to cut it though, Walter. Isn't there some machine now that you can use for harvesting?'

'Aye, I sometimes use a cutter for the reed, but never for sedge,' said Walter, taking a whetstone out of his pocket and stroking the edge of his blade. 'Them machines do more 'arm than good to the growth beneath. Look after the land, I says, an' it look after you.'

None of this information was new to Jack but his questions this afternoon were more to put the old man at ease. After a lifetime of working in their flat wet expanses, Walter had many a tale to tell, but the one Jack wanted to hear concerned far more recent events. 'Walter, I'm sure you know that Professor Rupert Stack was murdered the night before last.'

The old man turned his head and spat heavily and meaningfully into the drainage ditch. 'Yep, I did and God bless the man who done it. That bastard had it comin' to him for a long time now and I for one won't shed no tears for his passin'.'

'No, I know he brought a lot of grief to your family,' said Jack, nodding sympathetically, 'but I don't think the man they arrested is the man who murdered him.'

Walter grunted. 'Poor young Morecroft, you mean. Yeah, he's a bit of a wild 'un, that lad, but murder…' the old man shook his head, '… no, not young Pete.' He looked straight at Jack through eyes still sharp but holding more than their share of grief and heartache. 'So who do you think done it, Mr. Fellows?'

'I was hoping you could help me there, Walter. What were you doing that night?'

The marshman didn't hesitate: 'Out on the river with me gun.'

'For what reason?'

'To shoot Professor Stack.'

Jack had been expecting any answer but this one. When he did speak again, there was caution in his voice. 'Are you confessing to this murder, Walter?'

The marshman nodded. 'Yep.'

Through narrowed eyes, Jack looked for guilt in the old man's features and saw only resignation. 'Tell me about it.'

Walter shrugged. 'I jus' rowed to the broad and climbed aboard 'is boat. I told 'im what I thought of 'is throwin' young Charlotte out of 'er cottage, and said if 'e din't have no second thoughts on that, I'd kill 'im. 'E said 'e wouldn't, so I did.'

'As simple as that?'

'Yep, as simple as that.' Walter, though, hadn't missed the suspicion on Jack's face. 'You don't believe me, do you, Mr. Fellows?'

Jack smiled. 'On the contrary, Walter, I believe you completely … except the last bit. You didn't kill Stack.'

Walter almost looked offended. 'I did, I tells you. Why don't you believe me?'

Holding up a calming hand, Jack tried not to sound condescending. 'Walter, I spent a working life interviewing villainy and know guilt when I see it. I don't detect a glimmer in you.'

'Tha's 'cos I don't feel none.' The marshman's hand swept across his beloved marshes. 'I've killed enough vermin in me time not to care about clearin' the world of that particular article.'

'Okay; how did you do it?'

Walter seemed almost taken aback by this simple question. 'How d'you mean?'

Jack looked him even closer in the eye. 'I mean the details, Walter. How exactly did you carry out the murder?'

The old man stood blinking, knowing he was on thin ice but prepared to brass it out to the end. 'Like I says, I took me gun to shoot the bastard but in the end I jus' give 'im a good beatin' an' I guess, that was enough to finish the soft likes of 'im.'

'Good try.' Jack gave the old man a smiling slap on the back. 'You should have listened to the later news items, Walter. They would have told you Rupert Stack died from other causes.'

Defeat seemed to cloud Walter Giller's hardened features. 'Mr. Fellows, why don't you jus' let me confess to it an' save someone else takin' the rap. I've 'ad my time an' if the good soul who done the job I intended anyway can enjoy the rest of theirs, then why not?'

Jack stood in silence for a few seconds, imagining Walter Giller languishing in gaol with never a sight of the huge skies above his beloved marshes or the feel of fresh wind on his weathered skin. To such a man, even minimal custody would be as good as a death sentence.

'Forget that, Walter. I understand your feelings but the law is the law and the guilty must be punished. Tell me again, and truthfully this time, what happened that night?'

'I set off from 'ere in the dark with me gun and I intended to git that bastard to let Charlotte stay or finish 'im for good, an' tha's the truth,' said Walter, with feeling. 'But it din't work out like what I planned.'

'Go on.'

'Well, when I gets to the broad, it's jus' after midnight' an' blow me down if there ain't another boat alongside Stack's. I recognise it straight away as Stuart Thornton's, the artist bloke whose missus 'as been messin' with Stack. I can 'ear some shouting goin' on an' then I see figures crashin' an' bangin' around inside. Good ol' Stuart, I thinks, that'll learn 'im. Give the bastard what 'e deserve.'

'And he certainly did,' completed Jack. 'Stuart Thornton is at North Walsham right now helping police with their enquiries. So what did you do then, Walter?'

'I decides to stay clear until Thornton 'as finished 'is job. Far be it for me to stop anyone bashin' the good Professor Stack. So's I jus' row around the broad 'til I sees Thornton jump in 'is boat an' row away like he's got ol' Black Shuck hisself after 'im, an' then I goes an' gets aboard the *Aethelberht*.'

'How did Stack respond to that?'

Walter gave a chuckle. 'He weren't doin' too much respondin' to anythin' right then. Good ol' Stuart had bashed him good an' proper and 'e was still lyin' on the floor groanin' and whinin' an' lookin' at the smashed remains of 'is precious museum things. I pull 'im to a sittin' position an' ask 'im why 'e's throwin' Charlotte from 'er home. I tell 'im Alan's dead 'cos of him an' I'll make him the same if he don't change his mind an' quick.' The old marshman chuckled again. 'That put the frights up 'im, I tell you.'

'I bet it did,' agreed Jack, smiling. 'What then?'

Walter shrugged. 'At first 'e seem more obsessed with 'is own little bumps an' bruises, swearin' how 'e'll make sure Thornton pays for thumpin' 'im and the damage he done. I tells 'im that'll be nothing to what I'll do. Eventually, with my shotgun under 'is chin, 'e gets the message an', like the coward 'e is, crumples completely an' swears 'e'll leave Charlotte be.'

'And you believed him?'

Walter nodded. 'At the time I did an' I make it quite clear to 'im I'll be back with nothin' to lose if 'e don't stick to 'is word.'

'So then you just left and he was still alive.' Jack was trying to slot these new revelations into some sort of order.

'Yep, 'e was pretty knocked about and shak'n but definitely still breathin' when I left 'im.'

'What time was this, Walter?'

The marshman thought carefully, stroking his chin. 'Must 'ave bin a bit after one thirty. Took me over an hour to row 'ome an' just afore I got here the 'eavens opened, soaked me an' filled the boat. I din't care 'cos I thought I'd sorted it for Charlotte. When I 'ear on the news next mornin' that Stack's bin murdered, that make everythin' different.'

'So, why didn't you call the police?'

The marshman shrugged again. ''Cos I assume he died from the beatin' Stuart gave 'im. Though 'e's alive when I left, I thinks 'e must've 'ad some… what you call 'em?… 'ternal injuries… an' croaked it in the night. I don't want 'avin' to lay the blame at young Thornton's door so I choose to keep quiet instead. Even turned me own mobile phone off so Charlotte can't call me an' ask awkward questions.'

'Did she know you were going to see Stack?'

'I told 'er I were goin' to sort it.'

Jack could understand now why Charlotte Giller had shown such relief on finding Stack had been stabbed to death. She knew her father-in-law kept a gun and her first reaction on hearing of the murder must have been the thought that he'd used it. What was more disturbing was the thought that Walter had been with Stack so close to the time of the murder. The time-of-death given by doctors was always based on several variable factors and inevitably only an estimate. That could put Walter in the frame completely and, Jack had to admit to himself, Stuart Thornton and Peter Morecroft as well. The Ranger put another friendly hand on the marshman's shoulder.

'Walter, we're going to have to report this conversation to the police.'

The old man nodded with resignation. 'I understand, Mr. Fellows.' While Jack used his mobile to call DCI Hengrove, Walter gathered up his tools and lunchbag. After a longish conversation relating all they had discussed, Jack finally came off the phone.

'They're sending a police car to pick you up, Walter.' He gestured down the track towards the river. 'Why don't we go to your cottage and have a cup of tea while we're waiting?'

Walter nodded and together they made their way towards the marshman's home. When they reached it, however, Walter turned and asked, 'Do you think they'll be keeping me in, Mr Fellows?'

Jack shrugged. 'Hard to say, Walter. They might so they can have another good chat with you tomorrow.'

'Right…' the old man was looking beyond the cottage, '… in that case, Mr. Fellows, can we just go to the river first? I'd like to see it once more just in case I don't get back here for a while.'

'Of course.' Together they continued down until they were standing by the boathouse. It was a good time to ask another question that could have a bearing on the whole investigation. 'Walter, when you were rowing back here that night, did you pass any other boat or anyone, making their way upriver to the broad?'

'The real murderer, ya mean?' Walter shook his head. 'Not a soul, Mr. Fellows an' tha's the truth.'

'So, whoever he or she was, they were already on the broad,' said Jack, almost to himself.

'Look like you got yerself a good ol' problem there, Mr. Fellows.' The marshman sat watching the river flowing steadily by as it had since the dawn of time. 'If you'll take me advice, you'll jus' forgit it for now an' enjoy this bitta creation. I spend a lotta time jus' sittin' 'ere thinkin' 'bout the strange ways of life.' He nodded towards a family of mallards making their in-line way upriver. 'I knows all the birds an' creatures that lives 'ere. They's about the only friends I 'ave.' Suddenly he gripped Jack's arm and pointed to the far bank, at the same time whispering, 'Look… otter.'

Jack looked in vain. 'Where, Walter? I can't see one.'

'I can't neither, but I sees where 'e is.' The old man pointed to a line of bubbles running along the surface. ''e's jus' below 'em. They got two layers of fur: a long coarse'n on top and a short fine'n beneath. That under-fur trap air for ins'lation but it escape an' give 'em away with that there trail of bubbles.'

'What do they eat?' asked Jack, glad to divert Walter's thoughts into his abiding love of nature and away from the unpleasantness to come.

'Eels and the more sluggish fish.' Walter watched as the line of bubbles disappeared into the reedbed. 'Off to his holt; they're lazy eaters really and avoid any fast-movin' waterlife.'

'Which would explain why Peter Morecroft had one in his skirt-net on the night of the murder,' commented Jack. 'He reckoned it chewed a big hole in the pod which Peter was still mending when the police arrested him.'

Walter, nodded. 'They'll chew through a pod to git at them eels, the buggers. Not often they git in the skirt though. Tha' may 'ave bin the big'n I seen.'

'You saw an otter on the broad that night?'

'Not isself,' said the marshman, turning away back towards his cottage, 'jus'a line of bubbles but I remember thinkin' it must be a big bugger goin' by the size of 'em.'

Jack smiled. Walter Giller had such a love of the creatures that inhabited his beloved Broadland, but he had other loves too that would drive him to spend the rest of his life in prison for a crime he hadn't committed. As they walked he turned to the old man beside him. 'You were trying to shield someone in particular weren't you, Walter, when you said you killed Stack?'

The marshman just nodded.

'And that was Charlotte, wasn't it?'

He nodded again.

Walter Giller's daughter-in-law certainly had motive, opportunity and guts enough to commit murder, thought Jack. And she lived right on the broad. He'd talk to her again tomorrow. With all his heart, he hoped the old man was wrong.

Chapter Eleven

AUDREY FELLOWS WATCHED HER husband pour a gin and tonic and tried to think of something good to say. In all Jack's years in the police she had made a conscious effort to distance herself from his work and concentrate instead on providing a haven of love and calm into which he could retreat at each day's end. With this case, however, she sensed Jack wanted to talk.

It was, of course, a local crime that had gripped the whole neighbourhood and her husband's involvement was almost voluntary. At first she'd thought the chance to reapply his old detection skills would be an added bonus to his work as a Ranger. Now, as he replaced his tea-time cuppa with something stronger, she sensed a return of some of the stress and anxiety that had come with his old territory and driven him to early retirement from the Met.

'But you don't think Walter Giller did it?' It was as close as she could get to a positive comment after hearing Jack's account of the day's events.

'No I don't, Audrey, love. His original confession to me was just to take the rap for Charlotte, who he obviously thought was the real culprit.'

'But you don't?'

Again, Jack shook his head. 'No, I don't think she did it. Certainly Charlotte hated Stack, and he was about to have her evicted from her home but, on the morning of the murder, her surprise was genuine and her first reaction was that she had "never heard a shot". That tells me she thought old Walter had actually done the dastardly deed.'

'So we have a situation of father-in-law and daughter-in-law each thinking they're shielding the other,' said Audrey, pushing the plate of buttered scones nearer her husband. She wanted to get his thoughts into calmer waters and her home-cooking was always a handy tool. 'How was old Walter when they took him away?'

Jack shrugged. 'Resigned. Phil Hengrove sent his DC, young Bailey, and a constable to pick him up. They were gentle with the old boy. My guess is that they'll keep him overnight, charge him with "threatening behaviour" in the morning and then let him go.'

'I hope so.' Audrey shook her head. 'Peter Morecroft, Stuart Thornton and now Walter Giller. At this rate, the only ones left in the parish will be us and the vicar.'

'And talk of the devil…' said her husband, raising his eyebrows as the dog-collared figure himself came striding up their garden path and rang the bell, '… I wonder what he wants?'

'Ssssh, I don't know but don't use that expression for the vicar,' scolded Audrey as she went to answer the door. Minutes later she was showing the priest into the kitchen.

'Drink, padre?' asked Jack, gesturing the vicar into a chair.

'Er, no thanks but a cup of tea would be nice,' answered the Reverend Julian Jamieson, seating himself across the table from the Ranger. 'How are things with you, Jack?'

'Hectic at the moment…' Jack took a sip of his gin, '… this business with Professor Stack seems to have put a cloud over everyone.' Including the present company, he thought but didn't say. He liked Jamieson, a caring man in his sixties who had achieved much in restoring both the church and its congregation since coming to St Cuthbert's just a year previous. Today though, the vicar looked like a man weighed down by great worry and Jack could only guess it was the stigma of a murder within his parish.

'Ah yes, the murder,' agreed Reverend Jamieson, looking genuinely distressed, 'a terrible business.' He took the cup of tea just being handed to him by Audrey and nodded eager acceptance of the plate of scones also being offered. 'Actually, it's to do with Professor Stack's death that I've come to see you.'

'In what way?'

The vicar cleared his throat. 'Well, the fact is, his old academic colleagues at Cambridge have been in touch with me. They'd heard of the appalling crime on the national news and wanted to know when his funeral was, so they could come and pay their respects.'

'Funeral…' it was one aspect of this case that Jack hadn't even considered, '… I'm afraid it will be a long time yet, vicar. The coroner usually doesn't release the body until the police investigations are complete which, judging by how things are going, could be weeks.'

'Yes, yes…' the vicar nodded miserably, '… I realise there are … formalities… to be gone through but what we can do is hold a memorial service in lieu of the funeral to come. To that end, I have agreed to conduct such a service at St Cuthbert's the day after tomorrow.'

'Which means the church will have to be made ready,' injected Audrey, passing the vicar a buttered scone. 'How many mourners are you expecting?'

'Only half-a-dozen or so from Cambridge,' answered Jamieson, between mouthfuls of scone. 'That's one of the reasons I've come to see you, really: do either of you know of any relatives of Professor Stack whom I can inform?'

Jack and Audrey looked at each other blankly.

'From what I know, DCI Hengrove, the officer leading the investigation, has been unable to find any,' answered Jack. 'Lisa Thornton was Professor Stack's ... er ... personal assistant. Perhaps she knows of some.'

'No, she doesn't.' The vicar gratefully accepted a second scone. 'I rang her myself this morning and, as far as she knows, he has no family at all. She was very specific on that point. She said she would be attending herself out of duty, though she had no time for what she described as "religious nonsense".'

'Oh dear,' said Audrey.

'Well, that looks like *it*,' said Jack, surprised that a man like Reverend Jamieson, well-used to dealing with death and its aftermath, should find this whole business so unduly trying. 'I'm sorry we can't help you more.'

'Well, actually, you might still.' The vicar wiped his forehead with a large handkerchief as he strained to find words for what was obviously an embarrassing situation. 'You see, just asking around, it's obvious that none of our parishioners have the slightest intention of attending and paying their respects.'

'That's because no one round here had any respect for him in the first place,' countered Jack bluntly. 'The man was an obnoxious martinet who'll be mourned by no-one.' He was going to say more until he felt a dig in his back from Audrey.

'Oh my goodness.' The vicar shook his head before looking appealingly at his host. 'At least, would you attend, Jack? I've heard you're taking a professional interest in the case and trying to help poor young Morecroft.'

'I'm not sure I could get the time off work.' Jack had no intention of indulging in the hypocrisy of giving thanks for the life of a man who had ruined so many others. 'I'm spending enough time on the case as it is, without asking my employers for more.'

'Ah, well, there we should be okay,' countered the Reverend

Jamieson, brightening momentarily before continuing, slightly sheepishly. 'You see, I actually contacted the Broads Authority to see if they would send a representative, considering all the work Professor Stack had done promoting tourism on these waters. They suggested you and said you could attend on their behalf.'

'Did they now,' said Jack, sniffing slightly. 'Well, if I'm so ordered, I guess I'll be there.'

'Excellent.' The vicar swallowed hard as he prepared to push his advantage to the full. 'Is there anyone else you could bring, Jack, just to swell numbers? I'd hate Rupert Stack's old colleagues to walk into a virtually empty church. Colonel Etherington has agreed to come and represent the parish. Can you think of anyone else?'

'Yes, actually there is someone who'd probably be very interested in attending.'

'Good, good.' The vicar was looking even happier. 'Who's that, Jack?'

'The police.'

'The police?' Jamieson seemed shocked.

'Yep.' Jack finished his gin. 'Actually, it's almost standard procedure in these cases. Murderers often come to observe the results of their handiwork and the police like to have a good look at anyone showing even a sliver of guilt. What time is the service?'

'Twelve o'clock, midday.'

Jack glanced towards the phone. 'Right, I'll give Phil Hengrove a call and let him know.'

'Oh dear, I'm not sure about all this,' said Reverend Jamieson, getting to his feet. 'It's bad enough knowing there might be a murderer in the village without him attending St Cuthbert's and even … Lord forbid … being arrested there.'

'It's not a perfect world is it, padre?' said Jack, getting to his feet to see his priest out but, at the same time, feeling another poke in the back from Audrey. So, at the door, he said simply, 'I'm sure nothing will happen and Chief Inspector Hengrove will be the soul of discretion.'

'I'm sure he will.' The Reverend Jamieson's own soul seemed to be the one needing most consoling at this time but he quickly pulled himself together and shook his hosts' hands as he stepped outside, 'Thanks, Jack, for your help and thank you, Audrey, for the lovely tea and scones.' The mention of tea and food though had obviously recalled something else he'd intended to mention. 'Oh, by the way, the

Cambridge party have asked if we can provide refreshments afterwards in the church hall. They've agreed to meet the cost but I was wondering, Audrey, if...'

'... I could organise a spread,' his churchwarden completed for him, before smiling reassuringly and saying, 'Don't worry, vicar; I'll get the usual ladies to knock something up.' Audrey paused, noticing for the first time a gleaming new people-carrier standing just outside their garden gate. 'Hello, whose is that?'

The vicar turned, slightly embarrassed. 'Well ... it's mine ... actually.'

'Yours?' Jack was as stunned as his wife. 'But you've never had a car the whole time you've been here, padre. You told me yourself you preferred to get around on your bike.'

'Yes, I know but it will come in handy for church outings and for transporting the old and infirm.' The Reverend Jamieson smiled sheepishly. 'As it's for the benefit of the parish, I hope no-one will begrudge me my little extravagance.'

'I'm sure they won't, vicar,' said Audrey before her husband could say anymore. 'I'll call you tomorrow to confirm details of the service.'

'Phew, the Church of England must be better payers than I thought,' said Jack, closing the door behind him, pouring a second gin and easing back into his kitchen chair. 'Those new wheels of Jamieson's wouldn't give you much change out of thirty grand.'

'Yes, it is a surprise,' agreed Audrey. 'He's always seemed such a frugal man until now. Perhaps some rich relation has left him some money, and anyway...' she poured herself a fresh cup of tea, '... if anyone deserves a treat, it's the Reverend Julian, after all the fund-raising he's done for St Cuthbert's in just one year. You remember, Jack, what a state the church was in before he arrived? Well, look at it now: a new roof, completely re-wired and the church hall repainted as well.'

'Yeah, he's achieved miracles,' said Jack, nodding agreement and remembering all the financial worries the Parochial Church Council had agonised over before the arrival of Julian Jamieson. 'Those jobs alone must have cost hundreds of thousands and all from an anonymous benefactor, I understand.'

'Yes,' said Audrey pausing to butter herself a scone. 'Apparently he or she lived abroad but had links with St Cuthbert's and wanted to help.'

'And you have no idea who this mysterious, but very generous, person might be?'

'None at all.'

'How about the cheques…?' Jack's policeman's curiosity had been aroused, '… there must have been a name on those?'

Audrey shook her head. 'There weren't any cheques. According to Freddie Jenkins, the Treasurer, the money just appeared in St Cuthbert's bank account.'

'Hmmm…' Jack took a sip of his gin and stretched his legs under the table where Spike lay patiently awaiting his walk, '… and now our good vicar is driving around in the latest people-carrier. Did he know Professor Stack very well?'

'Jack, what are you saying?' Audrey put her cup of tea down with very deliberate force. 'You're not, I hope, for one minute even suggesting that Reverend Jamieson is in any way … involved in this murder.'

'No, of course not,' said Jack, retreating diplomatically, 'but we just don't know much about the vicar's past, do we?' He drained his tumbler. 'Where was he before St Cuthbert's?'

'No-one's quite sure and he's strangely reticent to discuss it,' admitted Audrey, reluctantly. 'Just missionary work is all he says when asked… which makes him all the more admirable in my book,' she added with emphasis.

'So why did he move here?'

'Just a desire for a Norfolk parish, apparently.' Audrey finished her tea. 'He is a bachelor, after all, with no family ties so it's not unreasonable that he's had an itinerant life.'

'No, of course not,' Jack agreed, again. 'Which university did he go to? Not Cambridge was it?'

'Why on earth do you want to know that?'

'Oh…' Jack shrugged, '…I was just wondering if he'd known Professor Stack in some other life. We have to check these things, Audrey.'

'What's this "we", Jack? You're retired from the police now, remember?' Audrey leaned across and took her husband's hand. 'Jack, I know you want to prove Peter Morecroft's innocence but don't you think you're becoming just a little … well… obsessed by this whole business? Now you're even suspecting our poor vicar just because he's got a new car. And you can leave that,' she scolded, just as Jack reached again for the gin bottle.

Jack withdrew his hand. 'Yeah, perhaps you're right, love. I'll take Spike for his run and then we'll watch some telly and get an early night. We've both got work tomorrow.'

'Yes, I've got to make sure St Cuthbert's is ready for the memorial service and organise the catering,' agreed Audrey. 'A bit of normal patrolling back on the river will do you good as well, Jack Fellows.'

'Probably.' Jack went and got Spike's lead. He never intentionally deceived his wife but perhaps it was better not mentioning that his first job on the river next morning would be Starcraft's yard, where he had more questions for Charlotte Giller. Better too, not to admit to Audrey that he was now looking forward to attending Stack's memorial service and the chance to find out more about the Reverend Julian Jamieson.

Chapter Twelve

AUDREY WAS RIGHT: it was good to be back on the river next morning. The day was slightly overcast, but the river scene as enchanting as ever. It seemed to Jack that, whatever nature's mood, these waters had an atmosphere and mystery all of their own. There was a keen wind blowing this morning but he still ran peacefully on electrics towards Starcraft's yard, savouring the scene but at the same time pondering on Audrey's words of last night.

Perhaps she'd been right about his becoming over-involved in this crime. Jack had discovered long ago that every murder turned up its own hornet's nests of bitterness, grief and scandal. This investigation was certainly producing its share of local misery and woe, but it was still a fascinating mystery that had got him gripped. Though still no closer to discovering the perpetrator, Jack knew his old stubbornness meant he would never give in until the truth was established. He just hoped other lives wouldn't be blighted along the way. Coming into sight now were two he especially wanted to protect.

Charlotte Giller and Colin Newell stood together on the quayside watching as Jack slid his launch once more into the boatyard dyke. He'd called ahead to check Charlotte was at work but there'd been anguish in her voice and now, even a boat-length away, he could see distress lining her pretty face. Nevertheless, she managed a brave smile as he came alongside:
'Hello, Jack.'

While Colin tied the launch, Jack jumped ashore and took both Charlotte's hands in his. 'Don't look so fearful, Charlotte. I just want to talk to you personally about old Walter.'

She was looking as appealing as ever in spite of paint-stained overalls and an errant lock of hair spilling over her eyes. She wiped it back and with it, an incipient tear at the same time. 'Is it true, Jack? That Pop's been arrested?'

'Not arrested, Charlotte; helping the police with their enquiries which, in spite of what people think, can mean just that.' Jack turned to the young boatbuilder now at their side. 'Colin, if you can spare the time, why don't we all go in your office for a chat?'

'Sure.' He seemed about to put an arm around Charlotte's shoulder before thinking twice and leading them inside.

Colin Newell's office was typical of his yard: unpretentious, functional and used. The one desk was buried under piles of unfiled paperwork, engine parts and tools. Atop the battered filing cabinet sat a magnificent model of a Broads sailing cruiser. That, and a few faded photos of boats built by the yard over the decades, were the only concession to aesthetics in the whole room.

While Charlotte went to get out of her overalls, Colin gestured Jack into a battered chair and sat down in his own. 'The poor girl's really taken it bad, her dad-in-law being taken in like that.'

'I can see.' Jack didn't say anymore until Charlotte returned in only moderately cleaner jeans and tee-shirt, shut the door and settled herself into the other chair. He turned towards her. 'Charlotte, I wanted to come and see you and explain that I was the cause of Walter spending the night at North Walsham Police Station.'

'What happened?' She was trying hard to keep her voice calm.

'I went to see him yesterday and he confessed to murdering Professor Stack.'

'Oh, no!' Charlotte's hand went to the side of her face. 'I feared this, Jack... I knew he might...'

'Charlotte...' Jack put a staying hand on her shoulder before she could say any more, '... he confessed but he didn't do it. In the end he admitted threatening Stack but that's all he did. However, apart from the murderer, he was probably the last man to see Stack alive and, for that reason, he is a valuable witness and that's why I told him to hand himself in. He might just get charged with "threatening behaviour" but my guess is that Phil Hengrove will give him a ticking off and send him home.'

'Oh, thank God.' Charlotte exhaled a lungful of relief and ran a tiny hand through her tangled hair. 'It was probably my fault. I'd rung him pretty upset when I found that Stack was having me evicted from Boatyard Cottage. I shouldn't have done really - he's had enough grief of his own to bear, poor dear - but I had to pour out my heart to someone. He said he'd "sort it" and when I heard that Stack had been murdered it was like a dagger going through my own heart. I was sure Pops had done it.'

'I know, and the crazy thing is that he thought *you* might have done it. That's why he confessed ... to take the blame from someone he holds very dear.'

'Oh, bless him.' She smiled and took Colin Newell's outstretched hand. 'Will Pops be all right, Jack? Will they have been easy on him?'

Jack smiled. 'He'll be fine. If I know coppers, he'll have had more fuss than he's had in a long time. I'm expecting a call anytime now to say he's been taken back to the marsh. I know you're working, Charlotte, but when he does get home I'm sure he'd love to see a friendly face.'

Charlotte gave Colin a questioning glance and he smiled and nodded. 'I'll drive you there now, Charlotte.'

'Before you do, there's a question I need to ask you … both of you.' Jack paused, steeling himself for words he didn't want to say. 'Where were you, both of you, on the night of Professor Stack's murder?'

It was Colin Newell who responded. 'Do we have to answer that?'

Jack shook his head. 'No you don't. I've no real authority in this case but if you choose not to, it'll be the police asking next and they won't give you that option.'

The boatbuilder went to say more but Charlotte squeezed his hand and gave a little shake of her head. Then she turned to Jack.

'I was at home all evening watching television.'

'And in the early hours of the next morning?'

'Asleep in bed.' Her answer was quick enough but Jack noticed the monotone of her voice and the fact that she glanced floorwards as she answered.

'How about you, Colin?'

The boatbuilder shrugged. 'I was here, working late in the yard until ten thirty. Then I went home.'

'Have either of you any witnesses to substantiate your answers?'

They looked at each other. 'No.'

Jack paused meaningfully, before continuing, 'You told me you'd had a dinghy "borrowed" that night, Colin. Presumably that was after you left?'

'Of course.'

'And it was back by the time you arrived at the yard next morning. How did you know it had been taken in the interim?'

'Because it was tied different to how I'd left it.' He leaned back in his chair. 'I always tie any boat the same way but that dinghy had been tied with different knots than I ever use.'

'Okay.' Jack could see this was enough interrogation for one day and it was time to change the subject. He smiled and said, 'I'm going to try and talk to Gwen Fosdyke now. I can ask her the situation as regards Giller's Yard, if you're still interested, Colin.'

It was Charlotte who answered. 'I shouldn't waste your time. The yard has already got a new owner.'

This was news to Jack. 'Who, for goodness sake?'

'Lisa Thornton.'

'Stack's PA-cum-mistress; how's she got her hands on it?'

Charlotte sniffed. 'By being Professor Stack's sole beneficiary. She told me so herself yesterday.'

'And she's going to have Charlotte thrown out just like Stack was going to, the stroppy cow,' completed Colin. 'It ain't right, Jack.'

'No it isn't.' Jack shook his head, unprepared for this revelation. 'Is it legal? Can an uncompleted sale be left in a will?'

'I don't know,' answered Charlotte, her voice weary with acceptance, 'but I'm sure Gwen Fosdyke will have found some loophole to screw me by.'

'But Councillor Fosdyke has always been such a defender of people's rights!' exclaimed Jack, trying to see a chink of light through these depressing trees. 'Why would she be party to anything questionable?'

'Because she was having her own fling with Rupert Stack and prepared to put her good name on the line to get him what he wanted,' responded Charlotte without hesitation. 'I told you I was sure that Stack's bid for the yard wasn't the highest and that Gwen Fosdyke, as Receiver, cooked the books in his favour. Having got him the yard, it was her position on the District Council that was going to secure him planning permission for its development. Now, it seems, even with her precious professor dead, she's acting for that little slut Thornton and going to have me thrown out anyway.'

'But why should Gwen Fosdyke help Lisa Thornton? If she was having a fling with Stack, as you suspect, then helping a rival mistress would seem the last thing she'd want to do.'

'I don't know,' was Charlotte's lame response. She'd calmed herself down now but that only served to emphasise the shock of her next words. 'There are a lot of things I don't understand about the relationship between Stack and Gwen Fosdyke but one thing I'm sure about: it was her that actually killed him.'

THIS WAS JACK'S MORNING for revelations and he took just a few seconds to take this one on board.

'What on earth gives you that idea, Charlotte?' he leaned forward, towards the young widow sitting beside him. 'Have you any proof?'

'No...' Charlotte shook her head, '... not solid but I know she telephoned him that evening and said she had to see him. She sounded really pissed off.'

'You heard her make this call? How?'

'Because I was in the office next door.' Charlotte's eyes lowered to the floor and her voice had just a hint of guilt. 'She didn't know I was there. Her office door was just ajar so I stayed quiet and listened to what she was saying.'

Jack sat upright. 'I think you'd better explain from the beginning.'

Charlotte turned to Colin Newell and it was the young boatbuilder's turn to nod and hold her hand ever tighter before she continued, 'I'm sorry I lied to you, Jack. I wasn't at home like I said. That night I was so upset by Gwen Fosdyke's call to say I was going to be evicted, that I decided to go to her office after hours, break in and find some evidence that she'd cooked the books for Stack. I took some tools and set off on my bike.'

'To break in? Commit burglary?' Jack didn't know whether to reprimand or admire this spirited girl. In the end he said, simply, 'Go on.'

'Well, in the end, I didn't have to break in because when I got there, I found her office still open but the staff gone. She was still in her office though, looking quite distraught; I could see her through the crack in the door. I thought this would be as good a time as any to have it out with her, and was about to go in when she picked up the phone and made that call.'

'To Stack?'

'Yes.'

'How do you know it was to him? Did she address him by name?'

'No. I just had the feeling it was to him.' Charlotte's mouth showed her conviction. 'I'm sure of it.'

'But without proof.' Jack sat back. 'What was said?'

'Just, "I need to see you tonight." The way she said it sounded like she was ready for anything.'

'Assuming it was Stack and they were lovers, why do you think she was so upset?' Jack asked.

'Perhaps she'd just found out that he was also knocking off Lisa,' answered Charlotte with no attempt at subtlety. 'Could be that she'd been expecting to be named in Stack's will and now found out that his little PA was going to get everything instead.'

'But Gwen Fosdyke was Stack's solicitor. If he had made a will in favour of Lisa Thornton, she would have known well before that night,' Jack surmised, almost to himself, before returning back to basics and asking, 'What did she do, having made this call?'

'Just got up to leave and that's when my own nerve failed me. I slipped out of the office just ahead of her. Next morning, when you told me that Stack had been murdered, my first thoughts were that Pops had done it but, in the back of my mind was the memory of that call and the steely resolve in Gwen Fosdyke's voice.'

'It certainly puts a new twist on everything.' Jack stretched his legs out in front of him. This conversation had become pretty intense and he wanted them all to loosen up. 'It's only surmise, Charlotte, but assuming Gwen Fosdyke was the murderer, how do you think she did it?'

'I don't know,' said Charlotte, shrugging, 'but the dinghy was taken from the yard that night. Perhaps it was Gwen, off on her own mission to kill.'

Jack shook his head. 'That doesn't make sense. She'd already told whoever she was calling that she needed to see them. There was nothing covert at that stage so why would she go nicking boats when, presumably, she could have just got Stack to pick her up at a staithe?' He got up to go. 'Anyway, I'm going to see her myself now and find out what I can. Obviously I won't mention how I know but I'll try and find out about that call.'

As the others got up to see him off, Jack's mobile rang. They could just hear him saying "Good" and "Right" before he rang off and turned towards them smiling. 'Some good news at least. Both Walter and Stuart Thornton have been released this morning. Stuart's been charged with assault but your father-in-law has just been told to save his shotgun for rats in future.'

'Great.' Charlotte's smile was good to see and Colin Newell seemed pleased to be able to give her a big hug.

Before starting the short walk into town, Jack had some final words for the pair. 'By the way, regarding your alibis for the night of the murder; when you say you were at home, Colin, I think you were telling the truth.' He turned towards Charlotte with just a twinkle in his eye. ' Would I be totally off the beam, Charlotte, in thinking that same home could be your alibi too?' Their silence and the gleam in their own eyes was all the answer he needed.

Walking into town, Jack pondered on Colin Newell's obvious deep love for Charlotte. Love like that could drive a man to the most desperate of acts. Perhaps Colin had used his own dinghy that night after all.

LOVE AND ITS CONSEQUENCES were far from Lisa Thornton's mind at that moment. She was six miles north, parked amongst marram grass and sandhills and trying not to think of the rolling expanse of the North Sea, unseen beyond the dunes. Turning up the volume of Radio One in a vain attempt to drown out the incessant squawking of seagulls circling overhead, she thought, 'God, what a dump.'

Lisa was not a creature naturally drawn to raw nature and it had taken quite an effort to prize herself from Professor Stack's apartment and out to this bleak desolate stretch of the coast. Sunshine and warmth might have eased her cynical outlook towards a scene that was as beautiful as it was wild, but today the chill wind and overcast sky mirrored her feelings towards nature in general. 'This has to be the end of the world,' she said out loud, before wondering mentally who, other than seals, brain-dead dog-walkers or boring birdspotters, would ever want to come to this dead-and-alive hole. Well today she hoped one other person would, one rather wealthy customer if all turned out as planned.

Having finally got through to Professor Stack's old contact, his response had been encouraging. The accented voice answering her call last night had been wary, initially, of even admitting dealing with Professor Rupert Stack, but a few well-chosen confidences from Lisa had convinced him she was a part of the scam and still eager to keep the supply chain open. He'd agreed to meet her but made it clear he wanted the same secrecy that he'd demanded in all his meetings with the late academic.

Lisa knew of the late-night contacts aboard *Aethelberht* at remote moorings. She'd been almost expecting this demand, though her late-employer's clandestine assignations and his violent demise weren't thoughts that naturally gelled. Secrecy, however, was what the buyer demanded and what he would get. The question was, where? Stack's apartment in town was too public and his boats were still under police jurisdiction. A meeting of cars seemed the answer, but Lisa shied away from trysts in the darkness with strangers working outside the law. In the end she had suggested a daytime rendezvous at this desolate beach where she now waited with a mixture of excitement and apprehension, while checking her watch for the umpteenth time.

Still half an hour to go. She'd arrived early, allowing plenty of time for eventualities but, unwittingly, also providing time for tension to build and nerves to stretch as the butterflies dancing in her stomach warned only too well.

Lisa told herself not to be stupid, to be uncompromising in the negotiations to come, perhaps even a little aggressive. Easier said than done though, as she stood on the threshold of her new and devious career. She checked again, the briefcase lying on the seat beside her. This morning she had obtained more of the merchandise, the goods her client was so eager to buy. But, much as he wanted them, Lisa knew he would do his utmost to beat her down in price. Seeking the resolve she knew she'd need, she glanced at herself in the mirror. Yes, she told herself, it was time to show that Lisa Thornton was more than just a pretty face.

A movement in the mirror beside that "pretty face" caused her to look behind. A car was pulling into the parking area. He'd arrived early. Lisa Thornton gripped the handle of her case, her own self-control and this moment in her destiny.

Chapter Thirteen

'I'M VERY GRATEFUL FOR you seeing me like this without an appointment,' said Jack as Gwen Fosdyke ushered him into her office and the chair in front of her desk.

'You were lucky, Mr. Fellows; I had a client cancellation.' The solicitor lowered her slim, still-shapely figure into her own chair. 'What can I do for the Broads Authority?'

'Actually, it's more what you can do for others,' said Jack, before explaining his supernumerary role in the investigation of Professor Rupert Stack.

'Yes, a bad business,' Gwen studied the letter-opener she was absentmindedly turning in her hand before suddenly becoming her old businesslike self and adding, 'but I'm not sure I can help you, Mr. Fellows. I only know what I've read in the papers.'

'Call me Jack,' said the Ranger. 'Nevertheless, Miss Fosdyke…'

'Gwen.'

'Right … Gwen … I'd like to ask you some questions; some personal, some legal, some perhaps impertinent, none of which you have to answer if you don't want to.'

Gwen smiled and nodded. 'Go ahead.'

'You were, I understand, the Receiver in the bankruptcy of Alan Giller?'

'I thought these questions related to the murder of Rupert Stack,' challenged Gwen, showing just a little irritation. 'What has Alan Giller's Receivership got to do with it?'

'Perhaps plenty,' answered Jack, unfazed. 'Yes or no?'

The solicitor paused again, obviously considering whether she should submit to this cross-examination. Perhaps she realised that answering Jack Fellows might be preferable than to the police because she then shrugged her shoulders and said, simply, 'Yes.'

'And the liquidation of Alan Giller's assets, namely his boatyard; how was that done?'

'The same procedure we invariably use in these cases: we invited bids from prospective purchasers and the highest was accepted.'

'Professor Rupert Stack's?'

'Yes,' said Gwen between slightly clenched teeth.

'Presumably, these were sealed bids. Who actually opened them?'

'I did, as Receiver. Naturally I relayed the data to the bank in question and they confirmed their acceptance.'

Jack nodded. 'What happened to the lower bids? Are they still on file?'

'No, they were destroyed.'

Jack raised questioning eyebrows. 'Is that normal?'

'Once the sale has been completed … yes.'

'But you were also Professor Stack's solicitor.' Jack pulled his chair just a little closer to Gwen Fosdyke's desk. 'Is it entirely ethical that your client is also the winning bid?'

Gwen sat upright in her chair. 'What, exactly, are you implying?'

Jack kept his eyes steadily on the solicitor before him. 'Just answer the question … if you feel you can.'

'I certainly can.' Gwen Fosdyke's cheeks were showing just the hint of redness. 'If the parties involved - in this case, the creditors - are happy, there is nothing to preclude it.'

'Understood,' acquiesced Jack, feeling it was time to resume normal relations. 'In a case like this, when the purchaser dies, what happens then to the property he was buying?'

'If the sale has been completed, as this one virtually has, then it passes to his main beneficiary.'

'Which, in the case of Professor Stack, is …?'

Gwen shook her head. 'That I can't answer, Jack. You know as well as I about client confidentiality.'

'Yes,' said Jack calmly, 'but if I offered the name, Lisa Thornton, would you deny it?'

Gwen swallowed slightly. 'No comment.'

'I'll take that then as confirmation that the beneficiary is Mrs Thornton.' Before the solicitor could protest, Jack sat back in his chair and said, 'Let's get on to the night of Professor Stack's murder; what were you doing that night, Gwen?'

'Working late, here in the office.'

'How late?'

'Very late … until about ten o'clock. I had a large backlog of cases that needed one hundred per cent effort to clear.'

'And then where?'

'Home … in bed.'

'And, while you were here "working very late",' Jack paused for effect, 'did you make any telephone calls.'

'Probably several,' answered Gwen, with diminishing patience. 'I really can't see…'

'Did you call Professor Rupert Stack?'

'No, I didn't. Why should I?'

'You might have several reasons,' responded Jack, 'legal or … personal.'

'What are you insinuating?' Gwen Fosdyke's irritation was turning to downright indignation.

It made no impression on the Ranger. 'That your and Professor Stack's relationship might have been more than professional.'

'How dare you!' Gwen Fosdyke stood up. 'If you've any more such questions, Mr. Fellows, I suggest you put them in writing so I can have them in evidence for any action I might feel fit to take.' She went to her office door and held it open. 'I shan't be making any formal complaint to the Broads Authority on this occasion, but if I hear one word…'

Jack held up a staying hand. 'Miss Fosdyke, I appreciate your time and help. I only wish you could have answered that last question.'

As Jack speed-walked back to Starcraft's yard and his launch, he mulled over Gwen Fosdyke's reactions. One thing very clear was that any romantic feeling she might have felt for Stack had definitely evaporated. Nonetheles she'd said something in that interview that nagged him even more but what? Perhaps it was just the fact that she'd lied, which was never a good sign.

MRS. MARJORIE PRENDERS ALWAYS walked her little Jack Russell terrier at the same place every day. It meant driving there in the car, but Popsie enjoyed running and burrowing in the sandhills, and Marjorie herself loved to stroll by the water's edge as the North Sea rollers came crashing ashore. This was a place she could find the solitude she needed to think her thoughts, both happy and sad. Marjorie enjoyed desolation and here you could walk a dozen times and never see another soul.

Perhaps not today though because the omens were bad before she'd even reached the spot she normally parked her little car. While still crawling down the potholed track to the shore, another vehicle had come speeding towards her, bouncing over the ruts and causing her to run into the verge to avoid what seemed an imminent collision. As the offending vehicle had bounced past, Marjorie had shaken a fist of protest at the driver, noting his flabby neck and stressed, panic-stricken demeanour. He threw her an anxious glance in return and, as his car accelerated away, Marjorie had just enough time to turn and note its registration. She prided herself on remembering details but just to be sure, she wrote this one down in the small notebook she always kept in her map compartment. Being a stalwart supporter of law and order, she never hesitated to report any driver she felt was a menace, and this flashy-looking one and his equally flashy car would certainly join her long list of offenders. Not that the police ever did anything about her numerous complaints, usually brushing her off with promises to "look into it" from which no results were ever forthcoming. Wondering, not for the first time this day, what this world was coming to, Marjorie slipped into first gear again and crawled onwards to the beach.

Arriving at her usual sandy space, she was annoyed to find it taken, and her little sanctuary also desecrated. Another car - a four-wheel drive thing - was parked, its radio blaring at full blast the hideous reverberations that these days so often passed as music. Well, we can do without that here, thought Marjorie, letting Popsie out to run free while she strode over to the offending vehicle.

The driver couldn't be seen at this stage, but Marjorie guessed she must be there, for surely no-one would have left the radio full-on while taking a walk. That the owner was female was very clear in Marjorie's mind. She rather fancied her own powers of deduction and surely this scenario of guilty-looking-man-hurrying-from-remote-location-leaving-lone-person-there meant only one thing in these immoral times: adulterous liaison. Prepared to give a short lecture on morality as well as respect for rural peace, Marjorie approached the vehicle and looked inside.

The occupant was certainly a woman and stretched across the two front seats, doubtless recovering from her immoral exertions. Without further ado, Marjorie wrenched open the passenger door. For a second, she stood staring, her hand going to her mouth to stifle a scream. Even as she slammed the door back closed, she knew the peace of mind that she always found in this remote and beautiful niche of the coast, had been ruined for ever.

JACK GHOSTED HIS LAUNCH back into its boatshed, content that his working day had ended. After his abrasive interview with Gwen Fosdyke, he'd decided to cruise home via Wyford's Mill, thinking that Stuart Thornton would probably appreciate a friendly chat.

It was not to be though, for when Jack arrived it was to find the old mill deserted. Home and comfort were the usual priorities of most released from police custody but Stuart obviously felt different. Perhaps Lisa's desertion had left too many memories at Wyford's Mill. Stuart's dinghy was also missing, so perhaps he'd escaped to the tranquillity of some marshy creek to sketch his next creation or just contemplate his future alone. With the thought of possibly meeting him downriver, Jack had set off home, but in this he was also disappointed for there was no sign of Stuart en route.

Mentally promising to try again next morning, Jack secured the launch in its boathouse, plugged in the charger, completed his paperwork and set off on the quarter-mile walk to his home. He was just passing St Cuthbert's Church and thinking of Professor Stack's memorial service on the morrow, when his mobile rang.

It was Detective Chief Inspector Hengrove. The body of a young woman had been found on the north coast and he wanted Jack there.

Chapter Fourteen

'ANOTHER MESSY ONE, JACK.' Phil Hengrove met the Ranger at the coloured tape that marked the boundary of those in authority and those not. There weren't many of the latter: just a couple of curious dog-walkers and the usual media. They were far out-numbered by uniformed police whose yellow jackets and the flashing blue lights of their vehicles were in stark contrast to the grass-covered dunes and ever-large Norfolk sky.

'If you were looking for a remote spot to murder someone,' said Jack, scanning the inland horizon and failing to detect the slightest sign of habitation within at least a mile, 'you couldn't do better than this.' He looked again to seaward where canvas screens hid what was obviously the scene of the tragedy. White-overalled crime scene investigators were already busying themselves in the immediate area. 'I take it, Phil, that we are talking "murder"?'

Hengrove nodded. 'Young woman, late thirties. She's lying in a Range Rover, throat cut from ear to ear but no sign of the weapon as yet.'

'I.D.?'

'The vehicle is registered to a Mrs Lisa Thornton.'

'Stuart Thornton's wife…' Jack had become used to murder and violent death in his years with the Met. but serious crime inflicted on people he knew was something else. He gulped back his shock and said, 'Are you sure?'

The DCI shrugged. 'Not yet and that's where I'd appreciate your help, Jack. You knew her.'

'Yes but…' Jack frowned. 'Does Stuart Thornton know yet?'

'No, and he won't until I've at least had a preliminary.' Hengrove absently scanned inland where the stumps of long-abandoned drainage pumps stood like centennials amidst the wild surrounding marshes. 'Just the same, I've got lads out looking for him but, so far, no joy.' He nodded again towards the canvas screens. 'Take a look, Jack?'

'Okay.'

At the tent-like structure, a constable pulled back the flap to reveal a familiar Range Rover, doors open and forensic experts crawling inside like collectors intent on some rare specie. The pathologist was examining something sprawled across the front seats. He stood aside to reveal the prone body of a young woman, eyes wide and staring and her blonde hair spattered with blood. That same blood had sprayed the windscreen and dashboard and stained the seats on which she lay. It wasn't difficult to detect its origin: across the victim's throat was a vicious gash that must have resulted in almost instant death. Amidst this destruction, Jack recognised the determined chin, petulant lips and oversize earrings of a young woman he knew only too well.

'That's Lisa Thornton all right.'

'Thanks, Jack.' Hengrove led him outside, leaving pathologist and forensic team to continue their grim task. Back in the open, the fresh sea air was like nectar after the stench of death within.

Jack inhaled gladly before turning back to the expressionless DCI.

'Time-of-death, Phil?'

'About three this afternoon.'

'Who found her?'

'A Mrs Prenders, busy-body dog-walker.' Hengrove nodded towards a police car where an elderly lady sat in the back, head bowed and a female officer's arm about her shoulder. 'Went to complain about the noise of the radio and found that decibels were the least of the driver's problems. A good witness though because she saw a man driving away at speed looking very upset. Gave a description and even a number.'

'And...?'

'Registered to one Max van Horsen, a coin-dealer with a shop in Tottenham Court Road. He's got previous for "handling and receiving". The Met. are trying to bring him in now.' Hengrove sighed. 'Hopefully, sooner rather than later.'

'What time did Mrs Prenders see him?'

'Just after three-thirty; walks her dog every day at the same time.'

'That's quite some time after death,' observed Jack. 'Considering he was "speeding away", there was half an hour between murder and get-a-way.'

Hengrove nodded. 'Yeah, I thought about that. Actually you can see the approach from here...' he pointed to where the rough track wound its way towards the beach, '... perhaps van Horsen suddenly saw Mrs Prenders driving towards here and decided it was time to do his bunk.'

'So, you think he did it?'

'I *hope* he did it,' said Hengrove with feeling. 'The most likely candidate is husband Stuart. With his missus doing the dirty on him, he certainly had motive and opportunity.' The DCI groaned. 'I'm praying he's got a good alibi. If it turns out he snuffed his wife just hours after I released him, the media'll have a heyday.'

'Well, at least you know who didn't do it.' Jack, felt the need to say something positive.

'Your mate Peter Morecroft, you mean?' responded the DCI. 'Well he certainly had a waterproof alibi for this one, but that young tearaway isn't off the hook yet.'

Jack shook his head. 'It's hard to believe these two murders are unrelated, Phil. After all, Lisa Thornton was Stack's personal assistant as well as being his mistress. By still considering Peter Morecroft for Stack's, you're stretching coincidence.'

The DCI nodded again. 'I know Jack, and I agree, there must be some link up, but I still can't believe Morecroft wasn't involved in Stack's murder. Neither he nor you can explain his initials scrawled in the victim's blood and those two coins we found in his dory.' Hengrove turned towards the Ranger. 'Norwich Castle museum came back to us with a make on those, by the way. Very interesting.'

'Go on.'

'Well,' said Hengrove, 'turns out they were from a hoard discovered four decades ago down in Essex. Workmen were digging some foundations and uncovered this urn full of sceattas which are Anglo-Saxon pennies minted in a variety of designs and types. There were about a thousand of them in this find, all silver and worth a fortune to any collector. The archaeology curator at the castle positively identified our two coins as belonging to that hoard. Apparently they had unique runic symbols spelling the name of the original moneyer who minted them. Runes are symbols…'

'Yeah, I know what runes are,' interrupted Jack. 'So how come these two … sceattas … got out of their museum?'

'Ah, there lies the story,' said Hengrove, obviously enjoying the satisfaction of imparting fresh information. 'Turns out the whole collection was sent on a tour of the country about ten years ago, but while they were on display in some museum in the Midlands, they got nicked.'

'Really… How?'

'Not easily.' Hengrove rolled his eyes. 'They were locked in the museum safe overnight but that didn't stop chummy. The casefile reckons he hid in the museum after closing time, got into the office, cracked the safe and then legged it over the rooftops with the complete hoard.'

'A pretty audacious villain.'

The DCI nodded. 'He was and you might even remember him, Jack: Freddie "Locks" Venning?'

Jack scratched his head, digging deep into his mental files. 'Venning ... "Locks" Venning ... Yep, I remember the name: ex-SAS corporal who could crack a safe quicker than Houdini. I never got to meet him but if I remember right, he got pulled in twelve years ago for the Croydon bullion job. It wasn't my case, thank goodness. I seem to recall they couldn't get enough evidence on Venning and let him go.' Jack gave a mirthless laugh. 'Sounds like he wasn't so careful with the coin hoard.'

'He wasn't. He left a print on the office door which matched those taken from him during the Croydon investigation...' Hengrove sighed, 'so Midlands Police had the evidence this time but no man.'

'You mean he was never caught?'

'No,' said Hengrove, shaking his head. 'Seems he dropped off the edge of the earth. Hopped it abroad and got himself a new identity, was one theory. That or some cronies from the Croydon job didn't get their cut and took him out. Either way, neither he nor the thousand sceattas have ever been seen since.'

'Until now.'

'That's right. Those two coins were the first ever recovered. The Museum Service are pretty excited about it.'

'And there were plenty more where they came from,' said Jack. 'You remember I saw piles of coins in Stack's safe as well as the gold brooches.' He slapped the DCI on the shoulder. 'There's your connection between these two murders, Phil; van Horsen is a coin dealer with convictions for "handling" and Stack often had a mysterious stranger visiting his boat at late hours. Chances are, van Horsen was that stranger. He might well have also murdered Stack during an illicit coin deal and cleaned out the safe.'

Hengrove started leading them back to the taped perimeter. 'But why kill Lisa Thornton?'

'Perhaps she knew too much and tried a little blackmail.' Jack held up his hands in supplication. 'Who knows? What we do know is that van Horsen was here this afternoon.'

'Well, let's hope the Met. pick him up soon,' said Hengrove with feeling, 'I could do with a nice clean solution to these two cases.' A white-overalled figure caught up with them. The DCI turned towards him. 'Anything more you can tell us, doc?'

The pathologist shook his head. 'Not until I get her back to the lab. It's pretty obvious that death was caused by the single wound to the throat that cut the windpipe and carotid artery in a single swipe. She was probably dead within seconds.' He pulled off his rubber gloves and took his own lungful of sea air. 'What *is* significant though is that it must have taken a fair-sized knife to inflict a wound like that.'

'What sort of knife?'

The pathologist shrugged. 'Hard to say but something more than your average penknife: a Bowie knife perhaps … something like that. I'd estimate at least a five-inch blade and with some serration on its edge too judging by the nature of the tissue damage.'

'So, we're talking premeditation,' said Hengrove, stroking his chin. 'This was no impulse job; someone came here fully intending that Lisa Thornton wouldn't see the sunset.'

As the pathologist left them for his car, Jack turned back to the DCI, 'Any evidence of theft, Phil?'

'Might be; not even a handbag left in the car,' answered the DCI, 'which is unusual for a woman motoring.' He paused and scratched his head. 'But it's more than simple theft, Jack. No-one cuts a woman's throat just for her handbag.' They'd reached the Ranger's car now. Hengrove looked at his watch. 'Lots to do, Jack. With all this, I'm not sure I'll even make Stack's memorial service tomorrow.' He shrugged again. 'If I can't, I'll send Bailey.' He glanced towards the half-dozen reporters and journalists converging towards them and grimaced. 'I have a feeling it's *my* throat this lot are after.'

Jack mentally agreed as he drove away leaving Phil Hengrove lost behind a barrage of tape-recorders and microphones. He was glad he hadn't told the DCI all he knew about Lisa Thornton. If Stack's ex-personal assistant really had inherited her late-boss's complete estate, that made her estranged husband the new beneficiary. Even more than Hengrove, Jack hoped Stuart Thornton had a good alibi.

Chapter Fifteen

'LET GO FOR'ARD!' In the graceful upturned bows of the replica galley *Raedwald*, Charlotte Giller obeyed Jack's command and slipped the head-warp while, on the other side, Jack's patrol launch produced a welter of foam as its engine went slow astern. With Colin Newell holding the fore-spring at *Raedwald's* stern, slowly and surely the galley's fine bows swung out from Giller's Yard. When they were pointing towards the open broad, Jack brought his engine control back to neutral.

'Let go, aft!' Colin Newell hauled the spring through the ring on shore, the launch went ahead and slowly the pair of boats glided out from the quay.

IT WAS AFTER ARRIVING home from Lisa Thornton's murder scene that the Reverend Jamieson had paid another call at the Fellows' cottage. Jack had barely had time to relate to Audrey the grim facts of this latest tragedy when the vicar's increasingly distraught figure had appeared at the door.

'Oh dear, I've just heard that the body of a young woman has been found on the coast,' he sighed, as Jack sat him down in the lounge and Audrey went to brew another tea. 'Have they any idea who it might be?'

'Next-of-kin have yet to identify the body but don't be expecting Lisa Thornton at tomorrow's service,' answered Jack, indicating without words, that this particular subject was not open for further discussion.

'Oh dear, oh dear. Such dreadful times for our little parish.' The vicar took the cup of tea from Audrey with grateful thanks. A few calming gulps seemed to steady his nerves before he looked up and said, 'Actually, I've come to ask another favour of you, Jack.'

'I'll help if I can,' responded Jack, keen to alleviate the vicar's worries in any way he could. 'What do you need?'

Reverend Jamieson took another satisfying sip of his tea. 'Well, it's the Cambridge academics actually, who have come up with an idea.'

'Another one?'

Reverend Jamieson nodded. 'Yes. You see, as Professor Stack's mortal remains won't actually be present, they thought it would be rather nice if his Anglo-Saxon boat was instead.'

'*Raedwald*?'

'Yes,' said the vicar nodding again. 'As the church is only yards from the river, they wondered if the galley could be brought to the staithe as a sort of symbol of what Professor Stack had achieved hereabouts.' As if reading Jack's thoughts he quickly added, 'I've already been in contact with the police who assure me the forensic examination is complete and they're happy for the boat to be released.'

AND SO, THE MORNING of Rupert Stack's memorial service found Jack towing *Raedwald* alongside his launch to the church staithe. As far as gestures went, he conceded it was probably quite a good one, though he could think of others that those less near-and-dear to the late professor would prefer to make. Nevertheless, when he'd telephoned Charlotte and Colin and asked them to crew the galley, they had, surprisingly, readily agreed. For Charlotte, the replica was still a living memorial to the skill of her late husband, while Colin seemed glad at the prospect of getting his hands on this unique wooden boat. Under way now and with sunshine glinting off the sparkling water, *Raedwald*'s clinker bow produced an enchanting chuckle as she cleaved the wavelets of the broad.

Charlotte and Colin stood together at the stern, the latter holding the replica's traditional steering oar. Jack gave them an encouraging wave and they waved cheerfully back. There was no doubt that this young couple found contentment in each other's company. Perhaps some would say it was early days after Alan's suicide, but Jack was always phlegmatic about happiness in the wake of extreme sadness. No-one deserved some more than Charlotte Giller and he wished them well.

This morning there was another factor influencing their contented frame of mind. They had voiced their shock at Lisa Thornton's violent demise but had been honest enough to utter no insincere platitudes of regret. Considering the deceased's gloating intention to still evict Charlotte from Boatyard Cottage, it was perhaps understandable. By the same token, those facts alone made the young widow a suspect.

But was this sweet girl capable of murder in such a ruthless way? Probably not, thought Jack, but Colin Newell had doubtless resented the pain Lisa Thornton was inflicting on someone he cared for very much. He was fit and strong and in love and that combination made anything possible. Added to that, Lisa Thornton had suddenly stood between him and Giller's Yard, a property he admitted to still be desperately wanting.

Jack looked again towards the couple smiling in the stern of the old galley. This was too fine a day to be harbouring such dark thoughts. He shook them away and looked ahead to the staithe just coming into view.

JACK WAS GLAD TO SEE that there was only one other boat at the mooring: Colonel Etherington's *Goosewatcher*. As Jack brought his small flotilla alongside, the old soldier himself caught the line thrown by Charlotte and soon *Raedwald* also was lying under the shade of the staithe's encircling trees.

'Morning, Fellows.' The Colonel always sounded as though he was addressing a parade. 'Lovely day.'

'It certainly is.' Jack made his way across *Raedwald*, jumped ashore and shook the Colonel's hand before glancing at his watch. 'You're here early, Colonel.'

'Yes, well, wanted time to have a chat with you.' The Colonel leaned confidentially closer. 'Just hoping you might give me an update on how the investigations are going into this damn murder. Understand there are two now. News this morning said that the second victim was wife of the artist chappie … what's his name? … Thornton.'

'That's right.' Jack had been relieved to hear on the morning news that Lisa's body had been formally identified by her husband. At least Stuart had been located and, hopefully, had established his movements at the crucial time. He turned back to Etherington. 'Early days yet, Colonel, but I'm sure they'll have some results soon.'

'Hope so,' said the Colonel. 'Damn awful business … gives the parish a bad name. Ought to hang the blighter when they catch 'im.'

'They should indeed, Colonel.' A car had just pulled up in front of the church giving Jack the excuse he sought to excuse himself from the old soldier's clutches. DC Bailey looked like a man who'd had little sleep of late but his greeting to Jack was cheery for all that.

'Morning, sir.'

'Morning, Bailey. Glad you could come.'

The young detective smiled. 'Actually, sir, it's good to get away from HQ for a bit. These murders have made life pretty fraught.' He glanced around at the grassy staithe, the weathered stone of St Cuthbert's Church and the river, flowing gently by. 'Not used to this sort of thing in these parts.'

'Thankfully,' added Jack, his expression becoming serious as he ushered Bailey to one side. 'Any developments?'

'Yes indeed.' The DC seemed relieved to have something positive to relate. 'Thornton himself went into his local nick just hours after the news conference. Apparently he'd been drinking in the local since we let him go. Got pretty worse for wear but at least there were plenty of witnesses to support his alibi.' Bailey nodded in the direction of the distant but unseen town. 'We got to check over Stack's apartment last night too. Hubby Stuart reckons that's where his wife had been hanging out since she left him.'

'And…'

'Evidence indicates she had. There were still some of her clothes and personal effects lying around. A couple of other strange things though…'

'What?'

'A book for starters, left lying open by his bookcase.'

'A book?'

Bailey nodded. 'Yeah, but not your normal sort. This was a big volume, part of a set, but only made to look like a book. In reality, it was a sort of box-file that had probably been used for hiding something.'

'Any idea what?'

The DC shook his head. 'No idea, sir; it was completely empty.'

'Hmm,' Jack stroked his chin. 'What else did you find?'

'Damage to a drawer in Stack's desk; looked like it had been forced and crudely too.'

'Any idea by whom?'

Bailey shook his head again. 'None, the only prints we found were Stack's and Lisa Thornton's. Experts reckon the damage was about a day old…'

'… which puts it previous to Mrs Thornton's death,' completed Jack, before lowering his voice further. 'What about van Horsen?'

'We got him.' There was even a note of triumph in Bailey's voice. 'The Met. picked him up last night and brought him straight to

Norfolk.' He smiled knowingly. 'DCI Hengrove intends to start questioning him in about an hour.'

'What's he like?'

Bailey grimaced. 'Shifty type and greasy with it; the sort who'd do anything for a quick quid.'

'Murder?'

The DC screwed up his nose. 'He's not the tough sort but, if there was enough in it for him, I wouldn't put it past him.'

'Right.' Jack didn't pursue the subject because expensive cars were now drawing up beside St Cuthbert's to disgorge a half-dozen be-suited luminaries and their fashionable wives. Jack nodded towards them and smiled. 'I think the academic brigade has arrived.'

In fact, the Cambridge contingent were a personable enough lot, making their introductions to all present, thanking Jack for bringing *Raedwald* and showing enthusiastic interest in the boat itself. While Charlotte and Colin answered probing questions, Jack noticed another car driven by someone he recognised, also drawing into the parking area. As the driver came to join them, Jack held out his hand.

'Miss Fosdyke.'

'Mr. Fellows.' Gwen Fosdyke was dressed in a black lightweight suit which showed her tall slim figure to perfection but there was little warmth in her hand or greeting which, considering the nature of their last meeting, wasn't surprising. Jack was initially surprised to see her, but on quick reflection, realised that it was perfectly reasonable that she should be there. Professor Stack had, after all, been her client and would be for some time yet, until his estate was wound up. Regardless of whatever other relationship they had enjoyed, ethics at least decreed she should attend his memorial.

Jack ushered forward the two other men at his side.

'Miss Fosdyke, you know Colonel Etherington?'

'Yes, of course. Colonel…' she shook the firm hand offered, 'How are you?'

'Well, thank you, ma'am.'

DC Bailey stepped forward and, as Jack was introducing him, the mournful tolling of the church bell came from St Cuthbert's. It was followed, minutes later by the full-robed figure of the Reverend Jamieson. There were more introductions and much hand-shaking at the church gates before the vicar led the whole assemblage from the sunshine of the staithe into the cool and hallowed interior of his church.

Audrey was at the door and showed the Cambridge academics to the front pews. Jack took one further back between Colonel Etherington and DC Bailey. After offering a short prayer, he allowed his thoughts to return to something he had just observed about the vicar. This was the first time that Jack had seen the incumbent of St Cuthbert's in his full vestments and was surprised at something the priest had stitched to the choir scarf over his surplice. Was it significant?

In the quiet sanctity of the church, Jack found his thoughts wandering between this revelation and the upright figure of Gwen Fosdyke kneeling just across the aisle. Were her prayers of thanksgiving or repentance?

As if signalling an end to such mortal thoughts, the church bell ceased its tolling and the Reverend Jamieson welcomed all to St Cuthbert's before leading them into the service of remembrance.

SEVERAL MILES AWAY, at North Walsham Police Station, DCI Hengrove was beginning a ritual of an altogether different nature. With a uniformed constable sitting to one side of the interview room door, he started the tape, recorded the details and then sat for a few seconds, studying the man opposite.

Max van Horsen had fleshy jowls, a red face, several chins and black thinning hair heavily glossed with cream. His expensive pin-stripe suit was creased from being slept in and its lapels liberally speckled with cigarette ash. The shirt beneath was stylish and open at the neck, exposing a medallion that matched in sheer gold weight the identity bracelet and watch on either wrist. If further evidence of wealth were needed, it sat by his side, a slick but obviously expensive lawyer who had sped from London at first light. He was the first to speak.

'Chief Inspector, I think my client deserves some explanation for his continued custody.'

Hengrove wasted no more time. 'As explained at the time of his arrest, I believe he can help us in our investigations into the death of Mrs Lisa Thornton.' He turned to van Horsen. 'We have evidence that you were with her on the afternoon of her murder. What have you to say about that?'

'I don't deny being there ...' van Horsen had a pronounced London accent with just an edge of arrogance in spite of a night in police cells. He glanced at his solicitor who nodded, '... but I do deny murdering her.'

'But you went there to see her.' The DCI paused again to study his suspect's face. 'Why?'

'Business,' replied van Horsen without hesitation.

'What sort of business?'

'I'm a coin-dealer.' Van Horsen glanced around the interview room, abstractedly before adding, 'I buy and sell old coins.'

'Yes, I know and you're not too fussy about the source of your "old" coins either,' said Hengrove, tapping a large file before him. 'Convicted eight years ago of handling property, namely some Roman coinage found to be stolen from a museum in southern Italy.'

Before van Horsen could answer, his lawyer leaned forward. 'My client was unaware that those coins were stolen property.'

'That's not what the jury thought.' The DCI flicked over a couple of pages in the case file. 'Sentenced to fifteen months and released in twelve.' He leaned forward. 'You can add at least a nought on that for a murder conviction, van Horsen.'

'I tell you, I didn't kill no-one.' There was just a hint of perspiration showing now between the streaks of the coin-dealer's thinning hair. 'She was dead when I got there.'

Hengrove sat in silence for a few seconds with a that's-what-they-all-say look. Then he said, simply, 'Okay; tell me the full story.'

Van Horsen paused to wipe his brow with a large white handkerchief. Once again, he glanced at his lawyer and once again got a silent nod in reply. 'Like I say, we'd arranged to meet on business. She'd rung me a couple of nights before saying she'd got these coins to sell. So we agreed a time and date to meet.'

'At one of the most desolate spots on the Norfolk coast,' added Hengrove. 'Pretty isolated for business, wasn't it? What was wrong with an office, her flat or even a pub?'

'I prefer things less public,' replied van Horsen, with lowered voice. 'I don't like the whole world to know my business.'

'No, I bet you don't,' commented the DCI before quickly adding, 'Go on.'

'So I turned up at the time agreed.'

'Which was...?'

'Three thirty in the afternoon.'

'You sure of that? Not half an hour earlier?'

'No,' said van Horsen with forcefulness, 'like I said, it was half three.'

Hengrove nodded. 'Okay, go on.'

Van Horsen ran a hand through what was left of his hair. 'Well, when I gets there, there's only one car, a Range Rover like she's described. She doesn't come and meet me so I park next to her and get out, thinking she must be having a kip or a walk or something. When I looks inside of the Rover, though, I sees her laying across the front seats and blood all over the place.' The suspect shook his head, his face pale at just the recollection of the scene. 'Gave me a right bad turn it did.'

'So, having discovered a murder, what did you do then?' asked Hengrove without showing any emotion of his own.

'Cleared off, just as quick as I could.' Van Horsen cocked his head towards what he assumed was the direction of the coast. 'Passed some old girl in a car as I scarpered. I guess she's your witness ain't she?'

The DCI didn't answer and instead asked, 'It didn't occur to you to report this serious crime to the police?'

Van Horsen shook his head but before he could answer, his lawyer again interrupted. 'I think it's very clear, Chief Inspector, that my client was in deep shock at the distressing scene he had just witnessed. He was, of course, going to report it but was arrested in London before being able to.'

'Or,' said Hengrove, leaning forward, 'his dealings with Mrs Thornton were of such an illegal nature that contacting the police would be the last thing on your client's mind.'

Even as the lawyer's chest swelled with mock indignation, there was a knock at the door and a young female constable poked her head inside the interview room.

'Met. on the phone for you, sir.'

'Right.' Hengrove left the room. Under the eye of the sole constable, any communication between van Horsen and his lawyer was limited to the odd raising of brows and rolling of eyes. After five minutes, the DCI returned, sat down, looked at his notes and then fixed the coin dealer with narrowed eyes. 'Mr. van Horsen, at nine o'clock this morning, the Metropolitan Police obtained a magistrate's warrant to search your premises in the Tottenham Court Road. In a safe there, they found thirty-five silver coins, identified later as belonging to the Anglo-Saxon period. Further investigation has shown them as belonging to a collection stolen from a museum in the Midlands ten years ago. 'Do you deny being in possession of these coins?'

This time, van Horsen looked only at his feet. 'No.'

'And these were the coins you stole from Lisa Thornton after you'd murdered her?'

'No…' the suspect was half on his feet before his lawyer's hand brought him back, '… I told you … I murdered no-one and I took nothin' … just saw her lying there an' beat it quick.'

'So, how did you acquire these stolen coins?'

The coin dealer sat in silence, mentally weighing his options before answering, slowly and quietly, 'I bought them from Stack.'

The DCI's eyebrows did a quick raise. 'Professor Rupert Stack?' He paused for just seconds. 'You are aware, aren't you, that Professor Stack himself was killed and some coins and artefacts stolen, only a few days ago. What do you know of that murder?'

'Nothing … nothing.' There was desperation in van Horsen's voice now. 'I heard he'd been bumped off but then that Thornton woman rings me and says she's going to continue handling the goods from now on.'

'The stolen goods?' The calmness in Hengrove's voice was in direct contrast to his suspect's. However, before the question could be answered, the lawyer leaned forward.

'Chief Inspector, my client has had enough for one morning. I'm asking you to curtail this interview so I may discuss the case with him further.'

'And perhaps get him to see some sense. Okay …' the DCI glanced at his watch, '… interview ends at twelve-fifty-five hours.' And with that, Phil Hengrove switched off the recorder and strode from the room.

AT THIS SAME TIME, the attendees of Rupert Stack's memorial service were emerging once more into the summer sunshine and walking the short distance between church and village hall. Inside once more, they found drinks and a light buffet prepared by Audrey's willing helpers. While plates were filled and coffee poured, Jack edged over to the young DC.

'Any thoughts, Bailey?'

The detective shook his head. 'Nothing that sticks out. How about you, sir?'

Jack glanced around the assembled mourners. The academics and their wives were mingling and chatting with Colonel Etherington and Gwen Fosdyke. He nodded towards the latter. 'That's Stack's solicitor though rumour has it their relationship was somewhat closer. If anyone has a grudge against Lisa Thornton for stealing both man and inheritance, it could be her. Try and find out where she was yesterday at the relevant time.'

'I thought she was with you, Sir?'

'I was with her, to be more precise,' corrected Jack, 'but an hour or so before the murder. Her office is only a few miles from the scene so she could have sped there, done the dreaded deed and still be back in her office before three thirty.'

'Which is the time van Horsen was seen driving away,' completed Bailey. 'My money's still on him, sir.'

'Except for that time gap.' Jack nodded towards Stack's solicitor. 'Go and find out where she was after seeing me.'

'Right.' Bailey wandered off to join the group while Jack found himself cornered by one of the academics.

He was a friendly enough man in his early sixties, white haired, deep voiced and with the slight unruliness of dress so often associated with the intelligensia. Under Jack's gentle probing, he explained he was a tutor and lecturer in Medieval History at Cambridge, and had worked with Professor Stack during his own university lecturing days. 'Did you know him well?' asked Jack, keen to know something of the Professor's pre-Norfolk life.

'Pretty well.' After checking to ensure that none other of the Cambridge fraternity were within listening distance, the academic leaned closer and whispered confidentially, 'Dreadful chap, actually. Don't know how you lot found him here, but we couldn't stand the sight of him.'

'Really.' Jack was genuinely shocked. 'I'm surprised you're all here then if you feel like that.'

The lecturer shrugged. 'Clan ethics I suppose and, anyway, whatever we felt about him, we had to admit he was quite outstanding in his field.' He glanced around again although it was probably more for effect than caution. 'He had a brilliant career ahead of him, you know. Would be with us still if he hadn't got into that spot of bother with the girl.'

'Oh, what girl?' asked Jack, intrigued.

'Young undergraduate.' The lecturer rolled his eyes. 'Went for a one-on-one tutorial with our good Rupert but claimed his intentions were in directions other than Alfredian Manuscripts.' He shook his head. 'The poor girl claimed she was actually assaulted.'

'So he was sacked?'

'Asked to resign,' said the lecturer with a little nod and a down-turned mouth. 'Actually, they'd been looking for an excuse to be shot of him for years since the funds went missing.'

Jack's eyebrows rose again. 'Funds?'

'Yes, some considerable research funds allocated to his department. Stack got through the lot in twelve months flat. He'd plenty of clever accounts to show they'd been spent on field work but the strong suspicion was always that he'd half-inched most of it into his own coffers.' The lecturer shrugged again. 'No proof of course so he got away with that.'

'Ah yes, proof,' said Jack nodding with understanding, 'Always the stumbling block in any conviction.'

'Talking of which,' said the academic, nodding towards DC Bailey, 'how are the police doing? Any idea yet who actually killed the old devil?'

'Not really.' Jack didn't want to go down that particular road and he had other leads to chase. By this time the lecturer's wife had joined them, giving the Ranger a ready excuse to slide away and join Colonel Etherington on the other side of the hall.

'How's it going, Colonel?'

'Fine, fine.' The old soldier nodded towards the chatting group. 'Seem a friendly enough lot, though haven't found one who had much time for old Stack. In fact they all seem to have detested the blighter if the truth be known.'

'Yes, so I've heard...' Jack turned as a familiar figure entered the hall, '… ah, here's the Reverend Jamieson.'

The vicar had divested himself of his robes now and was dressed in plain black working cassock. After helping himself to a coffee and sandwich, he came over.

'Good to see you, Jack.' He nodded to the old soldier. 'Colonel…'

'Jamieson …' Colonel Etherington was as loud as he was tactless. '… damn good service, padre. Glad you didn't dwell on old Stack's life too much. Liked the bit about having to see through the bad to find the good.'

'Yes, well,' said the Reverend Julian, coughing slightly and obviously conscious of his own delicate position, 'one does have to exercise diplomacy in these situations.' He glanced around at the little groups of academics still enjoying their snacks and chats. 'I'd better circulate a bit amongst our distinguished guests.'

'Did you know any of them before today?' Jack's question was put casually.

'No,' the vicar shook his head, 'why should I?'

'Just thought you might be an old Cambridge man yourself.'

'I'm afraid not,' Julian Jamieson smiled, ' Durham was where I got my degree before going on to theological college in Canterbury.'

'And where then?'

The vicar's eyebrows did a slight involuntary rise at this hint of a cross-examination but he answered, 'My curacy at St Benedict's Church in Hampshire.'

'Right.' Jack paused before asking, 'And did you go straight into the military from there?'

'Yes, I did.' The Reverend Jamieson paused to look at Jack through half-closed eyes. 'How did you know about that?'

'You wear a General Service Medal ribbon on your scarf.' Jack smiled knowingly. 'Army?'

'Yes, for just three years. ' The vicar braced himself just a little taller. 'I was chaplain to the Royal Leicestershire Regiment.'

'Infantry, heh,' said the Colonel. 'When did you leave?'

'1964, shortly after the Leicesters became the fourth Royal Anglians.'

'Ah, amalgamations; worst thing they ever did,' agreed the Colonel, shaking his head. 'Ruined many a good regiment. Decided to chuck it, did you?'

'No, actually they "chucked" me ... or at least the medics did,' added the vicar grimly. 'Malaria, I'm afraid ... couldn't serve overseas anymore so out I went.'

'Bad luck,' said the Colonel.

'Yes and no.' The Reverend Jamieson smiled philosophically. 'I was with the Anglians just long enough to realise that East Anglia was where I'd like a parish. It took a while but ...' he glanced in the direction of St Cuthbert's, '... here I am.'

'And here you are,' repeated Jack. 'So, where did you get your GSM?'

The priest paused for only a second. 'In Cyprus, actually. During the trouble there.'

'Good for you. So, what were you doing in the years before you came here?'

The Reverend Jamieson's expression was a mixture of suspicion and defence. 'Oh, moving around at the Lord's calling ...' once again, his eyes betrayed an inner conflict, ' ... why are you asking these questions, Jack?'

'Just interested ... I hope I'm not prying.'

'Not at all.' The Reverend Jamieson smiled a humourless smile. 'Please excuse me ...' he glanced again towards the rest of the group, '... I really must go and circulate.'

'Of course.' As the vicar moved off to receive the thanks of the Cambridge group and Colonel Etherington went to refill his plate, Jack turned to DC Bailey who had reappeared at his side. 'So, what did our good lady councillor have to say?'

The DC shook his head. 'Out checking some boundary in a land dispute. No witnesses, unfortunately.'

'For her,' completed Jack.

'Yeah, but it must be van Horsen, sir.' Bailey nodded over to where Gwen Fosdyke was chatting to an academic and his wife. 'That's one classy lady, Mr. Fellows. I can't see her resorting to *any* physical violence let alone cutting someone's throat, whereas that coin dealer seems the sort who'd snuff his granny for her Maundy shilling.' Further discussion ended with the shrill of the young detective's mobile phone. 'Bailey ... hello boss ...,' he said, as he left the hall with the instrument at his ear.

Seeing her husband alone, Audrey sidled up to Jack. 'Not the most crowded of gatherings.'

'We didn't expect it to be.' Jack held up a half-sandwich. 'The cheese and pickle are good though.'

'Well, that's something.' Audrey glanced at the small group chatting and eating. 'They seem to be making the most of the occasion.'

'People usually do.' Jack leaned a little closer to his wife. 'I'm taking a day off tomorrow to go into the city.'

'Norwich ...' Audrey had spent a lifetime vainly trying to anticipate her unpredictable husband, '... what on earth for?'

Jack shrugged. 'Bit of background research.'

'Research into what?'

'Just a few points that need clearing. I'll be going on to North Walsham then for a chat with Phil Hengrove.'

'Who'll be doing your job?'

'The Auxiliary; I'll clear it with Head Office.' Jack was spared further explanation by Colonel Etherington's return. 'Managed to break away again, Colonel? How are the Cambridge contingent doing?'

The old soldier smiled. 'Enjoying themselves, actually. Pretty interesting lot, by an' large but they're welcome to that academic life, what? Some cloistered university life might be all right for brainy types like them but always preferred the outdoors misself.'

'Same here.' Jack nodded towards Gwen Fosdyke, in deep discussion with two academics. 'She seems to fit in well with them though. Is it true our councillor might be putting herself up for MP at the next election?'

'Or even sooner if a seat comes up,' answered the Colonel. 'Party's damn keen to get her an' she's keen to serve, what with all her good causes an' suchlike.' He gave Gwen an approving glance. 'Damn fine woman that, Fellows. Make a great MP. One hundred per cent effort in all she does.'

'Yes indeed,' agreed Jack, without committing himself, before turning back to DC Bailey who'd just rejoined them. 'News?'

'Only that van Horsen wouldn't confess to anything other than going to meet Lisa Thornton on some shady business. The Met. have found coins from that stolen hoard on his premises. No brooches, I'm afraid, but it's enough for the boss to charge him with more "handling". At least that'll give forensics time to come up with something to connect him to the actual murder.'

'Let's hope so,' interrupted the Colonel, unashamedly listening in to all that the young detective had to say. 'Sooner this business is cleared up the better.' He leaned closer to Jack and lowered his voice. 'Wouldn't be surprised if this van Horsen chappie and that young scoundrel Morecroft weren't in it together, you know. Working a buddy system, no doubt.'

'Who knows, Colonel?' said Jack. He glanced at his watch. 'I'd better be getting the galley back to Giller's Yard.'

'Time for me to be off too,' said Bailey, finishing his cup of tea and following Jack to the door.

Outside, the afternoon sun and fresh air were invigorating. Jack took a deep breath and turned to Bailey. 'Tell Chief Inspector Hengrove I'll be calling to see him about midday tomorrow.'

The DC looked at the ex-policeman, enquiringly. 'Have you got something, sir?'

'Might have.'

'What, for crikey's sake?' Bailey ran a frustrated hand through his hair. 'If you have, sir, for goodness sake share it because I'm more confused than ever.'

Jack smiled. 'Just a few things that were said in there. Nothing specific, only conjecture until I can get some hard facts to back them up.'

'Right …' Bailey swallowed his frustration, '… well, we'll see you tomorrow, sir.'

As the DC drove away, the Ranger climbed back aboard *Raedwald* where Charlotte and Colin looked up from reworking a backstay.

'Paid your respects, Jack?' The boatbuilder's question came with a mischievous grin.

'In a way.' Jack glanced at the replica's rigging and the improvements worked while he was in church. 'You two seem to have taken this boat under your wing. How about crewing her again the day after tomorrow?'

'Love to…' Colin Newell met the older man's eyes enquiringly, '… for what reason, Jack?'

'Oh, just an idea. You wouldn't have to take her far; just out onto the broad and anchor.'

It wasn't the time or place to tell them that, for the first time since Stack's murder, the mists were ever-so-slightly clearing.

Chapter Sixteen

JACK PAUSED BEFORE THE wrought-iron gates that led across the dry moat to Norwich Castle's historic keep. Until 1868, condemned prisoners had been hanged at this very spot, a spectacle witnessed by thousands, brought by special trains from as far afield as London. How many would have come to see "justice being done" to Stack's murderer, Jack pondered as he strode across the moat bridge and into the museum's entrance.

With a ticket that admitted him to both the Castle and Royal Norfolk Regiment museums, he made his way first down the spiral staircase and through the dingy tunnel that led to the latter. Old iron gateways and a heavily studded door reminded Jack that a century earlier, this same route had been used for bringing castle prisoners for trial at the Shirehall. Now it led into an impressive reproduction of a World War One trench system, complete with sound effects, before emerging into the regimental museum proper. Here, amongst old uniforms, colours and drums, Jack spotted a female assistant rearranging a display cabinet. She smiled as he approached.

'Can I help you, sir?'

'Yes, I'd like some information on the Royal Anglian Regiment or, to be more precise, the other regiments that were amalgamated into the Anglians.'

'Right, I'll take you to the office.'

She led the way and soon Jack was shaking the hand of a surprisingly young man who introduced himself as the "Historical Curator". After hearing Jack's area of research, he dived willingly into the records and, within minutes, the answers were produced.

'That's all I needed to know,' said Jack, noting the facts in his pocket book with the satisfaction of a hunch confirmed. It had all taken far less time than he'd allowed, leaving some for a look at the main Castle Museum. He nodded back towards the way he'd entered. 'Can I get back into the keep that way?'

'Strictly speaking, you shouldn't,' explained the young curator, 'but I'll take you back myself.'

Back in the museum rotunda, Jack scanned the leaflet showing the location of all the museum's departments. One caught his eye:

Anglo-Saxon and Viking. He made his way up the stairs to the middle floor, a nagging instinct seemingly leading him to the displays depicting this most significant period in English history. Somehow he knew that here, amongst ancient shield mounts, figurines, coinage, spearheads and musical instruments, there lay the clue to the murder of a man who had devoted his professional life to their study.

Systematically, he worked his way around the display cabinets. There was much to see and considerable explanatory detail to read. Almost at the end, one particular section seemed to draw him in. Fascinated, he studied its content.

The display included a large tabulated definition and as Jack scanned the columns, so a light of revelation seemed to penetrate the thick castle walls. For contained within this remarkable material, was the solution to the strangest factor in the whole equation. Barely suppressing his excitement, he scribbled a copy of the relevant parts into his pocket book, uttered a quick prayer of thanks and headed for the exit.

Striding back across the moat bridge and into the sunshine, Jack rejoiced in his findings, knowing as he did now, precisely who had murdered Professor Rupert Stack.

CLOSE BY THE CITY'S magnificent cathedral, Tombland had a quaintness all of its own. After the medieval stone of the castle, the curving charm of Elm Hill with its overhanging timbered buildings and cobbled street, evoked a period two centuries on. Previously, these picturesque, gabled houses had been the homes of city merchants. Mercifully saved from demolition by just one vote in the 1920s, they were now places of commerce with art galleries appearing to predominate. Jack headed for one in particular.

A traditional bell rang as he entered, bringing forth a middle-aged custodian from the office within.

'Good morning, sir.' He was scanning Jack with an appraising eye and already marking him down as an unlikely prospect. Nevertheless, he asked, 'Can I help you?'

'Yes, I telephoned you earlier to confirm you had a Stuart Thornton landscape.' Jack looked around at the various works adorning the gallery walls before nodding towards a familiar style in oil. 'That's it there, isn't it?'

'"The Broad at Sunset", yes, a particularly pleasing aspect…' the custodian paused to almost imperceptibly wrinkle his nose, '… if you like typical Broadland scenes.'

'Actually, I do.' Jack smiled insincerely. 'How much is that one?'

'Six hundred and seventy-five guineas, sir.'

'Phew...' Jack blew out a whistle of surprise, '... too rich for my blood, I'm afraid.' He turned towards the custodian. 'Is the manager here?'

'I am the *owner* of this gallery, sir.' The answer came on a voice mixing mock offence with ill-disguised irritation. 'I deal in art.'

'Good. Then how about an offer: two hundred.'

'Good grief sir,' the dealer's contempt this time was totally genuine, 'paintings like this can't just be "marked down" like in some discount store.'

'Really.' It was Jack's turn to look down his nose. 'Do you actually own the painting?'

'No, of course not.' The dealer sniffed. 'We are purely the agents for the owner.'

'Then how do you know "the owner" won't accept my offer?' Jack nodded towards the office. 'Why don't you give him a ring and find out?'

The dealer went to protest, but changed his mind as Jack eased him towards his office where antique furnishing and rich carpets showed that lower bids were not something the gallery accepted very often. While Jack lay his notebook and pen on the Georgian desk, the dealer lifted the receiver of his telephone, thought for a second and placed his hand over the mouthpiece. 'Do you mind, sir...' he nodded towards the door, '... this is *my* office.'

'Ah yes ... of course.' Jack turned and went back into the gallery with the office door firmly closing behind him. While he casually scanned other paintings with prices in inverse proportion to their appeal, a well-dressed lady of formidable character entered the gallery and began her own perusal of the exhibits. Within a minute the dealer was back out, his manner even more dismissive.

'I'm sorry, sir; the owner won't even consider such a derisory offer. And now...' he glanced towards the lady customer with the air of someone who has had quite enough of his time wasted for one day, '... if you'll excuse me...'

'Right.' Jack moved off towards the door. Already the dealer was discussing the finer points of a very expensive period piece which the lady was obviously intent on buying. At the door though, Jack stopped. 'Oh no...' he was feeling the empty inner pocket of his coat as he turned again to the condescending dealer, '...left my notebook in your office.' He nodded towards the relevant door, '… may I?'

The dealer just nodded an impatient nod and a minute later Jack was back out and once again heading for the gallery exit. 'Thank you,' he smiled over his shoulder and received no thanks in exchange. He cared little; another piece of this strange jigsaw had just slotted into place.

'GOT SOMETHING, JACK?'

DCI Hengrove recognised the enlightened look on the Ranger's face: it was the quiet satisfaction of a case breakthrough.

'Might have.' Jack smiled, knowingly. 'How about you?'

The DCI shook his head. 'Nothing except a deepening mountain of villainy that matches another contradiction for every lead it produces.' Hengrove sighed. ' Van Horsen is going to get done for receiving but he swears he never touched Lisa Thornton and, between you and me, Jack, I'm inclined to think that possibly, for the first time in his life, he's telling the truth.' The DCI flicked shut the ever-thickening file before him with something akin to disgust. 'The times just don't gel.' He fixed his visitor with narrowed eyes. 'You, on the other hand, have obviously found something.' He sighed and leaned back in his chair. 'Care to share it with us, Jack?'

'Not just yet, but I need your help though.'

'Go on…'

Jack smiled. 'A few things, starting with the record file on that chummy suspected of stealing the coin collection ten years ago … what's his name…?'

'Venning …' answered the DCI pulling a file from his desk drawer, '… or "Locks" Venning as he's known in the underworld.' Hengrove flicked open the file. 'What do you need Jack?'

'Just a look at his mug-shot.' Jack nodded at the file, inverted before him. "The Croydon job was about twelve years ago, so it won't be the latest but it might just do. May I …?'

'Be my guest.' Hengrove spun the file around and watched Jack's face as the ex-Superintendent scrutinised the front and side profiles before him. Once again, he detected the glimmer of achievement. 'You recognise him don't you, Jack?'

'I think so … don't you?'

'No. Who is it?'

Jack shook his head. 'Let's do some more checks before we go hanging someone.' He closed the file and tapped its cover. 'Phil, I need an army service record and your police clout will get it quicker than I ever could.'

Hengrove nodded. 'Whose record?'

'The Reverend Julian Jamieson.'

'The vicar?' The DCI sat more upright in his seat. 'Strewth, Bailey told me you'd been giving the old Bible-basher the third-degree yesterday but surely you don't think…'

'I think nothing until I have some more facts.' Jack nodded towards the computer on the DCI's desk. 'Will you do that, Phil?'

'Okay.' Hengrove sat back again, wearily. 'Anything else?'

'Yes, I want you to telephone Stack's solicitor, Gwen Fosdyke, and arrange something for tomorrow.'

'Arrange what?'

'The reading of the Professor's will.'

'His will…' Hengrove shook his head in exasperation, '… what good is that going to do?'

'I'll explain later, Phil, but trust me.'

'I do…' Hengrove leaned forward, '… but Jack, if you suspect someone, I need to know.'

Jack nodded. 'Okay, Phil, but before I give you the gen and explain the plan I need one more thing.'

The DCI rolled his eyes but said simply, 'What?'

'A cup of coffee.' The Ranger sat back and smiled. 'I've been promising myself one all morning and if I don't get a caffeine shot soon I'll expire.'

While Jack awaited the blessed beverage, Hengrove relaxed a little, leaned back and said, 'This will reading tomorrow, Jack; where exactly do you want it done?'

Chapter Seventeen

'LET GO.'

As Jack's launch, with *Raedwald* alongside, gathered a little sternway in the middle of the broad, Colin Newell ran to the galley's bow and heaved over the heavy mudweight. Soon the anchor cable was taught and they were swinging to the slight breeze that rippled the sunlit water. The boatbuilder glanced across to the launch. 'She's holding, Jack.'

'Good.' Jack shut down his engine and climbed across the gap between the two boats. Standing in *Raedwald's* midships at the base of her mast, the replica galley looked huge. Shipshape too; Jack smiled approvingly at the reworked rigging and oiled woodwork, the result of Colin's and Charlotte's skilled attention. 'I can see you two have been busy. She looks good, Colin.'

'She deserves to.' The boatbuilder gave a slight scoff. 'I don't think Stack touched her from the day she was built, poor old boat.' He gave the sturdy gunwale a loving slap. 'Good for another hundred years if she's looked after though.'

'Alan would like that…' it was Charlotte, coming for'ard to join them, '… but I don't think he'd like this mission…' she paused to glance around her at the stacked oars, furled sail and coiled ropes, '… this lovely old boat being used for the reading of that dreadful man Stack's will.'

'What's the point, Jack.' Colin Newell shook his handsome head. 'Whatever that bastard's left, he got it by dishonesty and the less we know, the better. Do you really need us here?'

'I need *everyon*e here, Colin, *including* you and Charlotte and, if I'm not mistaken …' he shielded his eyes from the sun, peering towards the southern end of the broad where a long low boat was being rowed steadily towards them, '… here comes the first of the rest.'

'It's Pops!' Charlotte ran to *Raedwald's* stern and soon she was catching the marshpunt's painter and helping her elderly father-in-law on board. Jack went to greet the marshman with outstretched hand.

'Good to see you again, Walter.'

'And you, Mr. Fellows.' Walter Giller paused to take in the graceful lines of the replica galley his son had built. 'And good to be aboard this again now she's not owned by that vermin.' There was just a slight moistening in his eyes. 'Alan done a fine job of this boat an' she'll be around long after we're all gone.'

'Amen to that.' Jack took the old marshman's arm and sat him down on one of the thwarts. 'Thanks for coming, Walter.'

'It's no problem, Mr. Fellows, but what's it for?' Walter looked around him again and shook his head, 'Police rang me last night an' says we's all meeting on *Raedwald,* but they don't say why.'

'For the reading of Professor Stack's will.'

'His will...' Walter Giller looked towards his daughter-in-law but she only shook her head in equal mystification.

'More boats coming!' It was Colin Newell's call saving Jack further explanation for, out from the staithe, a small dinghy with raised gunwales and a throaty outboard was speeding towards them. Stuart Thornton, hand on helm, could soon be clearly identified, while in the bow another figure sat hunched in an anorak that failed to hide the clerical collar beneath. The Reverend Julian Jamieson threw the bow warp as they came alongside but it was Stuart who was first to jump aboard the galley. Jack went to meet him, one hand offered, the other on the artist's shoulder.

'Stuart, old friend, how are you?'

'Hi, Jack; okay I guess.' In fact Stuart Thornton looked anything but. The events of the last week had obviously taken a terrible toll on the artist, visibly draining him of the spark that had found its creative way onto so many canvasses. Before Jack could say more he turned to help the vicar, now struggling to follow onboard.

Once over the gunwale, the Reverend Julian stood rather shakily getting his bearings. Jack went and shook his hand also.

'Welcome aboard *Raedwald,* vicar.'

'Thank you, Jack.' The incumbent of St Cuthbert's looked down at Stuart's battered dinghy and back to the wake still showing on the broad's surface. 'I can't say I'm much of a nautical person myself and that is certainly a very small boat.'

'Perhaps you'd have been more comfortable in that one,' smiled Jack, pointing up the broad to where Colonel Etherington's *Goosewatcher* cleaved a white bow-wave towards them, her varnished hull and polished brass glinting in the morning sun. As they neared *Raedwald,* the Colonel stood up and heaved a line to be smartly caught by Colin Newell. Jack smiled to himself; there was always something strictly military in the way the Colonel handled his beloved boat. Soon, however, *Goosewatcher* too was safely warped alongside with her owner saluting from the cockpit.

'Morning, Fellows. Beautiful one it is too.' The same could also be said of his passenger. Jack had asked the old soldier to collect Gwen Fosdyke. The stylish cagoule she wore over smart blue slacks highlighted a coloured scarf that was almost gay, in direct contrast to the wearer's expression.

'This has to be the most ludicrous reading of a will that I have ever done.' The solicitor handed up her leather briefcase, ignored Jack's offered hand and nimbly sprang aboard the galley. 'I'm responding to a request from the police, Mr Fellows, but I rather suspect your devious hand behind this whole charade.'

'It was my idea to hold the reading here, yes,' admitted Jack. 'It's not unusual to read a deceased's will in their home, surely, so why not Professor Stack's on his boat?'

'But it is not usual to make it a public event.' Gwen Fosdyke glanced disapprovingly at the familiar but unwelcome faces around her. 'This ... audience ... presumably is another of your ideas?'

'These people are all interested parties in the estate of Professor Rupert Stack.' Jack's tone was unapologetic. 'When we're all here, we'll get started.'

'You mean there are others still to come?' Gwen's patience obviously had its limits.

'Only one more group ...' Jack glanced sternwards, '... and here they are.'

From the south entrance, an orange RIB was speeding towards them, rooster-tail wash pluming astern and blue-flashing light on her gantry mast.

'The police... my goodness.' The words were the Reverend Jamieson's but it was obvious no-one expected the Broads Beat to be present. With a roar of astern power, the RIB came expertly alongside, warps were thrown and soon she too was secure abeam the gathering flotilla of boats. While two uniformed constables remained onboard the RIB, and DCI Hengrove and DC Bailey transferred to the galley, a third familiar figure hopped nimbly across the gap between.

He looked as scruffy as ever and pale and drawn now from lack of sun, but the fresh air of the broad was having an immediate recuperative effect on Peter Morecroft's sorely-tried morale. He made straight across to the one man on board who had never lost faith in his innocence.

'Mr. Fellows …' The eel-catcher clasped the Ranger's hand in both his, '… great to see yer an' … this...' he glanced across the sparkling water and up at the blue sky before taking a deep breath, '… there was times I thought I'd never taste fresh Broads' air ag'in. I tell yer, it's right good to be free.'

'Not "free", Morecroft; released-in-custody,' corrected Phil Hengrove, before adding, 'We'll see about the other later.'

'I say, is this "on", Fellows?' It was Colonel Etherington stepping into the little gathering. 'One thing, old boy, to have us locals at Stack fellow's will thing but to invite his murderer is surely going a bit far.'

'Peter Morecroft has never been charged with that offence but he's certainly suffered in consequence.' Jack turned to all on board. 'If anyone has an interest in these proceedings, it's surely him.' He nodded towards the rowing thwarts. 'Let's get seated and started, shall we?'

One by one, all present selected a thwart facing the bow: Walter Giller between Colin and Charlotte, Peter Morecroft between Hengrove and Bailey, Colonel Etherington, the Reverend Jamieson and Stuart Thornton on a thwart each. Jack stood just to one side. Gwen Fosdyke made her way for'ard and sat facing them, an empty thwart between on which she placed her briefcase. While everyone sat in expectant silence, the solicitor opened her case, withdrew legal papers and cleared her throat.

'We are here today… in this unusual setting…' she cast a meaningful glance at Jack, '… to hear the last will and testament of Professor Rupert Stack. The will signed by Professor Stack and witnessed by … some friends…' Gwen glanced at the open document, '… just a few weeks ago, is a simple one. Without resorting to legal jargon, I can tell you that Professor Stack left his total estate to his secretary, Mrs Lisa Thornton.' There was a mixture of gasps, mutterings and the odd tut from those present, before Gwen Fosdyke closed the document, returned it swiftly to her briefcase and asked, somewhat brusquely, 'Are there any questions?'

'Yes.' It was DCI Hengrove. 'As we all know, Mrs Thornton herself subsequently became a murder victim. What happens to her inheritance now?'

Gwen Fosdyke cleared her throat again. 'As Professor Stack's will was in force from the time of his death, Mrs Thornton was indeed the beneficiary for the remaining ... few... days of her life. Her estate will therefore be settled in accordance with the wishes of her own will ... if there is one.' The solicitor looked questioningly at Stuart Thornton.

The artist looked up numbly, as though oblivious to all that was being enacted. Slowly, there came the realisation of what was being asked of him. Vaguely shaking his head, he said simply, 'No, Lisa never made a will.'

'In which case,' explained Gwen Fosdyke, businesslike as ever, 'as Mrs Thornton died intestate, her total estate passes to her husband, Stuart.'

Of all those present, Stuart Thornton seemed the least effected by this declaration of new-found wealth. To bring things to a quick conclusion, Gwen chose this moment to stand up and snap shut her briefcase. 'If there's nothing else, I think we can bring this reading to a close.' She turned to Etherington. 'Colonel, can you run me ashore now?'

It was Jack, however who responded. 'Sit down, Councillor.'

'I beg your pardon.' Gwen Fosdyke was unaccustomed to direct orders.

'I said "sit down", Miss Fosdyke; we haven't finished yet.' Jack walked for'ard until he stood beside his District Councillor. For a second, she too remained standing and then, with just the faintest roll of her eyes, resumed her seat. 'Thank you.' Jack looked at the faces before him: they were a mixture of incredulity and anticipation. He put his hands in his pockets. 'As we all know, Professor Stack was murdered and so was Lisa Thornton. One person was responsible for both crimes. That person is on this boat right now.' There were more gasps as he paused again to take in the wide eyes that were glancing from one to another. 'Before we leave today, I'm going to tell you who that person is.'

A motor-cruiser was passing through the broad, its wash causing *Raedwald* to roll and creak at her anchor. 'You're going to find out very soon,' said Jack, 'who committed both those murders.'

'EXCEEDING YOUR AUTHORITY a bit, aren't you, Fellows?' Colonel Etherington glanced towards the two detectives seated ahead of him. 'In my day, it was the police who sorted crime. What?'

The Colonel's protest found a ready ally in his vicar. 'Indeed; surely this is neither the time nor place for such recrimination.' The

Reverend Jamieson stood to expand his opinion but instead met the authoritative face of Phil Hengrove.

'Jack Fellows here has been helping me in my enquiries and has my full permission to conduct these proceedings.' Turning back to the Ranger, he said, 'Carry on, Jack,' and then sat down. The Reverend Jamieson hovered, obviously teetering on the brink of further protest before accepting the inevitable and reluctantly resuming his own seat.

'Thank you, Chief Inspector.' Jack waited until the muttering had died down before taking his hands from his pockets, folding his arms and scanning the rows of expectant faces. The murderer was looking at him right now but showing not the slightest indication of fear or guilt. It was disconcerting but he cleared his throat and pressed on.

'After Rupert Stack's murder, Peter Morecroft here was arrested for the crime. It wasn't an unreasonable suspicion; he had ample motive.' From the corner of his eye, Jack detected a shadow of alarm pass across the young eel-catcher's rugged features. He ignored it. 'Peter had spent thirty days in prison as a result of the Professor's flawed evidence. Not only had it cost him a month's freedom but also his boat and livelihood. He was struggling back but a flame of bitterness burned within him. He was bent on revenge for what Professor Stack had done to him and, on the night of the murder, he was determined to extract it.'

Everyone was now glancing at young Morecroft as he squirmed uncomfortably between the two detectives. There was a look of betrayal on his young face. Again, Jack pressed on unmercifully.

'Morecroft admitted being at the crime scene and not reporting it to the police. To make matters worse, the victim had scrawled PM in his own blood and some stolen coins from the treasure were found on Morecroft's boat. Not unreasonable, therefore ...' Jack glanced towards Phil Hengrove, '... that he was the police's prime suspect.'

By now, a combination of disbelief and desperation were beginning to overshadow Morecroft's already pale features. Jack knew it was time to lower his tone. He gave the young eel-fisherman a reassuring smile.

'But Pete was not the murderer. Indications are he arrived at the murder-scene an hour after Stack's death. None of the most valuable stolen artefacts, the priceless gold brooches, were found in his possession. Only two silver coins - stolen Anglo-Saxon sceattas - were subsequently conveniently discovered on his boat.' Jack paused to let that fact sink in. 'I'll explain how and why later. For the moment we have the other incontrovertible proof of Peter Morecroft's innocence. If we accept that both murders were committed by the same assailant, then Morecroft had the best of all alibis for the second by being in police custody.'

'But are you sure the murders were committed by the same person, Fellows?' Colonel Etherington was obviously enjoying the courtroom-like drama being enacted in the middle of the broad. 'We all know young Morecroft's a bad'n; gamekeeper caught him having a go at me own pheasants once, the little blighter. There are others here who had reason to take out the Thornton girl…' the Colonel glanced behind to Stuart Thornton, '… including her own husband. And anyway,' concluded the Colonel, aware now of the feelings of the artist sitting there in his own vacuum of misery, 'I thought some London coin-dealer chappie was in the frame for that one.'

'Max van Horsen has been charged with possessing stolen property,' clarified the DCI. 'I don't expect any other charges to be brought against him.'

'Hmmm,' was the Colonel's disapproving response.

'In fact, most here had ample motive to murder Rupert Stack,' said Jack, seeking to restore some order, 'some would say with justification. Walter Giller for instance.' He nodded towards the old marshman who faced him back with an expression of unreality. 'Walter lost a son through the financial wrangling of our late Professor. On top of that, he saw a much-loved daughter-in-law about to be evicted in pursuit of the same material ends. On the night of the murder, Walter took his gun and went to "sort it" with the man he hated more than any other in the world.'

'I told ya, I threatened the vermin but I never killed 'im,' protested Walter.

'If you're accusing Pops, you may as well stick the finger on me,' interjected Charlotte, visibly bristling. 'I had more reason than any to kill Stack.'

'Yes, and Lisa Thornton too,' agreed Jack. 'You were sure that Stack was in league with Gwen Fosdyke here in acquiring Giller's Yard from the receivers. However, with Stack dead, there was just the chance that that decision could be reversed. And then you find that Lisa Thornton, Stack's assistant who has also been having an affair with the Professor, is his sole beneficiary and just as intent on evicting you as her late boss.' He met Charlotte's bitter eyes. 'Killing Lisa

Thornton might well have been the act of a desperate woman.'

'Charlotte was with me, Jack.' Colin Newell had jumped to his feet now. 'I thought you were on our side and all the time you've been trying to frame us.'

'I've kept an open mind throughout,' countered Jack, well aware of the good relationships now being sacrificed on the altar of justice, 'including your own ample motives, Colin.'

'What motives?' The young boatbuilder was clenching his fists in suppressed rage. 'Why would I want to murder the wretched man?'

'Because you wanted Giller's Yard for your own boat-building and Stack beat you to it.'

'Yeah, I hated the man for that an' all but I had no reason to kill Lisa Thornton.'

'Yes you did, Colin, and for the strongest motive of all.' Jack was endeavouring to keep his own voice even and the latent violence of this whole procedure suppressed.

'What you sayin'?' By comparison, there was a shaking edge to Colin Newell's voice now.

'Love, Colin. You're in love with Charlotte and she loves you. You saw Lisa Thornton robbing her of her lawful rights and that alone would have been motive enough for you to kill her.'

'But I didn't. There are others here that could though.' Newell pointed to the man who had sat silently throughout this whole argument. 'There ... Stuart Thornton ... his wife was having it away with Rupert Stack. We all know how soppy he was on that cheating bitch of his. If you're talking about love and jealousy, he's the one who probably killed lover-boy and then did his wife in when she wouldn't take him back.'

'Don't you dare speak of my wife like that.' Suddenly, Stuart Thornton had emerged from his chrysalis of silence and stood, shaking in every limb. 'Yes, I knew Rupert Stack had seduced Lisa and yes, I went to have it out with him but he was alive when I left. And, as for Lisa ...' his voice wavered, '... I could never kill her ...' the anger was subsiding now into an outpouring of pent-up grief as the artist blubbed his final words, '... because I loved her.'

Stuart slumped back onto the thwart and it was Charlotte Giller who went and put a soothing arm around the slight figure that heaved with heart-powered sobs. She turned to Jack, anger in her voice. 'Can't you see what you're doing to us all?' Charlotte nodded in the direction of Gwen Fosdyke who, until this moment, had maintained a discreet silence. 'If you want to have a go at someone then ask her. She was Stack's fancy woman, wangling the bids for Giller's Yard and doing his every other bidding too, until Lisa Thornton stepped in and took him off her. "Hell knows no fury like a woman scorned" they say. I still say our precious Councillor killed them both.'

'How dare you!' Now it was Gwen Fosdyke who jumped to her feet and was facing Charlotte with blazing eyes. 'Rupert Stack was never my "fancy man", as you put it; I detested the man and wanted him dead but I certainly never killed him.'

'But I heard you … the night he was killed …' the sincerity of Gwen's outburst had drawn the heat out of Charlotte's anger, '… telephoning him from your office to arrange a meeting.' She shook her head with confusion. 'I was sure it was you who'd done the job.'

'You heard Councillor Fosdyke ringing someone, Charlotte, and assumed it was the Professor because you were sure the two were in league with each other.' It was time again to calm nerves and time also, Jack knew, to reveal the full story. 'Like the rest of us, you made the mistake of assuming that Gwen here was the Professor's mistress.' He turned and looked at the solicitor and District Councillor through sympathetic eyes. 'Yes, Gwen Fosdyke was deeply in love with someone, but it wasn't Rupert Stack.'

'You obviously know things the rest of us don't, Jack.' Colin Newell had calmed down now. 'If you really know which of us killed that bastard, then tell us and be done.'

'Right, Colin.' Jack rested a foot on the thwart in front of him and faced his friends. 'Here's the truth whether some of you like it or not.'

Chapter Eighteen

'I WAS A POLICEMAN and detective for many years,' began Jack, 'and even I made the classic mistake of basing my investigations on false assumptions. We all assumed that Gwen was Stack's mistress when she was anything but. We also assumed that the golden brooches were the key items stolen during the murder. They were a valuable haul for the murderer, yes, but they weren't the motive. In fact it was the old silver coins - the sceattas - that were the key to this whole story. It took me a while to realise these facts but, as soon as I did, then everything else very quickly fell into place.'

Overhead, a black-headed gull squawked its own shrill call before settling on *Raedwald's* mast truck. The sun was higher now and its rays starting to beat. Jack took his foot off the thwart and wiped a trickle of sweat from the end of his nose.

'Let's start from the beginning. Ten years ago, those silver sceattas were touring the country, a hoard of a thousand discovered on a building site in Essex. During that tour they were stolen by an audacious thief. He got away with the complete hoard but he made the mistake of leaving behind a single fingerprint. From that, the police knew his name. He was a man previously arrested in connection with a gold bullion robbery, a skilled safecracker and ex-member of the Special Air Service. Some would describe "Locks" Venning as a "likeable villain" but in reality, he was a man who would stop at nothing. Knowing he was facing a life sentence, Venning disappeared off the face of the earth and, to this day, has remained an enigma.'

'"To this day",' repeated the Reverend Jamieson, warily. 'You mean he's still around?'

'Oh, he's still around alright, vicar,' nodded Jack. 'In fact, he's on this boat right now.'

There was another gasp as, once again, suspicious eyes appraised their neighbour and more than one cast a reassuring glance at the police RIB alongside.

'And, presumably, this "Locks" Venning is our murderer?' asked the Reverend Jamieson through tightening lips.

'He is indeed, vicar.'

'You goin' to tell us who he is then?,' asked Walter Giller.

Jack nodded. 'In due course, Walter.' He put his hands back in his pocket. 'Let's first surmise Venning's life and actions after the sceatta robbery. The police know his identity so he needs to disappear. He's not short of cash: he's got his sceatta haul plus his share of the Croydon gold bullion. He may even have more than his share which is another good reason for disappearing. Scarpering abroad is one option but the world's a smaller place now and extradition a daily reality. What he really needs to do is become invisible and how do you do that?'

'By taking on a new identity,' answered Charlotte.

'Exactly.' Save for the lapping of wavelets against *Raedwald*'s oak planking and the creak of her rigging, not a sound could be heard as Jack paused in his story. Most were leaning forward now; only Gwen Fosdyke sat with lowered head while the Reverend Jamieson played nervously with a gold crucifix attached to his watchstrap.

'And so, did he do that ... become someone else?' It was Charlotte again, breaking the deafening silence.

'Oh, yes, and very successfully.' Jack wiped another bead of sweat from his face. 'Venning settled down, right here, in our village and would probably have continued to live as an impostor indefinitely except two things happened simultaneously.'

'What things?' asked Colin Newell.

'One was that he started to get short of cash. He'd used a lot of his gold in establishing his new identity and more went into the village itself.'

'The village ... how?' Colonel Etherington was struggling to follow some of this theorising. 'Not much here to spend your cash on, Fellows, what?'

'Oh there is, Colonel.' Jack nodded towards the village where the square tower of St Cuthbert's rose above the treeline. 'Our lovely church needed extensive repairs that were going to cost a fortune. Added to that, a second expensive factor had now unexpectedly come into our thief's life...' a sea of expectant faces asked the question but Jack answered it before it could be voiced, '... he had fallen in love.'

'With Gwen Fosdyke.' Charlotte Giller's womanly instincts were ahead of the men on this one.

'Yes, with our own District Councillor and she for him. Gwen fell for the loveable rogue who had suddenly brought romance and excitement into her lucrative but dreary legal practice. At some stage he told her his secret...' Jack turned and gave a questioning glance at Gwen Fosdyke beside him but the solicitor kept her eyes firmly down, '... and she agreed to continue the deception. She was, as we all know, planning to run for Parliament and even the hint of an alliance with a wanted criminal would scupper any chance of her being selected. In reality ...' he cast a sympathetic glance down at Gwen, '... she had little choice. The only problem was that the new man in her life was now in the hands of Professor Rupert Stack.'

'This has gone far enough.' Gwen was on her feet now and turning to the only other authority on board. 'Chief Inspector Hengrove, do I have to suffer any more of this slanderous nonsense?'

'I'm afraid you do, Councillor,' answered the DCI with calm forcefulness. 'You'll have your say later but until then, I suggest you sit down and listen.'

Gwen resumed her seat with unaccustomed submission.

'So Stack himself wasn't this "Locks" Venning?' It was Charlotte, still hanging on to her Gwen/Stack conspiracy.

'No, but it's to his mistress, Lisa Thornton, that much of what happened later is attributable.' Jack glanced at the late-secretary's husband, but Stuart's drawn face was expressionless. 'By this time, Professor Stack had arrived in our locality with his floating Anglo-Saxon museum and Lisa had become his secretary and also his mistress. Venning saw possibilities in the relationship. By this time his ill-gotten gains from the bullion haul were almost gone and the sceattas were so identifiable as to be unusable. How to fence them? He was probably unaware of Stack's flawed character but he knew Lisa as a woman ever-ready to further her financial interests, legally or otherwise. He gave her one of the sceattas with the request that she obtain a valuation from her boss. That probably turned out to be more than either of them expected and the seeds of an on-going scam were sown. Lisa may well have been unaware, initially, that the sceattas were stolen; Venning probably came up with some story about finding them himself. Stack, though, recognised them for what they were. He knew there was an underworld market for antique coinage and the dubious character who could handle quantities of them.'

'Max van Horsen,' stated DCI Hengrove. 'Stack was selling them on to him as fast as Lisa could supply them.'

'Which, I imagine, was a steady flow.' Jack nodded towards Peter Morecroft. 'Pete was suspicious of those late-night trysts on Stack's boat and had been trying to suss out what lay behind them as a way of getting back at Stack. On the night of the murder he went for a closer look and got involved in more than he bargained for.'

'So, Stack was selling coins for this "Locks" Venning?' Colin Newell was as intrigued as the rest at these revelations.

'Yes, but not knowingly.' Jack cast another glance at the still-silent Stuart. 'Lisa was a pretty street-wise girl and kept the identity of her supplier secret which suited Venning too. Remember, she was trying to promote Stuart's art business which may well have been how she met Venning in the first place. Whatever; unknowingly Stuart's art became the means to launder those stolen sceattas.'

'You mean a sort of three-way trade?' asked Charlotte Giller.

Jack nodded. 'That's exactly how it worked except it was more like four: Venning bought Stuart Thornton paintings from Lisa for silver sceattas. He then sold on those paintings through various art galleries around the country.' Jack nodded towards the silent artist. 'Stuart himself told me that all his paintings went to galleries but he was happy to leave all that business side to Lisa. He thought her nights away were spent negotiating the sale of his work whereas, in sad reality, the paintings were going to Venning and her nights were being spent with Stack. Lisa was quite happy to be accruing silver Anglo-Saxon coins knowing they had a ready market in Professor Stack. He, in turn, sold them on to his underworld connection, Max van Horsen, who got them distributed world-wide.'

'In other words, they were all making a packet.' Colin Newell shook his head. 'So how come it all went belly-up?'

'That happened when Stack discovered the real identity of Venning,' explained Jack. 'Don't forget that Stack was an acknowledged authority on the Anglo-Saxon period. It probably didn't take him long to work out that these coins he was handling were part of the Essex hoard stolen from the Midlands Museum. He delved into the case, probably secured old newspaper accounts including photos of the man wanted by the police and recognised the new identity of the original thief.'

'So, where did Gwen Fosdyke come into all this?' asked Charlotte with one eye on the lady herself.

'Good question.' Jack himself glanced down at the solicitor but Gwen Fosdyke remained silent. 'My theory is that Stack went round to Venning's place to confront him with his identity. It turned out even better than he'd hoped because I think that Stack discovered Venning in a compromising situation with our good Councillor. Stack's evil mind soon saw the great possibilities in this knowledge. He'd already put Alan and Charlotte Giller out of business by cheating them over this boat. Gwen Fosdyke had been appointed Receiver. By blackmailing her over her relationship with a wanted criminal, he managed to put in his own bid for the yard and have it declared the lowest.'

'I knew there was some shenanigans there!' exclaimed Colin Newell. 'I put in a good bid for that yard and by rights I should have got it…' he glanced at Charlotte, '… for both of us. So, why did this Venning kill off Stack? He might not have liked the bloke but they had a laundering scam going that was making money for them all.'

'Because Stack was now blackmailing Gwen, the woman Venning loved.' Jack shrugged his broad shoulders. 'Stack might have got away with it even then, but he made the mistake so common amongst the un-Godly; he got greedy. Not content to have used Gwen in her role as Receiver, my guess is he now asked her to abuse her position as District Councillor. He'd secured Giller's Yard, remember. For what? It can have only been to develop it and for that he needed planning approval. Gwen was in a position to wangle that for him too and so, turn-by-turn, the screw was tightening. Added to that, the knowledge that Gwen was now being put up for Parliamentary election must have made future possibilities almost unlimited. Gwen Fosdyke here is a lady who could have risen to highest office. Stack saw that and planned to use it. What he didn't realise was that, in so doing, he was signing his own death warrant.'

Sitting beside Jack, as he surmised all too accurately, the lady herself was only just hanging on to her self-control. She knew the truth of all she had just heard. What she was unprepared for was the reassuring hand coming onto her shoulder and the equally comforting words that came with it.

'Gwen, you found yourself in the hands of a ruthless man who could ruin your career if you didn't comply with his ever-more-unreasonable demands. You had only one person to turn to, a man who loved you and with enough martial skills to sort the problem once and for all. You called your lover, "Locks" Venning.'

'So that's who she was calling the night of the murder?' Charlotte shook her head. 'When she said, "We need to talk", she was arranging a meeting to plan the murder of Professor Stack?'

'I'm not sure if that was what she had specifically in mind,' said Jack, 'but she was at the end of her tether and prepared for extreme measures.' He gave a tender squeeze of the solicitor's shoulder. 'Is that right, Gwen?'

Gwen Fosdyke sat immobile, tears running down her cheeks. She wiped them away before slowly nodding her head.

'So why was the Thornton woman killed?' asked Walter Giller.

'Simply because she took over where Stack left off.' Jack glanced at Stuart, sympathetic of the artist's feelings and knowing he must progress carefully. 'Lisa probably sensed that Stack had sussed the identity of her coin-supplier. Doubtless she was about to be dumped like all who had served Professor Stack's purpose. Then he was murdered and a whole new world of possibilities opened before her. Lisa had the keys to his apartment. When the police searched it after her murder, they found a drawer in Stack's desk forced open and an empty secret volume in his library that was probably used to hide vital documents. My guess is that in those she found the means - probably photos - by which her boss had managed to blackmail Gwen. She also found, I'm sure, the contact details of Stack's underworld fence.'

'Van Horsen?'

'Exactly. She made contact with him and set up that meeting on the coast to sell him more sceattas supplied by Venning. Things must have looked rosy for Lisa. She'd left Stuart but that didn't matter because she didn't even have to sell his paintings anymore: the dirt she'd found on Venning and Gwen meant she had a bargaining power for hundreds of sceattas all of her own. Stack was dead so, almost overnight, two middlemen had been removed from the scam. This time it was Lisa, though, who didn't realise that men like Venning can only be pushed so far. Having been forced to supply her gratis with more sceattas, he probably sussed she was meeting with the fence and followed her to that lonely beach. Unfortunately for Lisa, the car she thought was van Horsen arriving early with her new wealth was actually Venning with the means of her demise. Van Horsen turned up on schedule for his wheeler-dealing only to find his supplier murdered and him the chief suspect.'

'Serve him right,' said Walter, 'but you ain't told us yet who this Venning character really is.'

'No,' said Jack, ' but I'm about to.'

Chapter Nineteen

'SO, WHAT CAN WE surmise about this Max Venning?' asked Jack. 'Well, from his record, we know he will now be in his middle sixties. We know he is also ex-SAS, so probably still reasonably fit. It's my experience that army men never really lose their military bearing and until recently, the only ex-soldier living locally was you, Colonel Etherington.'

'What the...' blurted the old soldier, but Jack held up a staying hand. 'I said "until recently" because at Professor Stack's memorial service I found there was another ex-army man living and working in our midst.' He looked towards the Reverend Jamieson and all the others followed his gaze. The vicar shrank back visibly.

'You're not saying? ... you're surely not suggesting?'

'Why not?' responded Jack. 'Before coming to this parish your background was hazy to say the least. What we do know though is that your accepting the living here coincided with very welcome injections of cash into church funds from some "anonymous donor". And now, just as priceless artefacts are stolen, we find you replacing your trusty bike with a very smart people-carrier.' Jack fixed his priest with steady eyes. 'I can't think of a better cover for a villain, Vicar, than the dog-collar of the clergy.'

'I must protest.' The Reverend Jamieson was on his feet now. 'It's true that there is a gap in my ecclesiastical career prior to my coming to St Cuthbert's but I can assure you it was time devoted to the work of our Lord.' He glanced around his parishioners. 'I have told no-one of this but prior to my accepting the living in this parish I was working amongst the homeless and dispossessed of our own inner-cities. Believe me...' there was spirit in the priest's words now, '... working amongst drug users, dealers and the lower strata of our society carries its own share of risk. My Bishop agreed that this period of my service should remain a secret; I had, after all, learned much that others might fear would be used against them. I was given this parish as a way of "disappearing", yes, but from the possible repercussions of gangland violence, not the law and society I have always upheld.' He looked around for support. 'I ask you all to respect the confidentiality of what I have just told you.'

'And so we shall, Vicar.' It was Jack breaking the stunned silence that had followed this revelation. He scanned the faces before him and received conditional nods in return. 'You can also be assured that I know you are not the man who murdered Professor Stack and Mrs Thornton.'

'But if it isn't the vicar…' even Stuart Thornton had succumbed to the drama of the scene and was voicing the thoughts of all, '… and you insist the murderer is an ex-soldier, then it can only be …'

'Colonel William Etherington,' completed Jack.

'What … what the blazes … have you gone mad, Fellows?' The Colonel was on his feet now, his neck red against the check flannel of his collar. 'You said yourself this bounder Vennage, or whatever he's called, is middle sixties. Good God, man, I'm in me late seventies.'

'Or so you act, Colonel.' Jack was unfazed by the officer's outburst. 'We've all remarked how remarkably fit you are for your age but, on what do we base that age? Grey hair: just as natural for a man in his sixties. Slight confusion: easily feigned. No, you had us all fooled, Colonel.'

'But I commanded the Jungle Warfare School in Borneo,' protested Etherington. 'Check my record, man; it's all there.'

'I have,' said Jack, 'only yesterday with Chief Inspector Hengrove in his office. There was indeed a Colonel William Etherington in the British Army and he did teach jungle warfare in Borneo. Quite a character, by all accounts, with a deep love of the jungle. So much so, he stayed on in Borneo after retirement, running the school on M.o.D. contract. As Corporal Venning of the SAS you must have benefited from his teachings yourself. Knowing this officer would remain in Borneo until the end of his days, he was the perfect man on which to hang your new identity.'

'Can you prove any of this, Jack?' Colin Newell was finding it hard to accept that their much-loved squire was not the man he professed to be. 'It's not impossible, surely, that Colonel Etherington decided to spend his final days in the old country?'

'Exactly. Well said, Newell,' added the Colonel.

'I'm afraid it is impossible,' responded Jack, evenly. 'The army haven't paid the real Colonel Etherington a pension for three years now for the simple reason that he's dead and buried in Borneo.'

The "Colonel's" eyes narrowed. SAS training had doubtless taught him to think on his feet and it served him well now. 'All right, Fellows, so I'm a blasted phoney. Yes, I used old Bill Etherington's

I.D…' he turned appealingly to the men and women he'd known as friends, '… but that doesn't make me a murderer. What?'

Jack's own eyes met his man's, unblinking. 'I'm afraid it does.'

'With what proof?' The voice sounded younger now with the need for imposture gone, but the spirit still remained. 'No-one on the river…' he turned and pointed a shaking finger at individuals, '… Thornton, young Morecroft, old Giller… saw me or any other boat on the water anywhere near Stack's that night.' He turned back to face Jack. 'If I wasn't there, how could I do it?'

'Because you weren't on the water, you were under it.'

'You're mad.'

'I think not. The SAS teach many skills and it's quite feasible that you trained as a scuba diver during your service with them. I've little doubt that a search of The Hall will reveal your equipment and other evidence as well.' Jack smiled. 'It puzzled me, I admit, working out how a murderer could go to and from Stack's boats with others coming from north and south and none of them meeting another. I had clues but I failed to recognise them at the time. There were those damp patches though, in *Aethelberht's* saloon, that we couldn't explain. And then Walter here said he saw the bubbles of a monster otter. It didn't occur to me that they were bubbles from a diver. Likewise, when the police first raided Pete's boats, they found him mending one of his nets. He thought an otter had chewed its way through them. Again, that was no otter. I suspect that on your return to The Hall, having murdered Stack and stolen the artefacts, you became entangled in Peter Morecroft's nets and had to cut yourself free.'

'This all sounds a bit far-fetched, Jack.' Colin Newell was still having problems with such a complex plan.

'To us, maybe, but not to a man who'd served with one of the best special forces in the world.' Even as Jack spoke, he noticed Hengrove make a discreet signal to the constables on the RIB. To keep attention in *Raedwald*, Jack continued his explanation. 'The Colonel, or Venning as we now know him, planned Stack's murder with military precision. It must have been a shock for the Professor when this rubber-suited diver climbed aboard *Aethelberht*. He was certainly in no condition to resist, having just had a good beating from Stuart here and being threatened by Walter. We'll probably never know exactly what happened on *Aethelberht* that night but we can have a pretty good guess. With the exhibition area wrecked and artefacts lying everywhere, I suspect it was a spur-of-the-moment decision to use an Anglo-Saxon dagger instead of the diver's knife he'd doubtless brought for the job.' He turned to the ex-SAS man. 'With Stack dead, you had ample time to open the safe and empty it of its contents but it wasn't really artefacts or gold that you were after was it?'

The man they'd known as "the Colonel" just nodded and said 'Go on.'

'What you were really looking for was the evidence used to blackmail Gwen, the woman you loved, hence the turned out drawers and cupboards. Of course, you didn't find them - they were hidden back at Stack's apartment in town where Lisa discovered them later - but you had the compensation of getting your hands on something else: a safe full of priceless artefacts.' Jack paused to give a mirthless smile. 'Ironic that you were stealing back the sceattas that you'd lifted a decade before. This time though, there was a bonus: the gold brooches. They had a double value to you: they made theft appear as the motive for the murder and gave you wealth enough for the rest of your life. Treasures like those would have been hard to fence but doubtless, Max van Horsen would have found a way. With them and the coins in the bag, you simply slid back into the water and headed home to The Hall.'

'Very clever.' Venning sat down on a thwart. For perhaps the first time in his life, he was feeling the dejection of defeat. By now the two constables were aboard *Raedwald* and placing firm hands on his shoulders. He shrugged them off. 'Give me a few more minutes. First I want to know how Fellows got on to me.'

'Quite simply in the end,' said Jack. 'Like the rest of us, there are words and phrases that you use all the time. A favourite one of yours is "one hundred per cent effort". When I had that chat with Gwen a few days ago, she used the same expression.' The Ranger smiled. 'Now, it's an endearing feature of close relationships that couples tend to adopt phrases used by the other - my wife and I do it all the time. When I came out of that meeting with Gwen, I knew she'd said something significant but I couldn't put my finger on it. And then you used the expression again after Stack's memorial service and I remembered where I'd heard it before. Only a small thing but it connected you and Gwen and as soon as I realised that it was you and Gwen Fosdyke that were the couple and not she and Stack, then everything else started falling into place.'

'Hmmm. They always said that "careless talk costs lives",' said Venning. 'I guess they were right.'

'And in more ways than one,' agreed Jack. 'It was another expression you used at that same memorial that first put me onto the diving theory. You were trying to forge a link in my mind between Peter Morecroft and Max van Horsen. You said that perhaps they were "working a buddy system". Now, I'm no diver myself but I've worked with plenty. For safety, divers often work in pairs and they call that a "buddy system". You using the same expression set me thinking that you'd been a diver yourself.'

'For several years in the mob,' confirmed Venning. 'Perhaps I should have stuck to diving instead of cracking safes.'

'Perhaps you should.' Jack glanced towards Stuart but the artist was only half-listening. 'That wound to Lisa Thornton's throat; it took a special knife to inflict that, a diver's knife if I'm not mistaken.'

Venning just nodded before adding, 'Planned to stick Stack with it but in the end used his own Anglo-Saxon dagger…' he paused and glanced again to that corner of the broad where the two boats lay on the night of the murder, '… seemed more appropriate somehow.'

Jack smiled in recollection. 'You know, Colonel… Venning, you made the same mistake when I met you on the broad, on the morning of Stack's murder, as you did just now but, at the time, I failed to pick it up.'

'Mistake, what mistake?' asked Venning, as intrigued as the rest.

'When you said "Bad business, Fellows", that morning, you nodded to where *Raedwald* and *Aethelberht* had lain at anchor. According to you, the only time you had been out that night had been in your dressing gown to get your mobile phone from *Goosewatcher* and saw Stuart Thornton rowing home. In fact, my guess is that far from being in your dressing gown, you were already in your scuba gear and about to set off on your deadly mission. By the time I met you next morning on the broad, we'd already moved Stack's boats to Giller's Yard, so how else did you know their position at the time of the murder? It was only later, when I began to suspect you, that I recalled the incident and recognised it as a clue.'

'But the initials… PM… scrawled in blood,' asked Colin Newell. 'Why did Stack try and lead us to the wrong man?'

'He didn't; he was trying to tell us it was the Colonel who'd murdered him but, in our ignorance, we didn't see the clue.'

'But PM stands pretty clearly for Peter Morecroft,' continued Colin, glancing sideways at his eel-fisher friend. 'I don't get it.'

'And neither did I until I visited Norwich Castle Museum,' continued Jack. 'Those letters had us all fooled from the start. What we should have remembered was Professor Stack's knowledge of the Anglo-Saxon period. He wanted to tell us Etherington was his murderer but, even in his dying seconds, realised that any clue he left would be simply obliterated by his assailant before he left the scene. Stack had explained runic symbols to me that very day when he showed me the artefacts. Even with that knowledge, I failed to realise he'd used Anglo-Saxon runes instead of modern-day letters. It didn't click until yesterday at the Castle. That's when I saw the explanation of runes and how P in the runic alphabet was W in modern day and M was E. By reverting to a subject he'd studied all his life, Stack wasn't writing PM, he was telling us it was WE … William Etherington.' Jack turned to the man he still thought of as "The Colonel". 'You probably saw those initials in blood and thought they were the delirium of a dying man. Nevertheless, they pointed to Peter Morecroft and so you left them as a false trail. Am I right?'

'Too true.' The phoney Sandhurst accent was slipping slightly now. 'Couldn't understand why he would blame Morecroft like that but I'd had my own run-ins with the tearaway over poaching so I thought, why not? Let Morecroft take the rap.'

'Cemented by dropping two sceattas into his boat,' completed Jack. 'When did you do that? After you cut free from his nets?'

'Yep.' Venning looked at the eel-catcher. 'Those nets gave me a bad moment, Morecroft, and with your initials left on Stack's boat I thought, what the hell; in for a penny, in for a sceatta and tossed a couple into that grotty tub of yours.' He shrugged weary shoulders. 'Almost worked too.'

'But not quite.' DCI Hengrove turned and faced his man. 'Frederick Venning, I'm arresting you on suspicion of murdering Professor Rupert Stack. You don't have to say anything but it may harm your defence…'

'All right, all right, I know the drill.' Venning turned to Gwen Fosdyke. Perhaps a wish for her to remember him as the man she'd loved caused him to revert to the well-modulated Colonel. 'Sorry old girl, made a bit of a mess of it in the end.'

'It was me who let you down, William.' There were tears rolling down her cheeks as Gwen Fosdyke put her arms around the only man she had truly loved. 'I'll stick by you … no matter what … always.'

'And in more ways than one,' said Hengrove, wasting no time on sentiment, 'because you're going with him for "aiding and abetting". Bailey ...'

The DC cautioned Gwen and then the two uniformed constables led them aft. Jack followed but as Venning went to climb down into the RIB, he paused and offered his hand. 'Bye, Fellows. Look after *Goosewatcher* for me.'

'I will ... Colonel. I enjoyed our chats.'

Gwen was the next to disembark. Before she climbed the gunwale, she turned and said, 'I knew there was more to this, Mr. Fellows, than just the reading of a will.'

'Ah, the will.' Jack leaned closer and almost whispered, 'I think Stack's estate will be in good hands with Stuart Thornton don't you?' He gave the solicitor a knowing wink. 'We'll just let the will stand as written, shall we?'

Her lips parted in just the hint of a smile before she winked back. 'Yes, I think that will be for the best.'

Hengrove and Bailey followed them down into the RIB. There was a roar of outboards and then the semi-rigid was curving away in an arc of propwash towards the village staithe where blue flashing lights already winked through the trees.

Over *Raedwald*'s high mast, a flight of Canada geese made their squawking way across the broad. The wind was strengthening now, swinging the galley at her anchor cable and sending rolling wavelets to slap at her clinkered sides. It would take more than man's iniquities to change this timeless scene thought Jack, as he made his way for'ard and rejoined the rest of the silent group.

Chapter Twenty

'READY ABOUT!'

In *Raedwald's* bow, Colin Newell let go the squaresail's tack.

'Gybe Ho.'

As Charlotte pushed the steering oar's tiller for'ard, *Raedwald* turned until her stern was passing through the wind and the fine curving bow was casting aside the wash of her own passing. Heaving on lines, Colin swung the sail on its yard through a full half circle until it was again on the leeward side and *Raedwald* was close hauled on the opposite tack. As the boat settled on her new course, the only sound once more was the eager sluice of water along her sides.

'Always better to wear ship than tack when short-handed,' said Charlotte, bringing the tiller back athwartships and glancing up at the burgee fluttering from the masthead. 'She's totally predictable though and handles so beautifully.'

'And so she should, Alan built her,' said Jack, looking astern at their furrow-straight wake. It was another glorious Broadland day and Charlotte had telephoned just the night before to invite Jack and Audrey to join her and Colin for this special sail. *Raedwald* was indeed sailing beautifully in the hands of this competent girl and her boat-builder friend, but this trip held special significance.

'How does it feel, knowing the boat is yours now?' asked Jack.

The beaming smile Charlotte gave in return was answer enough while she struggled to find adequate words.

'Wonderful beyond description, Jack. Stuart Thornton signing *Raedwald* over to us is unbelievable enough, but do you know he's paid off all the debts of Giller's Yard as well and had the ownership passed back to me.'

'So, Charlotte's going to lease the yard to me for my boatbuilding and continue living in the cottage herself,' added Colin, joining them once more in the stern.

'So, now *Raedwald's* yours, what are you going to do with her?' asked Jack, glancing down the galley's lean hull. 'A boat like this needs to earn her keep.'

'And so she shall,' said Charlotte, glancing aloft at the burgee and bringing the galley up closer to the wind. The replica heeled a little more as Colin hardened the mainsheet slightly. 'We're going to operate her together, doing eductional trips for schools. I think Alan would like that: teaching children something about the ways of wind and water and the beautiful wooden boats that used to harness their energy.'

'You'll make a good team, you and Colin,' said Audrey before adding, with a twinkle in her eye, '... in every way.'

Charlotte smiled as Colin put his arm around the fresh-faced girl at his side. 'We'll take things easy, Audrey, and just see how they develop.'

There was a fresh wind blowing down the broad this day, causing little whitecaps to curl and break. *Raedwald* seemed to be enjoying the sail as much as her crew, effortlessly punching her way through the wavelets with spray flinging on either side. Jack gestured to Audrey and together they made their way further for'ard on the windward side until they were close by the creaking mast.

'Just thought we'd give the lovebirds a little space,' he said, holding a shroud and leaning out over the side to watch the foaming bow wave slide past. 'What a great way to spend a day off.'

'Yes, and you've earned it, Jack,' said Audrey, leaning beside him. 'Whether you realise it or not, that whole horrible business took its toll on you.'

'Perhaps.' He continued looking out across the expanse of water, eyes on the distant reedbeds but his thoughts on the lives irretrievably altered in just the last week. 'I'm so glad things have worked out well for Charlotte,' he said, realising at the same time he was indulging in a spot of self-justification. He turned back inboard and looked aft to where the young widow was grinning with the sheer delight of life being lived once more. 'She deserves some luck, that girl and I know old Walter is content again, knowing justice has prevailed in the end.'

'Yes,' agreed Audrey, 'and what a wonderfully generous gesture of Stuart's. I'm so pleased the police are taking no further action against him.'

'So they shouldn't.' Jack shook his head. 'I truly believe he hadn't the faintest idea of what was going on.'

'What I can't understand,' said Audrey, turning inboard again herself, 'is why they used the art business anyway. Why didn't the Colonel just get Lisa to exchange the sceattas for cash without all that business of buying and selling paintings?'

'Because that's the trick with any laundering operation: moving on your loot while, at the same time, showing a legitimate income,' said Jack, folding his arms. 'The taxman needs to see a reason for large dollops of cash. The last thing the Colonel …Venning … wanted was any tax investigation. Dealing in art around the country was a very plausible front that served him admirably and probably made him a bit of extra profit to boot.'

'But what made you suspect that in the first place?'

'I didn't,' admitted Jack honestly. 'It was only after Lisa was murdered that I began to wonder about things that Stuart had said in our chats. I knew he was getting fed up with having to churn out paintings only to see them disappear to galleries he-knew-not-where. It all seemed a bit strange to me. As I began to suspect the Colonel, I remembered Stuart saying there was just one of his paintings in a gallery in Elm Hill. It only took a bit of telephoning to locate which one. I admit I was a bit devious. I paid them a visit, got them to ring the owner on the false pretext of making a bid and then made an excuse to get back into their office, press REDIAL and hear Colonel Etherington's unmistakable voice on the other end.'

'You're a sneaky devil, Jack Fellows,' said his wife, smiling. 'The really good news, of course, is that they found the artefacts at The Hall just as you predicted.'

'Yeah, and a full set of scuba kit as well,' nodded Jack, 'including a diver's knife which forensics are sure is the one that killed Lisa Thornton.'

'Poor Stuart,' said Audrey. 'I wonder if he'll ever get over all this?'

'He will. He's got a bit of cash now to pay off Lisa's debts and Stack's *Aethelberht* to go off cruising and paint Broadland landscapes to his heart's content.'

If his heart ever will be content again, wondered Audrey, but didn't say.

'Ready about!' shouted Charlotte again. Once more *Raedwald* gybed and Jack and Audrey moved across to the starboard side. They were nearing the north end of the broad now but to the south, just above the treeline, rose the square tower of St Cuthbert's Church.

'Poor Reverend Jamieson,' said Audrey, 'he's retiring you know.'

Jack nodded. 'So I heard. Has he given a reason?'

'His age, basically, but it's general knowledge that all the trouble hit him very badly. I think he feels that a new incumbent will give the parish a fresh start.' Audrey frowned. 'A really nice gesture is that he's signed that lovely big people-carrier over to the church.'

'Good,' said Jack. 'I told him to.'

Audrey turned sharply, unable to believe what she'd heard. 'You … told the Reverend Julian to give away his new car … for what reason for heaven's sake, Jack, and … when?'

'During a confidential chat before he left *Raedwald* on the day the Colonel was arrested.' Jack turned to his wife and, in spite of the crash of water against the galley's bow, lowered his voice. 'Audrey, what I'm going to tell you now is strictly between you and me … is that understood?'

'Of course, Jack … it's always been that way.' There was nervousness in her own voice, as though she were steeling herself for something she didn't want to hear. 'Jack, what are you going to tell me?'

'Something I've told no-one else.' Jack turned towards his wife. 'The fact is, Audrey, our good vicar is probably responsible for all that happened last week.' There was a cascade of spray as *Raedwald* sliced through the wake of some passing cruisers. Jack paused and then said, 'It was at Stack's memorial service that my suspicions were first aroused. The Reverend Julian was wearing the ribbon of a General Service Medal on his scarf. When I asked him about it over tea, he said he'd been awarded it for service in Cyprus.'

'What was wrong with that?'

'Nothing, except that Jamieson said he'd been invalided out for malaria.' Jack shook his head slightly. 'Malaria is a pretty horrible tropical disease but, as far as I know, was never in the Mediterranean or, at least, not in modern times. If our vicar had only served three years, as he said, then he must have contracted it elsewhere. So I went to the Royal Norfolk's museum in Norwich and checked on some regimental history. Sure enough, it was Borneo where the Royal Leicesters served during the Reverend Julian's stint, not Cyprus. Just to confirm it I got Phil Hengrove to check his army record. His GSM was issued "for service in Borneo."'.

'Good heavens.' exclaimed Audrey. 'Why would he lie about a thing like that?'

'To hide one very significant fact. Remember that the real Colonel Etherington ran the jungle warfare school in Borneo. The Leicesters would have gone through that school and Jamieson, as regimental padre, would have met the famous Colonel William.' Jack nodded towards St Cuthbert's church. 'You can imagine his excitement when he came here and heard that a man he admired from his army days was living just down the road as squire. He probably couldn't wait to cycle round to The Hall and renew an old friendship.'

'Only to find that the man calling himself Colonel Etherington wasn't the officer he'd known in Borneo.'

'Exactly,' agreed Jack, rolling his eyes. 'It must have been quite a shock for both of them.'

'But why didn't Reverend Julian expose him?'

'Ah, there, if I'm not mistaken, lies the reason behind much of what subsequently happened,' said Jack. 'I'm not saying our good vicar actually stooped to blackmail but it came as near as dammit. What I think happened at that meeting is that Venning, once he'd got over his own shock at being discovered as a phoney, made the Reverend Julian an offer he couldn't refuse.'

'Money?'

'Yes, but not directly. My guess is that good old Julian hinted that St Cuthbert's was badly in need of renovation and that generous donations would be more than welcome…'

'…and maintain his silence,' completed Audrey.

'Exactly, hence the very anonymous donations that could never be traced. That work probably drained Venning's coffers and was the reason he needed to start flogging off his sceattas which ultimately led to Stack's death.'

'No wonder poor Reverend Julian was so upset at the murders.' It was Audrey's turn to shake her head. 'He must have suspected the Colonel may have been responsible.'

'Quite,' agreed Jack. 'I think he probably went round to see Venning to find out the truth. That's when the people-carrier appeared.'

'You mean our vicar took a personal bribe to shield a murderer?'

'I think Venning probably forced it on him and told him to think things over. The church and church hall might have been brought up to scratch but there would always be work to do and he doubtless reminded the vicar of what would be lost if he blew his cover. Of course, as soon as the vicar drove that car away, Venning made it impossible for him to go to the police without branding himself as a bought conspirator. After that, things went from bad to worse, ending with Lisa's murder. Luckily for Jamieson's conscience, Venning was eventually nabbed without his having to renege on the arrangement.

'But it will come out now, surely?' queried Audrey, fearful that a man she had always respected might be exposed as a blackmailer or worse.

'I think not. ' Jack put a comforting arm around his wife's shoulders. 'Venning's no fool. Admitting bribing the vicar would win him no points at all in court. Instead, he'll get his defence to explain all the good work he's done in this village and money he's spent on St Cuthbert's, and doubtless earn himself a good reduction in sentence.'

'I hope so,' said Audrey. 'I liked the Colonel, in spite of his other life, and that people-carrier will be so handy for the new incumbent.'

'Indeed it will.' Jack allowed himself a smile. 'And riding his bike again will do the Reverend Julian far more good in his retirement.'

'Ah, "the Lord's ways..."' quoted Audrey, smiling herself. She nodded back to Charlotte and Colin in the stern. 'Let's rejoin the lovebirds shall we?'

Jack nodded. 'With all this fresh air, I'll sleep well tonight. An early one, I think.' He glanced again across the sparkling broad. 'After all, I do have a job to do tomorrow.'

Acknowledgements

Even a work of fiction requires much gleaning of facts and insights into the lives and skills of others. I'm grateful to the following for all the willing help they gave in turning *WATERPROOF* from an idea into a published book:

My thanks go to Ian Masters, who read the draft, made invaluable suggestions and then was kind enough to write the foreword. Publication is something of a mystery in itself but Jamie Campbell injected the whole process with enthusiasm and a sense of fun. Broads Authority Navigation Ranger Martin Joslin gave me an insight into the many aspects of patrolling these magic waters while Countryside Ranger Eilish Rothney provided enlightenment on the secrets of eel-fishing. Likewise, I'm grateful to Martyn Potter of the Norfolk Constabulary for all his help in explaining police procedures and the operations of Broads Beat. Thanks also to Sarah Rogers, for the illustrations at the end of each chapter. Finally, to my wife Sue for taking the cover photos, editing the draft and supporting me throughout.

Chris Crowther
Hoveton St. John

If you've enjoyed

WATERPROOF

You may want to read my other novel,

BLADESTRIKE

ISBN: 978-1-58736-773-1

BLADESTRIKE tells the story of helicopter pilot Mike Tempest. Fired from his job with a London air taxi operator, he's short of cash and excitement alike. Temporary salvation comes in the form of the vivacious but businesslike Miss Bird, who offers him one day's work. Though suspicious of her motives, he accepts and regrets it just as quickly when he finds himself on the wrong side of the law. On the run, but with large rewards in the offing, he embarks on a quest to hunt down the villains himself. Along a trail increasingly bizarre, he encounters spectres from his own past, romance in an unexpected quarter, and a plot far deeper than mere extortion. Could a century-old crime still threaten the destiny of a nation? As Tempest skims stormy waters en route to a climactic ending, he has only a vague idea of how to save a situation that began with a cappuccino at Tower Bridge.

Here's the first chapter to give you a taste...

The Bell 206 Jet Ranger helicopter is a great bit of kit. Its 420 horsepower turbine can hover over a spot or scoot along at a good hundred knots. Between the two it can fly at any old speed you want which comes in handy when the weather's lousy with low cloud, low visibility and rain. That's when you drop the lever, slow right down and hug the deck with the demisters screaming, tongue in cheek and eyes wide open for any masts and wires that could ruin your whole day.

It's probably not a very scientific way to operate in this high-tech age but when the chips are down there's still a lot to be said for scud running. It's hard on the nerves, bad on range and doesn't exactly endear you to livestock farmers or the Civil Aviation Authority but it does get you there and getting there was what it was all about that wet and windy November morning.

My name's Mike Tempest. I've been to a few places, done a few things and flying helicopters was what I'd done most. I'd built a fair amount of experience over the years and perhaps a bit of skill and I certainly needed it now as I ground my way through that hell-awful weather. Not for the first time in my life I asked myself what I was doing there and why? I knew the answer this time: I'd been suckered into it by that stroppy bitch at Tower Hill and I wouldn't even have met her if I hadn't gone into Ashmond's office and heard him say those magic words.

'YOU'RE FIRED TEMPEST'

Captain Ashmond was my Chief Pilot and not number one on my list of favourite people. *HELIJETS* was a four helicopter outfit operating from Denbridge, a grass airfield on the western edge of London. Small as our operation was, Ashmond liked to think he was running some international conglomerate and his desk was part of the fantasy. I sat down opposite its vast mahogany expanse.

'Really; why?'

Actually I knew the answer: our flying was mainly stroking the egos of yuppies from the city but fluctuations in the economy meant that many were down to their last millions and expensive helicopter transport was first for the chop, with me just a number down the chain. Not that Ashmond needed much of an excuse; he and the other two pilots had all served together in the Queens Bengal Helicopter Lancers or some such outfit and taking me on when they were short of pilots had been a constant thorn in his regimental side. Giving me the heave-ho was almost an act of exorcism.

'You just don't fit in here Tempest, you never have and you never will.' He settled himself back into his super-reclining chair. 'Your bush flying ways might have gone down well in the Third World but they're hardly appropriate in executive aviation.'

I pulled a cigarette and lit up. Ashford hated smoking in his office.

'So, I'm out on my ear?'

Ashford waved away some smoke that was invading his airspace.

'Yes, and with immediate effect. The chairman's quite adamant. Standard redundancy payment will be in the post.' He glanced dismissively doorwards. 'Sandra will take care of the details. Goodbye, Tempest.'

There are times when you have to bite your tongue and stay nice and leaving a job is one of them; you never know when you might be able to come back. So I just stubbed my cigarette on Ashmond's loveley desk, said 'Well stuff you, your chairman and your job', kicked my chair into the corner and door-slammed out.

'Oh Mike, how could you?' A slim girl with a thatch of close-cropped blond hair was standing by the filing cabinet with a sad expression. Sandra was secretary, receptionist, booking officer and operations manager rolled into one and as big an asset to *HELIJETS* as its helicopters standing outside. Unbeknown to Ashmond, we'd got pretty close over the last months and I'd promised to take her out for a Chinese this evening. A great girl Sandra, even if her ethics stopped short of listening at the boss's door.

'Could what? He did it to me.' I gave a poor imitation of a smile. 'Sorry Sandra, but you'll have to take a rain-check on tonight's supper. I need to sort things out. I'll give you a call.'

'I understand.'

She probably did too, knowing Sandra, but at the moment I neither knew nor cared as I stomped my way out to my old banger, gunned a bootful of revs and wheelspun off Denbridge for what I thought was the last time.

'Who needs a job anyway.'

I DID AND QUICK if my dwindling bank balance was anything to go by. My small basement pad was never going to feature in *HELLO* magazine but my severance pay from *HELIJETS* wouldn't run it for long and bills were already coming in. Mid-November wasn't the best time to start looking for a flying job but I dragged out my list of contact numbers and got calling.

The helicopter world is small and the jungle drums quick to beat and their message this time wasn't hard to guess: Tempest is bad news. No-one actually said that but two days of ringing around while the whisky level fell in inverse proportion to my phone bill produced only 'get in touch' promises that were unlikely as they were insincere.

The weather didn't help either. High pressure over the British Isles had enshrouded the capital in freezing fog that clawed at my windows like the creditors soon to come. With anti-cyclonic gloom outside and in, I was getting desperate. That's when the phone rang.

'Captain Tempest?' The voice was female, cool and businesslike to the point of being brusque.

'That's me; who's that?'

'You don't know me, Captain Tempest, but I'm calling to offer you some work. You are available at the moment, I understand?'

'I've just been given the sack if that's what you mean. What sort of executive position are you offering?'

She gave a barely audible sigh just to show my sarcasm wasn't appreciated.

'Not a position, Captain Tempest, just one day's work. If you're interested we can meet in town and discuss the proposal in more detail.'

This obviously wasn't going to provide for my old age but it could lead elsewhere and inject some interest into a so-far excruciatingly boring week.

'OK; where and what time?'

'Tower Bridge. There's a cafe down at bank level on the northwest side. They've got some outside tables. Meet me there at ten a.m. tomorrow.'

'I'll be there.'

I hung up. No need to ask for a description; there wouldn't be too many punters sitting at outside tables at this time of year. Besides, I wanted to show Miss Business Efficiency that I could cut the small talk just as sharply as her.

Perhaps I'd cut it too much; what was I getting myself into here and who was this self assured little madam? I tried a call back but the number was ex-directory...

I hadn't even got her name.

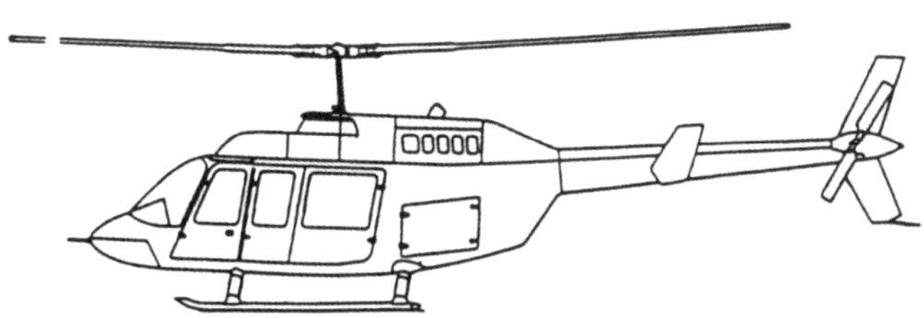

BLADESTRIKE
Chris Crowther